Shaman's Moon

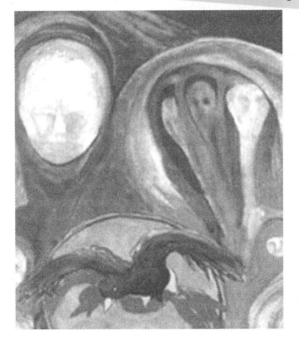

A Stoner McTavish Mystery by
SARAH DREHER

New Victoria Publishers
Norwich Vermont

Published by New Victoria Publishers Inc., PO Box 27 Norwich, VT 05055. A Feminist Literary and Cultural Organization founded in 1976.

Printed in Canada

Dreher, Sarah.
    Shaman's moon : a Stoner Mctavish mystery / by Sarah Dreher.
       p.   cm.
    ISBN 0-934678-91-X
    1. McTavish, Stoner (Fictitious character) - - Fiction. 2. Women detectives- -United States--Fiction. 3. Lesbians- -United States--Fiction. I. Title.
    PS3554.R36S48   1998   98-12883
    813' .54--dc21   CIP

To Donna and Jody
my friends and teachers

OTHER BOOKS BY SARAH DREHER

Stoner McTavish Mysteries

Stoner McTavish
Something Shady
Gray Magic
A Captive In Time
Otherworld
Bad Company

Novel
Solitaire and Brahms

Plays
Lesbian Stages

Chapter 1

Aunt Hermione insisted she was fine, but Stoner knew there was something wrong. She knew it by the slight, split-second hesitation in Aunt Hermione's speech, as if she had to search for the words to use before she spoke. She knew it by the light, waxed-papery, nearly-translucent quality of the flesh that covered her aunt's cheeks. Knew it by the tiny uncharacteristic sigh that rose from her as she got up from her chair. Knew it by the chill in her own bones and the tingling under her skin when she caught an unexpected glimpse of her.

Even Gwen, Stoner's lover and life partner, who had won three consecutive Olympic Gold Medals in Worry-freeness, was concerned. She didn't say much, but Stoner caught her glancing Aunt Hermione's way when she thought no one was watching.

Marylou Kesselbaum, their fourth housemate and Stoner's partner in the travel agency of Kesselbaum and McTavish, was the least concerned. "If there's anything wrong, she'll tell us," Marylou had said when Stoner had brought it up, and offered her an Easter green Snowball.

Stoner sat uneasily on the front porch step and watched the Deerfield River, a mile away but visible from their hillside home. Mortgaged to the eyeballs and struggling to keep the travel agency open through the winter, they'd lived in Shelburne Falls for seven months now. She loved the small-town western Massachusetts atmosphere, but she still hadn't gotten used to the quiet. Years of downtown Boston had, she thought, created the permanent hallucination of background traffic, which made silence seem noisy, and noise like silence.

It was a nearly perfect late spring day. A high crisp blue sky with a few wisps of cloud lay reflected in the sparkling water. The maples and oaks were in full leaf. The scent of apple blossoms drifted on the air. Bumblebees hung over the iris blooms, and a faint breeze made moving silver shadows in the tall grasses.

Another season. They'd all settled in well, actually. Aunt Hermione had found kindred souls and psychic counseling clients through the Psychical Awareness and Research Association and the Spiritualist Church, down in Springfield. In fact, after a lifetime of using only public transportation, she had made up her mind to learn to drive so she could visit her new friends more often. Last Candlemas a local coven had invited her to join after one of their members died and another moved to Oregon. She found it stimulating, being in a mixed-age group. But sometimes it exhausted her. "Young people," she told Stoner, "are so very exuberant."

Marylou, who was always looking for love in all the wrong places, had found it again. Her current flame was a Vietnam War veteran named Cutter. He lived somewhere deep in the woods, and spent his days in a Buddhist encampment out in the woods around Ashfield, where he did odd jobs and construction to atone for his sins. She'd met him one morning at McCusker's Market as she was checking out the day's whole grain muffin selections. Cutter talked very little, shaved his head, and most of the time wore Buddhist robes. Marylou found that attractive. He'd been to dinner once, but was so uncomfortable in their dining room he and Marylou had ended up eating on the back porch.

Stoner had the feeling Marylou was beyond rehabilitation.

Gwen had found work at Mohawk Regional School. Substitute teaching at first, then part-time, and by April had taken over a full-time position in History and Social Studies. She found it a little unnerving, being pink-slipped like a beginner after twelve years of teaching. But even though she'd be fired every May for the first three years, her superintendent assured her she'd be rehired if she submitted her application. The head of the school board's son had been her student, had developed a crush-at-first-sight on Gwen, and had raised his "D" in History to a "B" in one semester. Another school board member's daughter would be in her class this year. Information passed freely over the back fences and coffee cups among the members of the Mohawk Trail Regional School Board, good news as well as bad. They had already decided that Gwen Owens was good news.

And what about you? Stoner asked herself. The move had been easier than she'd expected. Of course, things were always easier than she expected. That was because she always made room in her mind for unanticipated disasters. Aunt Hermione was convinced that the problem was Stoner's latent and feared psychic ability, which caused her to have negative precognitions. "Undeveloped psychic ability," her aunt was fond of saying, "is an offense against Nature. The psychic drive is like sex, fine in itself, but you need to get a grip."

That was all well and good for Aunt Hermione. Aunt Hermione had been psychic all her life—several lifetimes according to her—and even managed to make a decent living giving psychic readings. She was equally adept at Tarot, clairvoyance and clairaudience, channeling—both trance and waking—and psychometry. Astrology, she declared, was too scientific once you go to transits, and beyond her ken.

Stoner believed in what her aunt did. She'd seen enough to be a fool not to believe. But when it came to herself, she wanted absolutely nothing whatsoever to do with it.

Her aunt wasn't surprised at her reluctance. Capricorns, she explained, often had a difficult time with psychic matters, being of a nature that liked things down-to-earth and do-it-yourself.

In the interest of being down-to-earth, Stoner periodically tried to remind herself that Aunt Hermione wasn't getting any younger—nearing eighty, in fact. Someday her health was going to fail. That was inevitable, and there was no sense trying to deny it. The healthiest people in the world eventually grew old. And…

Whenever she thought of her aunt's inevitable death, her mind turned to white noise. She couldn't think, couldn't move. Future didn't exist. There was a high wall at the end of Now and the beginning of Then, and nothing beyond that wall.

She really didn't know what she'd do when that time came. She'd lived with her aunt most of her life, since she was sixteen and ran away from home because her parents hated her for being a lesbian. Aunt Hermione had welcomed her into her arms and her life. Aunt Hermione had been more than an aunt, she'd been a friend, a parent, her family. Aunt Hermione held her hand through the ups and downs of adolescence and the whims of love. Cared for her when she was sick. Entertained her and loved her and sometimes made her crazy.

It worked both ways.

But someday Aunt Hermione wouldn't be there any more. No matter how vehemently she insisted she'd always be around in spirit, and make Stoner's life a living hell if she didn't behave herself… Someday she just wouldn't be there. Some morning Stoner'd come down to the kitchen and the air wouldn't smell of bacon and pie and reheats of last night's dinner.

Aunt Hermione's idea of breakfast was to browse the refrigerator and select whatever caught her eye, whether it had anything to do with a normal breakfast or not. "Think of it as brunch," she'd say when Stoner insisted it was much too early for meat loaf and spinach souffle.

Stoner never did get in the habit of desserts and leftovers hitting her stomach first thing in the morning. It just wasn't right. It wasn't done. It wasn't moral.

Aunt Hermione said Stoner had the sense of humor of a Lutheran.

At which Stoner realized she was being truly rigid and no fun at all.

Aunt Hermione had been married at one time—for about ten minutes, it seemed—to a "Gentleman of the Lutheran Persuasion." She insisted it had been one of the most soul-starving, hellish experiences of her life. After that she'd sworn off not only Lutherans, but religion, marriage, and men in general. Though she did have a brief affair with a minor member of the Kennedy family. There was, Aunt Hermione insisted, "nothing remarkable about that. Everyone does it."

In fact, her aunt considered the whole romantic love idea rather over-rated. That was until she met Grace D' Addario.

Grace was a Senior Citizen like Aunt Hermione, though a few golden years older. Grace was tall, kind, and terrifying, and a solitary practitioner of Wicca. Once Grace entered their lives, Stoner found herself flooded with humiliating emotions.

It was clear that Aunt Hermione had fallen head-over-heels for the woman.

And Grace returned the feeling.

They were, Stoner thought at the time in a condescending way, like a couple of kids. Holding hands in public. Even in restaurants. Bringing each other flowers. Talking on the phone endlessly.

"You're ridiculous," Stoner was shocked to hear herself say one evening quite unexpectedly. "You're too old to be carrying on like this."

Her aunt looked at her with utter amazement.

"Something really bad is going to happen, the way you behave." She heard her voice rise unpleasantly and couldn't control it. "You got arrested once, for God's sake!"

"Actually," Aunt Hermione said placidly, "I've been arrested several times. You just don't happen to know about it."

"Running around a cemetery NAKED !"

"Now, Stoner, you know what that was about."

She knew, all right. Whenever a person of a sinister nature died, Grace and Aunt Hermione would dance naked on his fresh grave in the dark of the moon, "to make sure he stays put." They did it to people they knew personally, like Gwen's husband who tried to kill her but Stoner got him first. They did it to people they read about in the papers—rapists and child molesters, wife beaters and "all-around nasty sorts." Sometimes they did it when they passed a new grave and "had a funny feeling about that one."

They never actually got arrested for naked grave dancing. Once they came very close, but the officer who approached them was young and couldn't bring himself to run in someone's grandmother.

Obviously, Grace was a terrible influence on Aunt Hermione. They were like dogs that run in packs, much more likely to make trouble together than apart.

And there was nothing Stoner could do about it. It made her feel as useless as the parent of a teenager.

So she worried and pouted instead.

Finally, even Gwen got tired of Stoner's moodiness, and one night sat her down and told her she was being a jackass. Except she was sincere about it, and when Gwen was sincere and annoyed she slipped back into her rural Georgia accent. She managed to make "jackass" a six-syllable word.

Stoner burst into tears, and as she was crying realized she was jealous and frightened. Frightened that her aunt, with a new and consuming love in her life, wouldn't need her any more.

She expected Grace to be angry, or at least to laugh at her when she confessed and apologized. But Grace listened very quietly, nodded, and said she understood.

"Besides," she said after a moment, "you're not losing an aunt, you're gaining a whole new set of problems."

A battered pickup truck rattled past the house. The driver peered nearsightedly at street signs and was obviously swearing to himself. He saw her and rolled down his window. "Hey!" he said.

It wasn't one of those, "Hey, there, how's it going, good to see you," sorts of "Hey!" It was a, "Hey, stupid, get off your lazy ass and tell me how the hell I get out of this jerkwater town that no one in their right mind would want to live in," kind of "Hey!"

Stoner pretended not to understand, and grinned and waved moronically.

Mr. Truck slammed his foot on the accelerator and burned one of his remaining three-quarter inches of rubber.

Maybe she should give Grace a call. Maybe she'd noticed something…not quite right…about Aunt Hermione.

But how could she explain what she meant by that? She couldn't put her finger on anything specific, nothing was clear. But there was an "off" feeling about her. Her aunt would call it disharmony between her chakras.

Stoner found herself watching her too closely, apprehensively. That wasn't right. Her aunt would say she was "feeding the forces of darkness with negative energy," or something like that. Stoner wasn't willing to go quite so far as to say that, but she knew she'd drive herself crazy if she didn't stop.

An oriole sang in a tree at the back of the house. She'd met a woman in the book store who called orioles "the avenging birds of Satan" because they built their nests near houses, had voices that could penetrate lead, and started up at dawn and went on all day. "Not only that," the woman said, "they seek out people with post-traumatic stress disorder and deliberately torture them." She grimaced as if speaking from personal experience.

Stoner hoped there weren't any orioles hanging around Cutter's campsite.

Still, she liked the bird. They hadn't had orioles in Boston. Except for the kind with a capital "O" who usually swept the home series from the Red Sox and weren't welcome in friendly Fenway Park. But this particular oriole, this flash of orange and black seen from the periphery of her vision, was a fascination. First, there was the color. City birds didn't have colors which startled. City birds were drab and gray, and if they'd ever been colorful had been drained by generations of city air until the color of concrete became part of their genetic make-up. Even the birds at the Franklin Park Zoo had a dull and defeated look about them.

And there was the song. Shrill, yes, but with a flute-like tone that could never be copied by human or human-made instrument. Once you knew the song, you would never mistake an oriole for any other bird.

Orioles had a presence. They were what they were, and nothing else. Stoner admired that quality.

Well, she'd better admire it from the office. During this slow season, she and Marylou were taking turns working morning or afternoon. Stoner preferred the afternoon shift, as there was no way she could be decent to herself or anyone else before ten a.m. Marylou was up and eager to embrace life at the crack of dawn, afraid something exciting might happen and she'd miss it.

Stoner was just as happy to miss it. Just leave her a note if there was anything she needed to know. That was as much excitement as she cared to experience these days.

She went inside the house to wash up. Aunt Hermione was bustling around in her study, getting ready to give a reading. She'd straightened the room, taken her crystals from the glass-fronted cabinet and arranged them on the table, filled a ceramic dish with water, and put a new candle in the holder. She was fussing over incense.

"What do you think, Stoner? Athena, or Mars? The client's a Scorpio."

Stoner went to look over her aunt's shoulder. The mingled incense odors tickled the inside of her nose. "I don't think Mars and Scorpio would mix well," she said. "Do you have any Kali left?"

"Of course," Aunt Hermione said. "The many-armed goddess for the many-armed scorpion." She looked pointedly at Stoner. "You do have more of a feel for these things than an average person would."

"It was logical."

"Oh, yes, the average person spends the better part of the day thinking about Sun Signs and incense," Aunt Hermione said wryly.

There were faint gray smudges under her eyes.

"You look tired," Stoner said.

"Oh, don't start." The older woman gave her an affectionate and exasperated look. "I'm fine. I've been fine since we got here, and I'm still fine."

"I hope so."

"Are you trying to drive me into an early grave with that kind of talk? Really, dear, it's very tiresome."

"I'm sorry. I just worry."

Her aunt patted her cheek soothingly. "I know you do, Stoner," she said. "Everyone you've ever met, and everyone who's ever heard about you knows you worry."

She felt herself blushing with embarrassment. "I'm leaving now."

"Have a nice day," Aunt Hermione said cheerfully. "Remind Marylou not to 'Yoo-hoo' when she comes in. It frightens the clients."

In Boston, walking to work had been a risky and fairly unpleasant experience. If you weren't mugged, or run down by one of the infamous Boston drivers, your brain and lungs were assaulted by noxious fumes. Your eyes were violated by ugly, glistening wet spots of suspicious origin on the pavements, and crumpled papers that attached themselves to your ankles like leeches. The weather see-sawed between cold, damp and miserable, and chokingly hot and humid.

But out here, the way to the agency took her through alleys and past back yards. Spots on the road were easily identifiable as oil, skid marks, dropped ice cream cones, or the remains of suicidal animals. And the worst smells were the lingering odors of decaying fruit and waxed cardboard banana boxes behind the super market.

The grass had greened up nicely in the past two weeks of cool air and rain. The river was high, swirling and churning over the glacial potholes, Shelburne Falls' natural tourist attraction. Shelburne Falls' unnatural tourist attraction was the Bridge of Flowers. This was a walkway between the Falls and Buckland, on the other side of the river. The good ladies of the town had turned an abandoned railroad bridge into a long flower garden that spanned both sides of the path. The flowers were lovingly cared for, healthy, and labeled to educate the young and the ignorant. They were changed with the seasons. At the entrance to the walkway a tiny gift-and-film store offered post cards of the Bridge of Flowers which looked as if they might have been photographed back in the '50s. Last Christmas, the two towns and the bridge between had been decorated with thousands of tiny bright lights that reflected in the black and sluggish river.

Anyone who had never seen it, she thought, wouldn't believe it.

Stoner took a deep breath of fresh air. She felt comfortable here. So comfortable, in fact, that she was constantly afraid Gwen and Marylou and Aunt Hermione really hated small town life but didn't let on because she was obviously happy here.

"Stoner..." She could almost hear the voice of Dr. Edith Kesselbaum, her former therapist and Marylou's mother. "Please, spare us your delusions of grandeur. Three people are not going to suffer just to make you happy."

Small towns could be good places. Sometimes. They had their dark side, too. Gwen had taken to rereading her old Shirley Jackson stories about small town life. She'd just about memorized *The Lottery*, and was into her second rereading of *We Have Always Lived in the Castle*.

Stoner hoped it wasn't a bad sign.

Stoner's own home town of King's Grant, Rhode Island, had certainly been an uncomfortable place. One of those self-consciously quaint New England villages with a village green surrounded by Colonial houses. King's Grant had about it the odor of money and pretense. It prided itself on its authenticity as a genuine eighteenth-century town, though, Stoner thought, if they were really going to be authentic, they should stop bathing and get rid of the electricity.

There were no malls or shopping centers in King's Grant. Even speaking the words was taboo. If the residents couldn't get what they wanted at the local grocery, they went "out of town," usually under cover of darkness, to the Super Stop and Shop outside Westerly. Westerly was also pretentious, but Twentieth Century enough to have a shopping mall.

Gwen had grown up in a small town, too, in Georgia. She seldom talked about it. Or about her childhood at all, as a matter of fact. All Stoner knew, really, was that her father had been abusive and her mother vain. Her brother had run away from home. Both parents were killed in a plane crash when Gwen was fourteen, and she had come to Boston to live with her grandmother. She and her grandmother had parted company when Gwen fell in love with Stoner and declared herself a woman-loving-woman. That had been more than five years ago, and Gwen hadn't heard from her since. Gwen claimed that Jefferson, Georgia, was the dullest place on the face of the earth. The only excitement there were the Klan's annual march through town, and the summer picnic sponsored by the motorcycle plant in the next county, where most of the Jefferson residents worked. She hadn't missed Jefferson a-tall.

Shelburne Falls wasn't Jefferson or King's Grant. It was hard to say exactly what it was, actually. In summer, the locals claimed, as soon as the schools let out, it would be jammed with tourists (for the glacial potholes and the Bridge of Flowers, of course) and hikers exploring the state forests around the Mohawk Trail. In fall it would be infested with hunters, and the gun and liquor stores would do enough business to get them through the winter. The citizens tended to look the other way when the hunters were in town.

Beneath its average-small-town exterior, Shelburne Falls had a whole other life. It was a haven for artists and craftspersons, a dinky little place where you could pick up a museum-quality painting from the original painter herself. Most of the artisans displayed their work at the Salmon Falls marketplace. This was an old wood building that seemed to have once been a depot for the Maine Central railroad, as a track and siding ran directly behind the store. There'd been talk about converting the old railroad yard into a skateboarding park. There was also the hope that the railroad business would pick up, and the yard would return to its former glory. A dream, Ethel who ran the Trolley Stop had told her, that Shelburne Fallers had been dreaming since the last century.

The basement floor of the marketplace was occupied by Turquoise, a store selling clothing, jewelry, books, incense, crystals, and various bits of New Age paraphernalia. It was owned and run by Diana, a trance channel who would "tune in to Spirit," and help you with any problem from life-and-death decisions to suggestions for gifts. Diana had been a tax accountant before she came into her powers—or whatever one did with powers. Stoner liked her, but felt a little uneasy around her, as Diana shared Aunt Hermione's view that Stoner was psychic and heading for trouble if she didn't do something about it.

Diana knew what she was talking about. She had, she said, "been tortured in mind and body, and brought to the doorway of death" before she accepted her psychic destiny.

Psychics, witches, pagans, and various alternative healers made up the other major group of citizens. You could take your pick of astrologers, clairvoyants, herbalists, massage therapists, Reiki practitioners, homeopathic physicians and veterinarians, Bach flowers specialists, aroma-therapists, Ayurvedic consultants—the list was endless. If you were looking for a new type of healing that wasn't in the local directory, you sent out the word and within forty-eight hours someone would surface who had what you needed.

Stoner wasn't alone in suspecting that, while most were sincere and dedicated, a few of these well-meaning souls added to their "specialties" with little more than a one-day workshop or an evening with a book-on-tape. This was, after all, America. Anything goes, as long as you make a buck and don't bend the letter of the law. If you were considering a certain kind of service, and you didn't know the practitioner personally, you simply stopped around at Turquoise and asked Diana. In Shelburne Falls, your reputation rested firmly in Diana's hands.

She hadn't seen any sign of a psychic lawyer yet, but she was certain there was one just around the corner. Channeling the spirit of Justice Learned Hand, no doubt. Or Clarence Darrow.

Interesting, she thought as she turned the corner onto Main Street. There aren't very many dead lawyers you'd want to channel. Among the living, lawyers were divided into two groups: those with ethics, and those who won. The Winners went into television and the Ethicals went into the Government, where they were quickly corrupted and became Winners.

Well, she thought, we are certainly in a lovely mood to start the day.

Passing the Trolley Stop Tavern, she exchanged waves with Ethel through the dusty window. Ethel was long past retirement age, but she kept the former coffee shop open even after her husband died. Townspeople still called it the coffee shop, the only coffee shop in the area, even though Ethel had acquired a partial liquor license and had laid in a supply of beer and wine. How she had gotten the license was open to much speculation and gossip, as it was well known that there were no more liquor licenses available for Shelburne Falls. But, as Ethel was fond of saying, in her enigmatic way, "There are more than two ways to skin a cat."

Why she had gone out of her way for the license was less puzzling. Shelburne Falls, like many towns in Massachusetts, had passed a "no smoking in restaurants" ordinance. Smoking was, however, permitted in bars. So Ethel stocked up on the beer, closed down for a week, and reopened as the "Trolley Stop Tavern." That's what the official papers filed in town hall said, anyway. Ethel never got around to putting up a new sign, and the alcoholic beverages that made it possible for her customers to hover over their coffee cups in billows of smoke and destroy their lives gathered dust and cigarette grease.

Ethel's regulars were an unhappy lot, the kind you expect to find in a cramped little store whose windows are opaque with grime and walls covered with the crisp remains of mummified insects. Seedy old coots with ragged shirts and three-day beards, they were all over seventy, and all retired—though they were hard put to tell you what they were retired from. "Retired from resting," Ethel was likely to say. They'd all been in The War, more or less. Some of the stories seemed to change with the retelling, and sometimes Ed would tell Malvern's stories as though they were his own. They all had aches and pains, despised young people, and had no women in their lives.

"Which should come as no surprise," Ethel said. "What self-respecting women would put up with them?"

Stoner had asked her once why she kept the Trolley Stop open. She didn't need the money or the work. Her kids were grown, her husband dead. Her daughter wanted her to come live with them in South Carolina. Said it would do her good to close the door right in the faces of those smelly, useless old sinners and find out what it was like to be around people who weren't mad at God.

"I don't know," Ethel said pensively. "Doesn't seem right. And where'd they go in the winter?"

Aunt Hermione suggested that Ethel's regulars might really be angels disguised as old coots, and Ethel knew what her path was, whether she knew she knew it or not.

The door to the travel agency closed behind her with a tinny jingle. She looked back. A small bell of tarnished metal hung over the lintel, where the door would strike it opening or closing.

"Cute," she said.

"Like it?" Marylou asked eagerly. "I picked it up this morning. At that antique barn on the Colrain Road."

"Well, nobody can sneak up on us now." She hung her pocket book over the coat tree and motioned to Marylou to surrender the desk.

Her partner laughed. "Stoner, no one could possibly sneak up on us. We have an 8 by 12 storefront in a defunct laundromat, one door, and windows that let us see everyone on the street, and everyone on the street see us."

"So why the bell?" She shoved the book she had brought along into the desk drawer and switched her running shoes for loafers.

11

"For the tourists. To give the place an air of authenticity. You know, old colonial country store and all that."

"Marylou." She shook her head at her affectionately. "In the first place, I doubt they had travel agencies in colonial times. And second, tourists are already where they want to be when they get here."

Marylou grunted. "We could offer some kind of special trip thing. Like charter bus tours of the local haunted houses."

"Are there any local haunted houses?"

"This is Massachusetts! Of course there are haunted houses!"

Suddenly serious, Stoner looked at her. "Are we in trouble? Financially?"

"Not yet. But it's time to think of a gimmick."

It had been a little frightening at first, agreeing that Marylou would handle the business accounts. Marylou went through life like a roller-coaster at high speed. The ups were exhilarating, and the downs were heart-stopping. It all averaged out to anxiety.

But the fact of the matter was, Marylou knew where she was going, and never jumped the track.

Besides, Stoner lived in nearly-irrational terror of official business with the Government. Like taxes. She was certain she'd make a terrible mistake and spend the rest of her days in the Women's Prison in Framingham. It was enough to make her mind go blank whenever important-looking letters arrived at the agency.

Marylou took a different view of it all. If they made a mistake, she assured Stoner, the Government would rather get the money owed them than spend taxpayer dollars feeding and clothing a pair of travel agents. Marylou felt about tax inspectors the way Stoner felt about cats—they were strange, kind of cute, and perfectly harmless if you didn't play too rough.

Face it, Marylou knew how to deal with men in general. As far as she was concerned, aging hippy or IRS, they were all alike under the skin.

"What do you think?" Marylou asked. She opened her change purse and began counting coins to see if she had enough to stop by McCusker's for a treat. "Should we do it or not?"

"Do what?"

"Sponsor the women's softball team?"

"What women's softball team?"

Marylou emptied her wallet on the desk in front of Stoner and poked in the corners with one finger. "There isn't any women's softball team. Not unless we sponsor them. Or they find someone else. The only other offer they have is from the taxidermist, and they don't feel comfortable about that."

Stoner shoved her hands through her hair. "I never even heard of any women's softball team around here."

"Well, you've certainly seen them. The baby dykes who hang out across the street waiting to catch a glimpse of you."

She blushed deeply. "I don't know what you're talking about."

"Sure, you do." Marylou gestured toward the window. "They hover over by the post office."

Yes, she had noticed them. A rough-and-tumble bunch, in their early twenties for the most part. They lounged around on the post office lawn in shorts and sleeveless tee-shirts, looking peppy and eager, and jostling one another with their elbows.

"That has nothing to do with me," she said. "It's just where they congregate."

Marylou shook her head as if Stoner were too impossible to be believed. "If you were here in the morning, you'd see them flutter in and perch, one by one, when it gets toward noon. It's like a scene out of *The Birds*."

"They're on their lunch hour. That's where they spend it. Across the street..."

"From our agency," Marylou interrupted and finished for her. She got her pocket book and dumped the contents onto the desk top and stirred through them. Life savers, lip gloss, mascara, a small notebook. Sunglasses case, empty. Appointment book, out of date. Three ball point pens stolen from motel rooms, one without a cap. A pack of condoms. Shredded tissues. The receipt from a bank transaction...

"For God's sake, here." Stoner got out her wallet and offered her money. "Take what you need."

Marylou looked over the selection of bills and chose a five. "That should do it. Unless you want something from the store?"

"I'm fine. Are you going to tell me about the softball team?"

"Oh, right." Marylou swept her life's detritus back into her pocketbook and settled one hip comfortably on the desk. "They want to start a softball team. Feminist, as we used to say without fear of offending. Noncompetitive, everyone gets to play, just to have a good time. They can join the women's league out of Northampton if they have a sponsor."

"And what does that involve, being a sponsor?"

"Pay for their tee-shirts, go to a couple of games." She shrugged. "Mother them, I guess."

Stoner laughed and rolled her eyes. "I can see you mothering a softball team."

Marylou tilted her chin as if insulted. "I can do that. You ask how they're doing, bring cookies to the games and 'tut-tut' if one of them gets hurt."

"Yeah," Stoner said. "It'll be the only team in the league with cookies made with Godiva chocolate."

"And what's wrong with that?"

"Unless times have changed, at least half of them probably don't even eat sugar. Much less exotic chocolate."

Marylou jangled her silver bracelets, a definite sign she was about to make her discussion-ending point. "It would be advertising, Stoner. We need to do things that'll get us known around the area. The softball team would be perfect." She moved in for the kill. "Think of all the women who go to those games. And every one of them would think of Kesselbaum and McTavish first when they need a travel agent."

There was no disputing that.

"You realize we might become identified as a lesbian travel agency," Stoner pointed out. "How does that sit with you?"

"Not a problem for me. Is it one for you?"

"Why would it be?"

"I could be a problem, not being one of the tribe. Unless you want to make me honorary."

Stoner grinned. "We could present you as my assistant in het-as-a-second-language."

"You might need a straight consultant from time to time, Marylou said, serious and musing. "We could make me vice president in change of non-alternative lifestyles. Of course," she went on slyly, "we can scrap the whole idea and continue with the Chamber of Commerce and Rotary Club luncheon talks. I've run out of slide shows, incidentally. You'll have to come up with something for the June meetings."

Stoner covered her head with her hands. "All right, all right. We'll do the softball team."

"Great." Marylou gathered up her things and went to the door. "You won't regret this."

"Famous last words."

Stoner watched as she crossed the street and said a few words to the baby dykes. They were clearly waiting to hear from her, and excited. She wondered how many meetings there had been between them and Marylou before Marylou had just "happened" to mention it to her.

My God, she thought as their very own lesbian softball team surged across the street toward her, now what have we gotten ourselves into?

If the child weren't such a worrier…

Hermione mentally gave herself a slap on the wrist. Stoner wasn't a child. Hadn't been for a number of years, if she ever had been. Sometimes it seemed her niece had been born grown up. Not all that unusual for an only child, of course. But in Stoner's case it was complicated by parents who were…well, to be perfectly honest about it…as loving and warm as rocks. In addition to her many talents, Helen, Hermione's sister to her great dismay, was a snob, a social-climber, and a label-peeper. Dishes, coats, blouses, shoes, you name it. Helen could always find a way to get a peek at the label.

It was one of the joys of Hermione's life to catch her at it. "Sister, dear," she used to say, "anyone with real taste would know what brand it was without having to look at the label."

Helen would claim she found that ridiculous, and usually said something lame like, "What would you know, you gypsy?"

Which was true, but definitely not a term of endearment on Helen's lips. Hermione had been a gypsy several times. Not surprising, considering she had been psychic for as far back as she could remember. Italy, Rumania, Bulgaria, Hungary, even the Isles of Britain. Sometimes male, sometimes female. Many lifetimes, in quick succession. She'd enjoyed those lives, what she could recall of them. They were hard, short lives, but filled with passion. Lust, rage, love, revenge, fury…each with its own color and taste. Rage was red and sharp as peppers. Fury was black and oily. Love was the blue of robins' eggs, and bore the taste of almonds. Lust burned with orange flames, and smelled like hunger. But revenge, that was the most complex. Revenge was mercury, silver-gray, taking shape to fit the container, impossible to catch and hold. Always in motion, changing, but mercury never the less.

She'd never lived so vividly as when she was a Gypsy. But it was exhausting, which was probably why those lives were short.

Hermione was a sort of gypsy even now, if by "gypsy" you meant a free spirit who was never very impressed with the kinds of things most people are impressed with. And who didn't give a damn about their opinion of her.

It was all those hundreds of lifetimes, she often thought. After a few turns on the karmic carousel, all that hoopla over things and status took on a very false ring. She couldn't remember exactly in which lifetime it had happened to her. In the pre-Christian Roman one, maybe. Or when she served in the court of the Empress of China, who, she was firmly convinced, was now her sister Helen in another incarnation.

The Empress had been a thoroughly nasty, bloodthirsty individual with well-developed and famous sadistic appetites. By comparison, Helen had come a long way. But she was no Mother Teresa.

At least the Empress had had the good grace to give away her children. Helen preferred to drive hers away.

The only time Hermione had ever seen Stoner be a child was that morning when she had opened the door to find her sixteen-year-old niece huddled on the step of her Boston brownstone, tired, dirty, hungry, eyes deep with anxiety.

"Please don't make me go back," was all she'd said, and Hermione fell into a case of mother-love from which she'd never recovered.

Stoner's child phase had lasted only one day. By the next evening she had made arrangements to finish high school and applied for early admission to B.U., and had found herself a part-time job. She insisted she had no intention of grubbing, and wanted to do her share toward expenses.

It was the lesbian business, of course. Helen had—not quite accidentally—found Stoner's journal and read it. In it, she expressed some rather charming feelings toward a particular teacher—social studies, if she recalled correctly—who was clearly female. That threw Helen into a state, and whatever nasty and hurtful things she hadn't already said to her daughter, she said to her now. Stoner had borne it for a few weeks, but finally couldn't take it any more and had run to the one member of the family she could trust—her Aunt Hermione.

It was, Hermione thought, the best and luckiest day of her own personal life.

She blew out the candle and folded the fringed table cloth she used for her readings. She was wandering again. Marylou's mother, 'the eminent Dr. Edith Kesselbaum' as they called her affectionately, would pronounce her "loose and tangential." But it was an occupational hazard. She had to follow her thoughts wherever they led, because that was where intuition lay.

The trouble was, lately she was having trouble thinking in a straight line when she needed to. And she was forgetful, and clumsy. A chronic state of PMS, except that she had passed far beyond the point where PMS was a possibility, and hadn't been bothered by it much when she was of the age. It felt a little like being in a fog, where you didn't notice things until they were on top of you, and then they scared you half to death.

She supposed it would pass, but until she was certain it wouldn't, she wasn't going to worry Stoner with it. It would turn out to be some seasonal ailment, an allergy, perhaps. She wished she could remember her herbology from her lifetime as Blue Mary the healer, but some of them didn't stick as well as others, and herbs had been her bugaboo of record from her current life.

If they all knew how she was feeling, they'd probably start treating her like an old person. Raising their voices and speaking in simple sentences and fetching and carrying.

Hermione Moore had no intention of being fetched and carried for as long as she could assume a vertical position.

The worst part of being treated like an old person, she thought, was the loneliness. She'd had friends who aged, and clients. Loneliness was the one thing they had in common. "It's not that I'm neglected," Laura, a Virgo, had told her (and if there was anyone who would know when they were being neglected, it was a Virgo), "but they treat me as if I were a chapter in a book on how to handle your aging parents. It's all 'old people need this,' and 'old people like that.' They never ask you what you need. If it's not in the book, you don't need it."

Laura was living in Boston with her daughter at the time. Hermione advised her to run away and change her name. The last she heard from Laura was a postcard from Las Vegas. It turned out that she had a previously-undetected knack for remembering numbers, and was doing quite well at the blackjack tables. In fact, one casino had offered her a job as a dealer, just to get her on their side. It wasn't exactly what Hermione had in mind, but it was an improvement.

She heard the back screen door slam, and smiled. That would be Marylou, coming in the back so as not to disturb her, then letting the screen door slam.

"Marylou," she called, glad to be brought out of her own rambling, "would you like some tea?"

Chapter 2

"They probably don't even know who Lucy B. Stone is," Stoner said.

"But they know who you are," Marylou insisted.

Stoner laughed. "All fourteen of them know me. And a few close friends. Not exactly name recognition."

What in the world were they talking about?

Hermione patted her mouth with her napkin and arranged the knife she hadn't needed so its handle was exactly perpendicular to the table edge. She must have drifted again. A minute ago they'd been talking about...about... Damn, what had they been talking about? They'd discussed the weather, the tourists who were beginning to filter into town, Gwen's job, and...what?

She couldn't remember eating, either, but her plate was clean. She remembered cooking, but not what she'd cooked.

"What do you think, Aunt Hermione?" Stoner asked.

Oh, dear. "I think," she said, covering, "it would be a risky idea. But if you really want to do it..."

They all looked at her.

She felt herself go pale.

"It was your idea," Marylou said.

"Well, that's true. But it was only an idea, after all. Not a requirement."

Gwen was watching her in that quiet, concerned way she had. Seeing through her. Gwyneth was all too good at seeing through people.

"I have to agree with Stoner," Gwen said. "Most of these kids wouldn't know who Lucy B. Stone was, much less want to name their team after her."

Ah! "It was a good enough name for my niece," she said. It ought to be good enough for a softball team." She put a touch of crotchety into her voice and sniffed a little. Maybe they'd think she'd drifted away on a cloud of despair for the younger and definitely unpolitical generation. "But it seemed like a good idea at the time," she added with a rueful smile. "Too bad the time was nearly forty years ago. Though, as I recall, nobody knew who Lucy B. Stone was then, either, at first." She touched Stoner's hand. "Just think, dear, I named you for a shadowy historical figure."

"Better a shadowy one than a shady one," Stoner said, returning her touch. "Besides, by the time I was old enough to care about who I was named for, we were in the middle of the Women's Movement, and everyone knew who she was."

Hermione let her mind drift to those sweet days, when they were raging feminists together, Stoner the teenager and her middle-aged aunt. They went everywhere, to rallies and conventions and sit-ins and pot-lucks and candlelight vigils, "Take Back the Night" marches, and side trips to protest nuclear power. Washington, Miami Beach, Wall Street, Atlantic City—and Boston, of course, picketing movie theaters and other dens of sexism. The two generations of "libbers," glorying in the unexpected delight of being women.

It wasn't an insult then, to be called a "libber" or a "bra burner." You could say "feminist" without apologizing or explaining what you meant. Even the people who didn't agree with you knew you stood for change.

In the '70s, change was needed and change was in the air.

Gwen's life and marriage, for instance, were perfect examples of why they'd needed a Women's Movement. Oppressive traditional father, totally self-centered traditional mother, and an untraditional but sociopathic cad for a husband. Went into teaching because it was a safely "feminine" thing to do. And the grandmother, a Southern Lady who cared only about appearances and—the last Hermione had heard—was drinking herself into oblivion because her granddaughter was a lesbian. Liberation material if she'd ever seen it.

She liked Gwen. Always had. And took a secret pride in her part in bringing her and Stoner together. It had required a little manipulating, but Hermione didn't think she'd incurred a serious karmic stain for throwing a few opportunities in her niece's path.

Gwen was the quietest of them all. Not out of shyness or introversion, but because it was her nature. Her body was quiet, her mind was quiet, and her heart was open. She was content to let things and people—especially people—unfold in front of her. Every new day was a new life to her, and she let her feelings tell her who to trust and who to avoid.

Sometimes she was wrong. She was usually right.

She was like a radio telescope, Hermione thought, waiting for the signal from outer space that might or might not come.

Stoner, on the other hand, was sonar. Constantly sending out 'beeps,' listening for 'pings' to return. Gwen might wander into trouble. Stoner plunged into it with her eyes wide open and checking for the exits. Because it was the right thing to do.

Not many people did things these days simply because they were the right things. Hermione was grateful to be related to someone who did.

"Well," said Marylou as she licked a bit of jelly from her spoon, "I still like my idea."

Gwen smiled. "Of course you do. You always like your own ideas."

"What kind of a no-self-confidence jerk would I be if I didn't?"

"I usually like your ideas, too," Stoner said. "I just wonder if 'Guts and Glory' is the kind of message we want the softball team to send."

"Doesn't sound like a good idea to me," Gwen said. "It sort of makes me think of a plane crash."

"Personally," Hermione ventured, "if you don't think the feminist motif is appropriate, I'd suggest you go with a travel image. Preferably a positive one."

"Yeah," Stoner said and slouched down in her chair. "But what?"

Hermione stroked the stem of her wine glass with one finger. It wore her out, having to play catch-up with the conversation. And filling in the gaps in her memories of her day with activities which sounded plausible and couldn't be checked.

"Confabulating," Edith Kesselbaum would call it.

It was a symptom of a wide range of mental problems, none of them desirable.

Alzheimer's, she thought, and shuddered. There was no way she was about to share a diagnosis with Ronald Reagan.

"Aunt Hermione?"

Stoner was looking at her with that troubled expression.

"Sorry. I was wool-gathering."

"Where were you?"

"Thinking about Ronald Reagan."

"That does it," Marylou said, and flipped her napkin onto the table. "I don't know what you were burning when I came in, but it's reduced your IQ to double digits."

"It was Kali," Stoner said, still looking at her aunt.

"Really?" Gwen asked. She turned to Marylou. "I thought the house smelled like a high school bathroom. Are you sure it wasn't marijuana?"

"Not unless Cutter's ship has come in."

"Does he...?" Stoner began.

"No, he doesn't 'do drugs.' Sometimes he smokes a little, when he can get it. It helps him sleep. His nerves are shot."

Hermione nodded, glad to be on safer ground. "They used to call it 'shellshocked' back in World War II. Somehow that seemed like a more accurate description than this post-traumatic business. When you heard shell-shocked, you knew it was about the war. It put the blame where it belonged."

What were they all thinking? Did she sound rational, or as rambling as she felt? There was no person in this house who needed a lecture on the evils of war.

"Well," she said, dabbing at her mouth again so they wouldn't see the trembling at the corners of her lips, "I, for one, would like to go to a movie. Anyone care to join me?"

"I don't know," Gwen said, "by the time we drive to Greenfield and back it'll be pretty late."

"I was thinking of the show over at Pothole. I believe it's the last one of the season."

Pothole Pictures had been started by a group who wanted to bring movies back to Shelburne Falls. They'd found space in the old Memorial Hall, and showed old and slightly arty films on Thursday and Friday nights. Sometimes the films were followed by a discussion. It was, the locals agreed, a good way to spend the months between half-past hunters and ten minutes to tourists.

"Stoner?" Gwen asked.

"You go on," Stoner said. "I've seen the movie."

"Dear God, it's not *Gone With the Wind*, is it?" Gwen asked in horror.

"*The Maltese Falcon*."

"Everyone's seen that one at least three times," Marylou said. "See it again."

"I don't want to see it again. I hate seeing movies twice."

Marylou raised an eyebrow. "Really? I thought you'd seen *The Sterile Cuckoo* five times."

"That's different."

"She's never seen *The Wizard of Oz*," Hermione offered.

Stoner slouched down further in her chair. "I've seen the previews a dozen times. They're creepy."

"Now that you mention it," Gwen said, "The movie's pretty creepy, too."

"Personally," Hermione said, "I'd love to see *The Maltese Falcon*."

She knew what Stoner had been thinking by the way she glanced at her. Quickly. Irritated. Guilty. She'd been hoping to get her aunt alone to have a talk.

We know each other so well we can read three emotions in one glance.

She wanted to wink at her in their usual conspiratorial, tell-you-later way. But she couldn't let herself do it. Until she knew what this… thing…was, she couldn't risk the intimacy. It would make her fall apart.

"What about it?" she asked them all in general. "I'll buy the popcorn."

"That does it for me," Gwen said. She got up and reached for their dishes. "My turn. I think I'll just heave them out the back door."

"You will not," said Marylou, pushing back her chair to help. "There could be bears out there. We don't need to turn our back yard into a Yellowstone campground." She started making a pile of the plates.

"My grandmother would kill you," Gwen said. "Stacking and carrying."

"Your grandmother," Marylou pronounced, "is something out of a Tennessee Williams play." She pretended to fan herself. "Ah swear ah shall perish, just perish from this heat."

"Go right ahead," Gwen said as she pushed through the swinging door to the kitchen. "Don't start depending on the kindness of strangers. You tried that at Disney World, and look where it got you."

"The ride I was on there," Marylou said as she pursued her through the door, "was a whole lot more exciting than the ride you were on."

So now they were alone in the room together. It was the last thing Hermione wanted. "I think," she said quickly, "Marylou has a short memory for trauma."

"Aunt Hermione…"

She avoided Stoner's eyes. "I recall her complaining heartily about being 'snatched', as she so colorfully put it."

"Aunt Hermione…"

She couldn't take it any more. The hovering, the questioning, her own guilt. "The only thing wrong with me," she snapped, "is that you don't give me a chance to breathe."

She got up, shrugged into her coat, and left the house.

The glass panes in the door rattled behind her slam.

Did it again, damn it.

Stoner tossed the unread newspaper to the floor in disgust. Finishing the dishes hadn't helped. Kicking furniture hadn't helped. Staring at the wall hadn't helped. And the time was creeping along. Still only 8:15 and they wouldn't be home until 10 at the earliest.

You just have to keep pushing and pushing until you go too far, don't you? she berated herself. Never satisfied to wait. Never willing to leave well enough alone. Other people get scared, and they live with it. They don't make fools of themselves and annoy everyone around them.

You need professional help.

She sat up.

Yes! Call the eminent Dr. Edith Kesselbaum. She helped you before, she can do it again.

Stoner picked up the phone and hoped this wasn't Edith's night to work late. She stayed at her office one evening a week, so people who were gainfully employed wouldn't have to take time off every week for their shrink sessions.

It also fit in quite nicely with Max's schedule.

Max was Edith's second husband and a retired FBI agent. Once a week he and his cronies from the "old days" got together to reminisce. Wayne—Edith thought it was the one called Wayne, but it might be Stewart or even Carl—was obsessively unable to let go of a murder he hadn't solved ten years ago when he was working for the Bureau. Still thinking he had missed a vital clue. Still thinking, if he went over it all often enough it might come to him.

There wasn't a Fox Muldur in the bunch. If there were, Edith might have stayed home.

The phone rang three times, and a low, breathy voice said, "Kesselbaum."

Stoner felt better immediately. "Hi, Edith. It's Stoner."

"Stoner! How are you? Is anything wrong? Is it a crisis?"

"Maybe."

"Excellent," Edith said.

Stoner couldn't help smiling. "There's nothing you like better than a crisis, is there?"

"I suppose not," she said thoughtfully. "It's so energizing. Do you think it's a sickness? Do you think I should get help?"

"No, but I think I should."

"Of course. I'm sorry. You called in a maybe crisis. How can I help?"

Stoner took a deep breath, feeling a little guilty and disloyal but desperate. "It's Aunt Hermione," she said.

Edith Kesselbaum waited for her to say more but she didn't so Edith prompted, "Hermione."

"Yeah." She ran one hand through her hair and felt foolish. "There's something wrong with her."

"Is she ill?"

"Yes. Well, no. I'm not sure. She's just not right."

Edith treated her to one of her throaty chuckles. "Nobody in your family's 'just right,' Stoner. I need to hear more."

Now Stoner couldn't help laughing. "If your colleagues could hear you, you'd be kicked out of the American Psychiatric Association."

"I would, wouldn't I? What a dreary bunch. Are you going to tell me the problem, or are we playing Twenty Questions?"

"I don't know what's wrong," Stoner said. "She says she's fine, but she doesn't seem fine. It's as if she's…" She felt herself choke up. "…not really here. Sometimes I think I could almost see through her."

"Oh, dear. That must be terrible for you."

The tears were spilling over now. She let them come. "I'm really scared, Edith, and I don't know what to do. She won't talk to me and I start pushing and tonight she said I wasn't letting her breathe…"

"You probably weren't, Stoner," Edith said very gently. "You know how you get."

For some reason, knowing it was just how she did things, knowing people knew that about her and still cared for her, knowing it was really okay, made her feel better.

"I find it impossible to believe," Edith went on, "that Hermione won't confide in you eventually. She always does."

"I guess," Stoner muttered.

"And we know how Hermione can be, too. Stubborn and self-sufficient, just like you. It's a genetic trait. Do you think we should try an intervention?"

Oh, sure, she could really picture that. All of them clustered around Aunt Hermione, the doors locked, telling her how much they cared about her and how much she was hurting them. And then what? Tough love? Throw her out and don't let her back until she talks?

"I don't think so, thanks," she said.

She could hear Edith jotting something down on the pad of paper she always kept by the phone.

"What are you doing?" Stoner asked.

"Sorry. I was making a list for Max. He's on his way to Burger King." She turned from the phone and made kissing noises and turned back. "My God, I thought he'd never get on his horse. I'm starving. What did you have for dinner?"

Stoner tried to remember. She couldn't. "I don't know. Nothing. Not much. I was too upset."

Dr. Kesselbaum "tsked" a little.

"Don't 'tsk' at me," Stoner said. "You just ordered from Burger King."

"It may not be the healthiest food in the world, but it stays with you. You don't faint if you miss a meal. Unlike the crunchy-granola you health freaks are so fond of."

The thought of them as health freaks was too much for her. She laughed out loud. "The day your daughter goes in for crunchy-granola will be the day after hell freezes over."

"I know," Edith said. "Isn't she lovely?"

"A pity she's straight."

"I've often said that, myself." Edith cleared her throat. "So. My advice to you is, be patient and call me in the morning."

"That's not going to be easy," Stoner said.

"Calling me?"

"Being patient."

"Well, you'll just have to. Do something to take you mind off of it. Have sex."

Stoner was shocked. "Edith!"

"Eat, then."

"All right, I'll eat." She could hear the disappointment in her own voice.

"Go get a Big Mac."

"We don't have that kind of thing in Shelburne Falls. This is rural."

"Stoner, I know what you're feeling. I know you thought I could be more helpful. I can't from here. But if she's not better by Sunday, or you're still feeling desperate, I'll come out there for a few days and beard the lioness in her den—whatever that means. It's nearly summer. My patients expect me to be erratic."

"Thank you," Stoner said. "It's really nice of you."

"Nice, schmice. Does it help?"

"Yes, it does."

"Then that's what matters."

"I'm sorry I get so carried away."

"It's my fault," Edith said. "I should have fixed you better."

Stoner smiled. "You couldn't. It's genetic."

"You're right on the verge of going too far," Gwen said.

"I can't help it, I'm really worried."

Gwen took off her reading glasses and put her book down. "She'll tell you, sooner or later. She always does."

Stoner rammed her hands behind her neck and stared at the ceiling. "It might be too late."

"What do you think's going to happen?"

"I don't know. Something awful."

Gwen pushed herself up on one elbow and looked down at her. "Is this a real intuition, or just a Stoner worry?"

Stoner glanced at her impatiently. "You mean you haven't noticed anything?"

Gwen gave a non-committal look. "Sure, she seems a little off. But I really don't think we're at a crisis..."

"You never do," Stoner groused, "which is why that man almost killed you."

Gwen frowned in puzzlement. "What man?"

"Bryan Oxnard. Your husband."

"My late husband, unless memory deceives me."

"He would've killed you, if I hadn't gotten there..."

Gwen sighed. "Love, we've had this conversation a million times. We both know you go off like a cannon at the first hint of danger..."

"Do not," Stoner interrupted in a mutter.

"And I could be walking down the railroad tracks and wouldn't know a train was coming until it was too late."

"That's right."

"Which is why we need each other." Gwen bent down and kissed her.

Her hair, falling against Stoner's face, felt like the touch of hundreds of daddy longlegs. She shuddered.

"What?" Gwen asked.

"That tickles."

Gwen threw herself back onto her side of the bed. "Okay."

"Okay what?"

"You. You're so jumpy it wears me out just to be around you."

"I'm not doing it on purpose," Stoner pouted.

"Sometimes I just wish you didn't have such a stranglehold on life. Ease up a little."

Stoner felt her temper flare. "Look, if you want to have sex, say so."

Gwen put her pillow over her own face and groaned. "I could kill you when you're like this," she said after a silence.

"Like what?"

"Impossible."

"I don't even know what we're talking about. I'm not sure what I'm talking about, and I sure as hell don't know what you're..."

"Your MOOD!" Gwen said loudly and vehemently, slamming the pillow to the floor. "I'm talking about your lousy mood, which has gone on for days, maybe weeks, maybe I can't even remember a time when you weren't in it."

Stoner made a calming gesture. "Take it easy. You'll wake the whole house."

"So what? I haven't slept in nights, with you tossing and turning and mumbling. Let everyone else have a bad night for a change."

"You know," Stoner said icily, "just once in my life I'd like to be concerned about something and not have everyone tell me how stupid I am for being worried."

"And I," Gwen retorted, "would like to not be concerned, and not have you tell me how stupid I am for not being worried."

She turned on her side, facing away from Gwen. "Good night, then," she said.

Gwen flipped off the light and turned on her side, away from Stoner. "Good night," she said tightly. "I hope you're in better shape in the morning."

I doubt it, Stoner thought. I'll be in worse shape. Something awful is happening with Aunt Hermione, and nobody wants to deal with it but me.

She felt horribly, achingly alone.

Sure, I get carried away sometimes. Sure, things have looked bad and turned out all right in the end. But isn't everyone wrong some of the time?

Shit.

She felt tears crowding behind her eyes.

We have a real crisis on our hands, and all they do is walk around with their heads up their...whatevers.

She drew back and looked at herself. Oh, boy, only seconds away from truly pathetic.

But I need to be worried about, too, sometimes. I try really, really hard to take care of everyone else. No one ever wants to take care of me.

Now that's truly crazy. Gwen tries to take care of me, but I won't let her. I can't let her. I know that. I know it's my fault. But I can't help myself.

That made it worse. She felt trapped, trapped in herself, by herself. There was no way out of that.

Maybe I need to go back into therapy. But not with Edith. Not since I'm business partners with her daughter and live with her daughter and call Edith my friend. Having her for a therapist now would be too...too strange.

But I can't think of anyone else I want to talk to. Not in that say-anything-that-occurs-to-you-and-to-hell-with-what-people-think way.

Therapists aren't supposed to think like other people.

Except that some of them do. Some of them think exactly like other people. Some of them are other people.

I'd probably get one of those cheerful types that talks about "challenges" when you're talking about tragedy.

Maybe Edith would know someone. Stoner couldn't remember her ever talking about another therapist with her particular twist of mind, but then one of the twists Edith's mind took was to be wary of other therapists. "Half of them are still Freudians whether they know it or not," she often said. "Another thirty-five percent are behaviorists, and the rest live in California where their feet don't touch the ground."

"Do you have any idea," Gwen said suddenly, "how oppressive it is to be treated like a ninny?"

"No more oppressive than being treated like a neurotic, impulse-driven adolescent."

"Well, you act like one."

"And you act like a…" She couldn't bring herself to say "ninny." It was too much. "…someone who's never been out of the house."

"Look," Gwen said after a pause, "let's not do this, okay?"

I don't want to do it, Stoner thought. Oh, God, nobody knows how much I don't want to do it.

She didn't dare say anything out loud.

"Tell you what," Gwen went on. "I'll spend some time tomorrow with Aunt Hermione. Just the two of us. Maybe I can get her to open up."

"Why should she open up to you when she won't open up to…"

"Because," Gwen said, and turned over and stroked her shoulder, which made Stoner want to cry, "you go at her like a charging goat…"

"I am a goat," Stoner muttered. "I'm a Capricorn."

"You and Marylou both," Gwen went on, ignoring her. "Maybe if I can just be with her for a while, she might be less self-protective."

"What you're saying," Stoner said, "is that I'm a bully."

"You are," Gwen said softly, squeezing the back of her neck. "Sometimes. When you're worried, or frightened. Especially frightened."

"I think I love you," Stoner said, and turned to face her.

"My, my." Gwen leaned over to run her hand through Stoner's hair. It put her breasts dangerously close to Stoner's face. "What a surprise. I had no idea."

Stoner pulled her down closer and nuzzled her. She smelled like Jergen's lotion, a vanilla/cherry/almond odor out of Stoner's childhood.

They all used the same soap and the same laundry detergent, but only Gwen managed to smell of Jergen's lotion. "Hold me?" she asked. "Please?"

"It would be the greatest pleasure." Gwen slid one arm under her neck...

"Hey, kids."

...and collapsed in a heap on top of her. "Marylou, what the hell do you think you're doing?"

Gwen's body had landed on her just the wrong way. She couldn't breathe.

"Popcorn," Marylou said cheerfully. "Want some?"

"You had some at the movie, for crying out loud."

"It was awful." Stoner could feel Marylou settle herself on the edge of the bed. "I think they got it out of one of those big plastic bags at the supermarket. Maybe at Wal Mart."

It was getting on time to take a breath. She hoped Gwen would decide to move.

"You ate it," Gwen accused.

"I was desperate." She crunched loudly. "And it's not politically correct to waste."

"That was during World War II, when there were starving children in Europe." Gwen moved a little, and then made sounds like taking a handful of popcorn from the bowl.

"Hey," Stoner gasped.

"Is that you in there?" Marylou called.

Gwen slipped off of her, letting in fresh air. "We were just talking."

"Interesting position for a chat," Marylou said, and gave Stoner a salacious wink.

Gwen tossed a piece of popcorn at her.

"So," Marylou said as soon as Stoner had a mouthful of popcorn, "what were you two arguing about?"

Stoner shook her head and said, "Mumph."

"We weren't," Gwen translated. "We were discussing."

Marylou smiled. "I stand corrected," she said pleasantly and without an ounce of sincerity.

"About Aunt Hermione," Stoner said.

"Uh-huh."

"We don't know what's the right thing to do. What do you think?"

Marylou tossed a kernel into the air, caught it in her mouth, and murdered it. "Tonight?" she said. "Go to bed."

She left the room.

"Know what I think?" Gwen asked when they'd finished off the pop-corn.

"What?"

"We should all try to be more like Marylou."

Cutter sat cross-legged on the ground, arms folded across his chest, and watched the lights in the house of the four women. He could see only the bedrooms of the old one and the pair from where he sat, and the bathroom. Not Marylou's, she slept at the front of the house. But that was all right. The ghosts weren't interested in Marylou. Ghosts didn't like people whose lives sparkled in tiny lights around them. Ghosts were afraid of so much life energy.

He hoped it wasn't his fault that the ghosts had come to this house. He'd tried not to show them his interest, but they could read his mind and sometimes good feelings crept in before he could catch them and paint them over. Sometimes the ghosts picked up on that good feeling and it made them hungry.

It had been a long time since he'd felt this particular good feeling, this bit of warmth that settled in the center of his spine. Not since 'Nam. Not since his buddies. That was when the ghosts had found him. That was when his buddies died.

Since 'Nam he felt mostly shame. Shame at the things he'd done, and the things he'd left undone. Shame for the Vietnamese people and his part in their suffering. Shame for his country. Shame that he'd lived.

Shame had become an old friend to him. Not a pleasant friend, but one that could be counted on. That was important. Having something to count on kept you going forward.

The light was still on in the old woman's room. But he could see them, inching their way up the side of the house and around the window. They were growing bolder. Or hungrier.

Cutter watched and waited.

She wasn't going to sleep tonight. That was one thing she was certain of. They'd apologized to one another, "made up" as they used to say. But she knew it was only a truce. She knew Stoner knew it, too. They were both simply too upset and exhausted to argue any more tonight.

Besides, she had enough on her mind. Not that you could really say there was any one thing on her mind for more than a few seconds these days. She'd no sooner get a thought going than it'd disappear into thin air.

Or one thing would lead to another until she couldn't remember where she'd started. And, she noticed, other people were beginning to become just as loose-brained as she, after only a few minutes of conversation with her.

The movie was the thing that capped it. She'd seen *The Maltese Falcon* at least four times, in the original and on television and even at a film festival. But tonight, as she sat in the dark and semi-gray of the theater, not a single image appeared on the screen that she had ever seen before. It had to be *The Maltese Falcon*. It was right up there on the opening credits and on posters both inside and out. And no one mentioned it being a different *Maltese Falcon* From the median middle age of the audience, she knew darned well she wasn't the only person who'd seen this movie before. But she was the only one who thought there was something peculiar about it.

At one point she'd become so bewildered she'd leaned over to Gwen and said, "There's something not quite right about this film. Do you think Ted Turner's gotten his hands on it?"

Gwen shook her head. "It looks like the same one I've seen before on TV. And it's not colorized. Definitely not a Turner operation."

So whatever was wrong with her had wiped her memory cells clean, as completely as if lightning had struck a computer. Trouble was, she didn't know the slightest thing about rebuilding the desktop in her brain.

Hermione sighed and turned off her bedside lamp. Okay, it was time to "get a grip," as the kids said these days. Or was it "get a life?" Well, get something.

She pulled up the blankets and tucked them around her shoulders and gave herself a little pat, just as she always had, as if she were tucking herself in. An odd habit. She had no idea where it had come from. A past life, maybe.

Hermione grunted a little. People were so concerned with their past lives these days, they didn't stop to watch where they were going in this one.

Sometimes lately she found herself wondering about dying. How it would happen, and when. And why so few souls seemed to have that information. Was it something they didn't decide for themselves before coming into life, the way they did about the kinds of lessons and experiences they wanted? Or did they really plan ahead of time but forget?

Well, there were the ones who chose to be born just to prove something about dying. You could tell which ones they were, though. They always had that tentative, slightly appalled look about them. As if they could be contaminated by life if they weren't careful. They didn't engage.

Like Jesus, for example. He knew what he was here for, and he sure didn't engage. Did a lot of good things and a lot of talking, but he never got down and dirty in a relationship. He wasn't about to get himself involved when he knew he was leaving pretty soon.

Jesus was always doing things like that—getting himself born just for the sake of dying and making a point. Like the time he decided to be Socrates. You'd have thought he'd have gotten the picture after that. Fat chance.

He was a stubborn one, too. Once his mind was made up—and that didn't usually take long—you might as well wind him up and watch him go. Try to argue, and he'd just say God had told him to do it, and that was it. Nobody was going to argue with that.

They even had a saying in Spirit, to describe a soul skilled in the art of persuasion. "She could convince Jesus to change his mind."

Rambling again, and turning morbid. Maybe that was what she was going to be from now on. Morbid. Morbid as a dead shoe on the highway.

And sarcastic.

Hermione really hoped she wouldn't end up sarcastic. She'd always hated sarcasm. Thought it was a sign of limited intelligence. Couldn't think of anything clever to say, so you just took what was there and skewed it. Easy.

Not as easy as contemporary street language, though. You didn't need a thesaurus to express yourself these days. Just sincerity.

Her heart was beginning to annoy her with its pounding. Thinking wasn't making her sleepy, just stirring her up.

And when she tried not to think, she could hear that irritating high-pitched hum in her ears. It reminded her of electricity saying, "Rice."

Turn your attention outward, she told herself firmly.

She listened in the darkness, sorting and classifying all the outside night sounds.

And made a mental note to ask Stoner to see what she could do about that tree branch that had recently started scraping the house just under her back window.

Chapter 3

He seemed like a nice young man. A nice, very young man.

She took another peek at the diplomas on his waiting room walls. According to her calculations, he'd been practicing medicine for nearly twenty years, which was impossible from the looks of him. Either he'd been a child prodigy and graduated from medical school at the age of twelve, or he was an impostor. Or Doogie Howser, M.D.

She hadn't heard much about Doogie in quite some time, not since the show went off the air. He had shown up in a few made-for-TV movies but, judging by his behavior in those, he had certainly taken the left-hand path. The result of too much responsibility too young, no doubt.

She hoped that wouldn't be the case with Travis Kolek.

He'd come out of his inner sanctum a few minutes ago to collect his phone messages, and had scampered away as if he didn't see her.

The receptionist, as thin, young, and peppy as a Barbie doll, assured her, "Doctor hasn't forgotten you. He'll be with you in a minute."

She hated that "Doctor this," and "Doctor that" business. It always sounded breathy and awe-filled. Why not refer to him as "Dr. Kolek?" Or "Travis?" Or "Dr. Travis?" Or "Doogie?"

The receptionist—Hermione saw by the name plate on her desk that her name was Jill, nothing else, just Jill, nobody was anything but their first names these days, as if they lived in a sorority house instead of a society of hundreds of millions, it struck her as rude—stood and stuffed a few files into the cabinet, then approached her in a briskly efficient manner.

"Suppose we get you ready while we're waiting."

"Thank you," Hermione said in a coolly dignified voice, "but I think I can get myself ready, if you'll tell me what to do."

Jill smiled at her a little twitchily and held open a door to an examining room. She stood aside. "You'll find a gown there on the table. Strip completely, and put it on with the opening in the back." She hesitated at the look of horror on Hermione's face. "Naturally," she added quickly, "you may keep your panties on if you prefer."

"You're very kind," Hermione said as sweetly as she could. More sweetly, actually. More sweetly than anyone could. Much too sweetly.

The receptionist caught the implied threat of an imminent eruption in that sweetness. She edged toward the door, her peppiness fading fast. "If you need any help, just press that little button over there, and I'll be right here."

"Splendid," Hermione said to the closing door, and went to put her purse and coat on an empty straight-backed chair.

She hated these first meetings with new male physicians, she thought as she settled into the only other chair in the room. They weren't so much consultations as territorial pissing-on-the-fence-posts disputes. What are your rules, what are my rules, who makes the rules and how far can we push against them...?

The problem with male physicians was, they didn't seem to realize there was a struggle going on. They didn't know their patients had rules, and if they knew they didn't care. Patients knew doctors had rules, and they themselves had rules, but they didn't dare express them. That was how it was supposed to be played. That was the first rule.

When the patient refused to play by the rules, thereby pointing out that there were, indeed, rules, it could get very interesting.

Hermione took a book from her purse and opened it and waited. She read one chapter and started another.

When she heard his footsteps—or the flapping of Doctor's angelic wings, Jill might say—she eased a serene smile onto her face.

Doogie popped his head in, and blushed. "I'm sorry," he said. "I didn't know you weren't ready."

Hermione waved him inside. "Don't be embarrassed, young man. I'm perfectly ready."

He glanced at the unused hospital gown, then at fully clad Hermione. Then at the lack of a proper chair for himself to sit in. He said, "Uh..."

"When I was growing up," she responded pleasantly, "I was taught to keep my clothes on in front of someone to whom I hadn't been properly introduced. Especially a male someone."

He struggled with his rules for a moment, and then threw back his head and laughed. "You're absolutely right." He held out his hand. "Travis Kolek, M.D., at your service."

She took his hand and shook it firmly. "Hermione Moore. I'm pleased to make your acquaintance."

"Thank you," he said, "I look forward to being pleased to make yours." He pulled a stool from under the examining table and sat in front of her. "Now, then, what can I do for you?"

It wasn't a terrible way to spend an afternoon, as visits to doctors' offices go. Young Doctor Kolek took time to explain what he was doing. Did all the necessary but simple things—like drawing blood and taking blood pressure and pulse—himself, a rare thing these days. And seemed happy to chat.

Probably doesn't have many patients, Hermione thought. That didn't bode well. Still, she couldn't help liking him.

They joked around about birth control. He said, delicately, he assumed it was no longer an issue, as she had moved on from the risky, fertile years. She told him it hadn't been an issue in decades, that she had learned she preferred the one truly safe method. She only slept with women.

He didn't bat an eyelash.

During the taking of blood, she diverted herself by accusing him of practicing medicine without proper training, on account of his youth. Bought his M.D., no doubt, she said.

He replied if he'd known such a thing was possible, he wouldn't have wasted all that time and anxiety in school.

She remarked, if he had indeed earned his degree in the usual way, they were certainly making doctors young these days.

He replied he hadn't noticed, but didn't the police look terribly young all of a sudden.

She said just wait, the next to be young were lawyers, and then he'd get to thinking the same thing about doctors.

"And politicians," he said as he neatly labeled another vial of her blood and propped it in a beaker. "One day you look up and think, 'My God, those babies are making decisions about my life.' Keep that gauze where I put it and don't fiddle."

"Sorry." She bent her elbow again. "If you're between police and politicians, you certainly must have robbed the cradle when you married."

"Jill looks younger than most people her age."

"Aerobics and granola?"

"It runs in her family."

"She looks like teenager."

"Thirty-one." He made a note in her chart, and noticed her peering at him suspiciously. "I'm writing down the date and time I took the blood sample." He held out the clip board. "No secrets. Want to see it?"

Hermione shook her head. "You must think I'm paranoid."

"No," he said, "I am. Who knows what you'll jump on me about next."

That pleased her. "Am I that intimidating?"

Travis smiled a little. "Just very, very particular."

They were so easy together, they must have known each other in the past. But she had no sense of having met him before. That was sort of unusual, since she was one of the souls who liked to remember old friends and enemies. She couldn't remember them all, of course. There must be thousands. If she remembered them all, she'd never get the grocery shopping done—stopping every two minutes to chat and reminisce, "remember the time we…where was that, Crete?…no, Alexandria, in the library, before the fire…"

And there were those she'd just as soon not recognize. Like the bleached blonde from the Barbary Coast. Little Miss Ruin Your Life and Skip Away Humming and Whistling and Pretending Nothing Happened, while you were left behind to try to put it back together again.

She supposed one of these lifetimes she'd have to work things out with that one. Not that she was sure she wanted to. But it was considered the thing to do. Not a rule, but good manners. She sensed Jesus' hand in that. Sometimes she suspected that Jesus had incarnated as Emily Post, he could be such a fanatic about manners.

Some of the souls on the Other Side—as they called Spirit when they visited material form, because they couldn't think of anything else to call it that most incarnates could pronounce and understand, and Spirit was too indefinite, incarnates were always wanting to define it—though once in a while a soul would come up with an exotic sounding name and plant it in some channel's ear just to see how fast it spread. Some of the souls thought Hermione was out of her mind to want to carry around memories of past lives. And sometimes she had her doubts, too. Particularly when she ran into someone she'd loved and was so glad to see, and they didn't remember her at all. That hurt. It was hard to keep her balance then.

Her memories weren't complete, though. Sometimes they were nothing but an intense feeling, repulsion or attraction. Sometimes she'd meet a new person, and the knowing was so deep and clear, she wanted to pull that person aside and warn her, "You shouldn't go around in public with no skin. They'll kill you." Later she'd realize it wasn't that at all, it was because she'd known her before.

Sometimes they were quite precise. Sometimes she could almost predict what that person was going to say next, as if they'd been together not only yesterday but all the days between then and now. Assuming there was a "then" and a "now," which only seemed to be true at a certain evolutionary level...

"Mrs. Moore?"

Hermione jolted out of her train of thought. If you could call it a train. More like a shotgun blast. "It's happening right now. That thing with the thoughts."

"Excellent. You can describe it?"

"I'll try. First I was thinking about...about...something about you, I think." She frowned with the effort.

"Relax," Travis said. "Let your mind go slippery. It'll come to you."

"That's the trouble. My mind is slippery. Like a nest of eels." Maybe if she started at the end and worked her way back to the beginning...

Absolutely nothing came to her.

He must have noticed the look of distress on her face. "Can't get it back?" he asked.

She shook her head.

He looked through her chart for the fifteenth time. "I don't know what to tell you. I've given you every quick-and-dirty neurological test I can, and nothing fits a pattern."

"Try Alzheimer's," she said softly.

"Nope. Far as I can see, you don't have Alzheimer's. Or Old Timers', either. Do you ever find yourself sitting around longing for the good old days?"

That made her laugh out loud. If she ever got sentimental over the days gone by...well, she could come up with a lot of days gone by. "Hardly."

"What's so funny?" he asked.

"It's too complicated."

He shrugged and said, "Well," and looked at the blank back of the chart as if he might find inspiration there.

Hermione was reminded of her third grade school teacher, who would ask a question and–if anyone gazed at the ceiling while thinking–loved to say, smugly, "The answer's not up there."

Ah, yes, she could remember her primary school teachers, all right. She just couldn't remember what she had for lunch.

If the problem was with her short-term memory, she ought to know what she had for lunch last month.

But she couldn't remember last month at all.

"Are you worried about anything?" he asked. "Other than your memory?"

"My niece, a little."

That perked him up. "Tell me what about?"

"Because she's too worried about me. She always has been. We've lived together since she was sixteen. She thought I was about to die of old age then, and she still does. Though she does admit she was wrong back then."

"Tell her I said to stop worrying. You'll probably outlive her."

"I probably will."

"Her worry's perfectly understandable, of course."

She felt a moment of anxiety. What wasn't he telling her? "Would you care to explain that?"

"It's what they do," he said. "I have an aunt who can out-think all of us, and will probably outlive us all. It's only natural that I'd worry about her. It's our job."

Hermione smiled. "How old is your aunt?"

"Eighty-three and still living independently."

"Ah. Married?"

"Never."

"Lesbian?"

"Could be. I never thought about it."

"That explains it, then," Hermione said. "Men wear you down."

"I have the feeling," Travis said, "I'd better not respond to that. Are you living together now, you and your niece?"

Hermione nodded. "And with her lover, Gwen, and Marylou, her business partner. They've been friends for years. Stoner and Marylou. Marylou's mother was Stoner's therapist. It was sort of like the blind leading the blind, to tell you the truth. But they had fun."

"Stoner and Marylou?"

"Stoner and Edith. They were a perfect pair: one with her head in the clouds, one riveted to the ground."

"I take it the therapist..."

"Edith."

"...was the riveted one."

"No, my niece. She's a Capricorn, after all. I don't think there's a sign for what Edith is. Probably a touch of Pisces, definitely some Gemini, and a large helping of Taurus. Good Goddess, her appetites."

He laughed and said, "You know some interesting people."

"I should hope so. Where I come from, the biggest sin you can commit is to be boring." She stopped short of telling him that, being out of body, it was about the only sin you could commit.

"Would you like me to have a talk with your niece? Stoner, is it? Maybe I could reassure her."

"How? You haven't reassured me."

He scratched his head. "Maybe we'll know more when we get the test results. But, frankly, I doubt it."

So do I, Hermione thought. Whatever's wrong with me, I don't think we're ever going to find out what it is. I'll spend the rest of my life with Creeping Uselessness until they put me away. Which, knowing Stoner, will be a long time after they should.

The worst thing she could think of would be to be kept around out of a sense of duty or guilt—or even love—until she became such a pain in the ass they forgot the person she'd been and could only remember her as pathetic and burdensome.

"Hello?" Travis said.

Hermione felt herself redden. "Sorry. I was wool-gathering again."

"Do you often go off like that?"

She nodded. "Often. And I can't seem to control it."

He tapped the eraser end of his pencil against her chart. "How would you feel about a referral for a complete neurological work-up?"

"I didn't know that was the sort of thing you were supposed to have feelings about," she said defensively.

"I don't have dire expectations," he said quickly. "But a woman with your level of health…"

"At my age," she interrupted.

"At any age. I wish I were as healthy as you at my age."

"Flattery," Hermione said, "will get you everywhere."

"Seriously, Mrs. Moore…"

"Oh, please. My ex-husband was a fool and a ne'er-do-well. If I'd known strangers were going to connect me to him for the rest of my life, I'd have opened a vein before I ever married him. Ms. Moore will do. 'Hermione' will do even better." She stared him straight in the eye. "Especially since you've spent the better part of the afternoon peering at and into me."

As she'd expected, he was struck dumb with embarrassment.

"I wasn't married long," Hermione said as she slipped into her coat. She was pleased to see he didn't jump up to help her as if she were feeble and had lost track of her arms. "Young and foolish. BWM."

He looked at her questioningly.

"Before Women's Movement."

"My aunt talks about those times with great fondness."

Hermione picked up her hand bag. "It probably wasn't as much fun as we remember. I recall having the compost scared out of me more than once. But it was a lot more fun than the War Between the…" She caught herself. "Well, most things I can think of."

"I have something to tell you," Aunt Hermione said a few days later over after-dinner coffee. "I went to a doctor and there's not a thing wrong with me. The blood tests came back today, everything normal."

Stoner looked around the room. Gwen and Marylou were smiling as if they'd just heard good news. Aunt Hermione seemed pleased with herself. My God, Stoner thought. Don't they realize this is worse than finding something? She still looks awful, and they don't know why?

"What kind of doctor?" Stoner asked. "A real doctor, or one of those New Age types that sniff your navel and charge you two hundred dollars?"

Her aunt turned to her. "A real doctor," she said in a voice so calm it hurt, "the kind that refers you to someone else, who performs unnecessary and life-threatening tests, and charges you two thousand dollars. He referred me to a neurologist."

"A neurologist? You say there's nothing wrong and he's sending you to a neurologist? They don't send people to neurologists for nothing."

"Actually, he's sending me to one for about six hundred dollars."

Stoner gripped the edge of her chair and tried not to scream. She forced herself to lower her voice to something close to her normal range. "He must have given you a reason."

"The reason was, he couldn't think of anything else to do."

"I don't believe you," Stoner said in a tone of finality and dismissal. "People don't do that sort of thing."

Aunt Hermione stared at her defiantly. "That's what they said when Hedda Gabler shot herself."

"Oh, please," Gwen said. "Will y'all just let it go for once?"

Uh-oh. When Gwen said "y'all" it was a warning that something truly unpleasant could very easily happen.

It was grocery shopping night. Tuesday. Stoner's turn. She was just as glad to be getting out of there. Even glad for Marylou's company. It would keep her mind off of things. And she couldn't nag Aunt Hermione if she wasn't even in the same place.

Ever since the Mohawk Trail Big Y World Class Supermarket in Greenfield had gone to twenty-four-hour openings, Marylou had been convinced that homeless people were using it as a shelter. It was perfect. Restrooms, magazines, flowers, and even a halfway decent deli and wine department. With no rent to pay, you could splurge at the deli. She was on a mission to find someone who was living there. Not to make trouble, just to talk with them and ask them what it was like, living in a Super Store. What kinds of people came in? Who was friendly and who was nasty? What clerks had been hired or fired? Were any of them under age and should the management be reported? And, especially, what was the gossip?

Marylou loved gossip. Not in a uncouth or spiteful way, but because it was like reading about someone's life without worrying about the book coming overdue. And you didn't have to listen to the day-to-day grind, the way you would if you made friends with them. You just got the high and low points. It was perfect.

It wasn't safe to trust what she passed along, though. Marylou had a talent for creative embellishment. The story was usually exciting but indistinguishable by the time she was through with it, and she generally forgot who she'd heard it from or who it was really about.

"Now, remember," she warned Stoner as they pulled into the parking lot, "they'll talk to me more easily if I'm alone, so stay away from me until we come out."

"Really?" Stoner asked, big-eyed. "You're finally coming out?"

Marylou hit her on the wrist. Her collection of silver bracelets sounded like wind chimes. "Stop that. You're too old to be corny." She gathered up her huge tote bag.

"That thing's going to cripple you some day," Stoner said as Marylou hefted the bulging bag over one shoulder. "What in the world do you keep in there, anyway?"

"Things I might need. Cosmetics, aspirin and other emergency supplies, appointment book, notebooks, whatever I happen to be reading at the time, and another book in case I finish that one while stranded in a remote and boring place."

"And your lunch?"

"Well, of course not, just a snack." She started away from the car and turned back. "Don't forget, give me a five-minute head start. I want to be able to blend in unobtrusively."

Stoner grinned. Marylou had as much chance of blending in unobtrusively anywhere as a Mexican festival at a Quaker meeting.

"And, when you see me at the other end of the aisle, don't jump up and down flailing your arms like a demented dervish, the way you usually do."

"I do not," Stoner said.

"You do. You'd think I was your long-lost something-or-other."

"Okay, okay. So it makes me happy to see you unexpectedly. Even if it's just in the frozen food aisle. It's like a nice surprise. But I do not flail."

"Well…" Marylou said, "maybe not exactly flail…"

"It hurts my feelings when you say things like that."

Marylou patted her head. "I'm sorry. I didn't mean to do that. Forgive me?"

Stoner thought it over. "Okay, but you owe me a free pout."

"Good. Take it while I get a head start."

She swung away from the car before Stoner could stop her again.

Hermione glanced up from the Tarot spread she was contemplating to snatch an unnoticed hard look at Gwen. She liked the woman. Always had liked her. Of all the people Stoner could have brought into her life—and she had brought more than one unsavory sort in her youth—she was glad Gwen was the one who seemed to be sticking.

She couldn't recall having met Gwen before in any form. She liked that, too, meeting a new soul and one she was drawn to. The spirit formerly known as Yogananda was fond of hanging around souls who were about to incarnate and reminding them not to waste their time on souls they'd never met before, but stick to the ones they'd already worked things out with. As if they'd remember his uninvited advice once they were carnate.

It wasn't bad advice, but rather narrowing. Yogananda was like that, always thinking about how to avoid the obstacles to evolvement. As if all you were interested in was getting there as quickly as possible. As if the only way to get to a particular point were a straight line. Like your typical man with control of the car. Hermione herself enjoyed the scenic route, even if it meant delays, errors, discomforts, and all the rest. Yogananda was single-minded, and sometimes she wished he'd concentrate more on raising his own vibration and leave the rest of them alone. Or just go on up to the next level, where things were calmer and more contemplative. Hermione and her bunch weren't through with disarray quite yet.

Gwen glanced up and saw her watching and smiled.

"Final papers?" Hermione asked.

Gwen nodded. "The last batch for this year, thank God. Sometimes I get a little sick reading about things I already know."

"I thought you had a teaching assistant to grade papers."

"I do, but he has college finals. And I figured I'd better be a little familiar with these since we have parent conferences." She paused briefly. "How are you feeling?"

Hermione looked down quickly at her Tarot spread. "Better than these cards imply. If I believe them, I've been dead for years."

Gwen took her reading glasses off. "Is it a bad reading?"

"It's completely flat. All minor arcana and mostly pentacles. It seems there's nothing going on with my soul at all."

"Maybe it just needs a rest."

"It's getting one," Hermione said. She raked her cards together and shuffled them three times and started to lay out a Tree of Life spread. After the first four cards, she gave up. "Nothing."

Gwen got up and came over to the table. "Want me to try it?"

"It's not the cards, it's me." Suddenly she heard herself say, "I'm driving Stoner crazy, aren't I?"

"A little." Gwen took the community pack of Tarot cards and sat at the table. "How about you?"

"Me?"

"It has you a little crazy, doesn't it?" Gwen asked as she shuffled the cards, not looking directly at Hermione. When Hermione didn't answer, she said, "If I felt as terrible as you seem to, and they told me there was nothing wrong with me, I'd be out of my mind."

Hermione smiled. She knew exactly what Gwen was doing, drawing her out, without making too much of a big deal about it. She didn't mind. In fact, she was rather relieved. If there was anyone she could count on not to become emotional or pushy, it was Gwen. "I think I might be, slightly."

Gwen shuffled the cards again. "What's it like?" she asked.

"Going a little crazy?"

"Yeah."

Hermione contemplated how to put it into words while Gwen started flipping through the cards, one at a time. "Well," she said at last, "the closest I can come is how you feel when you take an antihistamine right before you go to bed, and it hasn't worn off when you wake up."

"Thick in the head and flannel-tongued," Gwen said.

"Flannel-everythinged. Not quite here, disconnected, as if there's a wall of water between me and the rest of the world." She watched as Gwen removed the Queen of Pentacles from the deck and tossed it to one side.

"Stoner," she explained, indicating the rejected card. "Let's see how it reads without her."

"Good idea. It's a struggle for Spirit to get through her anxiety."

Gwen glanced up. "She doesn't mean to be difficult. She's just…" She shrugged. "Impossible."

Hermione had to laugh. For a Pisces, Gwen could be amazingly clear. But Pisces could be like that. When they came up for air, they glinted silver in the sunlight.

"And there's the memory problem," Hermione said as Gwen started in on a new layout. "Sometimes I can remember in such detail, and other times I'll go into a room and can't for the life of me think of why I did. I suppose that can be advancing age…"

"Hardly," Gwen interrupted. "You don't lose your memory from one week to the next. Not without a severe trauma to the head." She leaned back in her chair. "Look at that, would you? Not a single major arcana."

Hermione looked. It was nearly identical to the reading she'd gotten. "It happened suddenly?" she asked. "The memory thing?"

"About a month ago. One day you were fine, the next you seemed to have trouble remembering anything at all. And losing weight. Your energy seemed to drain right out of you."

"You noticed."

"Everyone noticed. They just didn't know what to do. I mean, we all kept asking you how you are, and you kept putting us off. We got the message. At least, some of us did."

Hermione felt a deep burning behind her eyes, along with a sense of relief and regret. They'd all known, of course, all this time. And she'd felt so alone, so frightened, and there was comfort so close all she had to do was reach out…

She began to cry.

Gwen came and put her arms around her. "You're not in this alone, Aunt Hermione," Gwen said, and stroked her hair. "We're your family and we're right here."

Hermione let herself be held until she was comforted.

It wasn't getting any better, Cutter thought. Not that he'd expected it to. Ghosts didn't get bored and wander off. When they wanted you, they wanted you, no two ways about it. And these ghosts wanted the old woman.

They started showing up just after sunset now, before it was even totally dark. Growing braver. Arrogant. They even knew he was here, and it didn't bother them one bit. They knew who he was, and that he knew who they were, and it didn't even slow them down. Tonight one had come so close to him he could almost see its face, staring directly into his. But he didn't see its face. He never let himself see their faces. Back in 'Nam, if they showed you their faces you were dead.

What was he going to do? They weren't afraid of him. He couldn't knife them or shoot them or strangle them the way he'd been taught. He knew that from bitter experience. His hands'd gone right through them when he tried to pull them off his buddies.

He wondered why they never attacked him.

Maybe they were like the old Roman legions. Leave one of the enemy alive and mangled, so he'd go home and tell about how vicious the Romans were. So they wouldn't even try to fight the next time.

Maybe he'd been left alive in the jungle because he was supposed to come back and warn people about the ghosts.

There seemed to be more of them tonight, but they weren't doing anything. Not yet. Just kind of congregating under the old woman's window.

Cutter waited.

At times like this, he often found his mind going back to a kid he'd known, before he'd let himself be drafted. The kid'd been a soda jerk in the local drug store. A nice kid, friendly but serious at the same time. He knew where to find everything in the store, and how much chocolate syrup you liked on your chocolate, marshmallow, peanut sundae.

The kid had wanted to be a pharmacist after college. Cutter grunted. If he'd been in 'Nam, he'd know more about drugs than he'd learn in a thousand years of college. But the jungle probably would have broken him, his mind, his body, both. He was the kind of kid the jungle could break.

Cutter wondered what had happened to him. He hoped he'd slipped across the border to Canada. He could be back home now, because of the amnesty. Sometimes he wondered what his own life would be like if he'd done that. It had made sense, even at the time, even thinking you'd never come home.

His Dad would have disowned him, of course. His Dad was one of those flag-waving veterans of the Second World War who never talked about it. That wouldn't have bothered him much, to have his Dad disown him. They'd never had much to say to each other, anyway.

But his Mom, his Mom would have been ashamed. He couldn't do that to her.

The old woman was about the age his Mom would be now. He wondered how she was doing. He'd wanted to go see her right after the war, but he was too fucked up, he couldn't let her know what had happened to him, she'd have blamed herself. And now it just didn't make sense.

But he still wondered about her, and hoped she was all right, and wished he could do something for her.

Well, he could still do something for this old woman.

He slipped around to the front of the house through the deepest shadows. Marylou was out tonight, with Stoner. It'd be easier with just Gwen and the old woman there. Still, his heart pounded and his mouth was desert-dry with anxiety. He stood for a moment at the bottom of the steps, hidden in a pool of night, and watched them.

He avoided talking to people when he could. It frightened him. Frightened him more than his drill sergeant had, or even the Viet Cong. Everyday people could catch you off guard and cut you. Even if they didn't mean to, they could say something that seemed perfectly unimportant to them, and it would slice right through you. Words like "family" and "loyal" and "kids." Sometimes even the dumbest words you could imagine—like "sour cream," which was the stupidest thing he could think of to name something you wanted people to eat—sometimes even innocent words like that could stab and sting. It depended on what they ran up against. And he wasn't sure what there was inside him that they shouldn't touch. So even the most innocuous conversation, about the weather or baseball or the price of tea in China, could leave him bleeding.

Cutter took a deep breath and straightened his shoulders. He had a job to do. Like in 'Nam, when you had a job to do you did it. Otherwise your buddies could get hurt.

He fixed his eyes on the door bell and forced his feet to follow.

"Ma'am," he said when the old woman answered the door, "excuse me for bothering you so late, but someone's trying to steal your soul."

Chapter 4

Stoner supposed it was possible. Stranger things had happened to Aunt Hermione. Stranger things had happened to her, as a matter of fact. She'd run into an unsavory collection of beings during some of the adventures she'd fallen into. A few of them could be said to be definitely not of this world, or so it had seemed in the fear and confusion of the moment. In retrospect…well, it was hard to tell.

And as far as soul-stealers went, she'd encountered more than a few of them in her time. Maybe not ghostly entities that lurked in the wisteria to snatch your spirit while you were sleeping, but energy-draining, manipulating vampires none the less. As a matter of fact, she'd been lovers with at least one. Maybe even had one for a mother. They were all around.

So if things were looking a little odd…well, it was just one more oddity in her life.

But she knew, absolutely knew there were other, more mundane explanations for Aunt Hermione's problems than hungry ghosts. They hadn't even scratched the surface of real life, everyday possibilities.

Marylou was out in the first base coaching box, shouting the Blue Shirts through their wind sprints. They had finally settled on the name when the mother of one of the young women, a potter of some regional renown, had been coerced into doing the laundry. Maybe she had just experienced an inspired creative moment and was preoccupied, or maybe she didn't notice what she was doing or didn't know any better, or maybe she just plain didn't want to be asked to do it again. At any rate, she'd washed the tops and bottoms of the uniforms together, new white tees in the same hot water as the new discount-house blue shorts. The result was a softball team that looked tie-dyed.

Which put an end to their endless discussions about uniforms and names that made a political statement.

"Come on, girls," Marylou yelled. "Pick 'em up and put 'em down."

Stoner winced. "I wish she wouldn't call them 'girls.' They're young women."

"They don't seem to mind," Gwen remarked.

The second base woman sprinted past Marylou and grinned and made a rude gesture. Marylou laughed.

Young lesbians and softball. It was a rite of passage, she supposed. One of those spontaneous traditions that sometimes surfaced in a subculture that didn't even know it had traditions. Women's Music Festivals was another, though lately women's music had been co-opted by the mass culture. Not that she minded, it was great to see women finally getting some of the rewards they'd done without for centuries. And when the fickle populace found new fads—which was inevitable—they could go back to the old, original Women's Music Festivals.

Young lesbians, she thought, would never forsake softball. She'd even joined a team herself, when she was first coming out. It was what you did, to make friends and be around your own kind.

Her team had started with the same philosophy as the Blue Shirts, too. Most of them did. Winning didn't matter, as long as every woman had a chance to play and learn and could feel good about herself. Sometimes the within-game schedules were more complicated than the league schedules, so everyone could play the position she wanted and the one she wanted to learn, all in one game.

It worked, too. Morale was great, the camaraderie was touching. Every game a celebration of sisterhood the way it ought to work.

Until they started to win.

Then suddenly it mattered who played second base because it was such a vital position. And they'd have to field their best team against the Hot Shots because they'd lost every game to them last season and they were tired of being laughed at. And, anyway, it was only for one game.

Except that it was never only for one game. The less talented, less athletic members would complain a little, reluctantly for fear of being accused of jealousy, and then begin—one by one—to drop out.

She wondered how long it would be until it happened with this team. When her own team had gone in that direction, she'd left along with the others on principle, even though she was a pretty decent player and scheduled to play every game. But if they were going to play that way, she wasn't interested. It was wrong, and unkind, and she wasn't going to treat her sisters like that.

Some of the original "good" players never spoke to her again.

She sighed and glanced over at Gwen, who had never been in the softball racket and would be beyond middle age before she'd been 'out' longer than she'd been 'in.' There was that familiar sudden tightening in her chest, as if someone had just knocked the wind out of her. After all this time, Gwen could still do that to her. It wasn't that she was pretty in the world's eyes–though to Stoner she was just plain drop-dead gorgeous. It was the calmness about her, as if there was nothing in the world to be afraid of, and nothing that couldn't be handled if you just took your time and thought it through.

Stoner, who believed that there was a great deal in the world to be afraid of, and seldom time to think it through, could have moments of the same calm just by being around her.

Gwen, she thought, is like the goat they put in the stall with a nervous race horse.

Which, while not flattering on the face of it, was absolutely the best thing Stoner thought you could say about anyone. It was, as Gwen was inclined to say about the aura of animals, "so very Zen."

Marylou had decided to join them on the grass while the team chose sides for a practice game.

"How do they look?" she asked brightly.

"Fine." Actually, they looked a little scraggly, but she didn't want to hurt Marylou's feelings. Marylou had adopted the team as her personal project, and had become so identified with them that if one of them cut herself, Marylou bled.

"There's a lot of potential there," Gwen said.

Marylou scowled at her. "I haven't fallen for that one since I was six." She pulled a two-quart plastic bottle of Big Y brand unflavored seltzer from her tote bag. "They have a few rough edges, that's all."

"Uh-huh," Gwen said.

Marylou handed her the seltzer and stood up, cupping her hands around her mouth. "Hey," she yelled at the women on the field, "this isn't rest hour. Let's see some Charlie Hustle out there."

Gwen unscrewed the cap from the water and took a swig. "My God," she gasped, "that's potent stuff." She recapped the bottle and handed it back to Marylou. "I didn't know you were a fan of Pete Rose."

"Who's that?" Marylou asked, squinting toward the field.

"Pete Rose? The baseball guy. The one that got kicked out for gambling."

"What's that got to do with Charlie Hustle?"

"They called him that."

"Why?"

"Because he was so aggressive. Especially on the base paths. He'd make a dive for home plate that would mangle anyone who got in his way."

Marylou looked over at her. "Well," she said indignantly, "that's a fine example to set for young people. No wonder the world's gone to hell in a handbasket. Gangs, drugs, random vandalism and poorly thought out violence. And we make heroes out of people like this Hustle person."

"She has a point there," Stoner said.

"Poorly thought out violence?" Gwen asked. "You prefer well-thought-out violence?"

"It's better than crashing into some poor working stiff just because he's standing where you want to be when it's where he belongs in the first place. Yes, compared to that, give me a good old gangland execution any day. At least that's about something."

Gwen said she "saw."

Stoner didn't say anything at all.

Maybe it wouldn't hurt to see what Diana had to say about their predicament, even though Aunt Hermione adamantly refused to run it past the other women in the coven. She didn't know them well enough yet, she insisted. And some of them weren't psychic, just devout. A few would probably think she was accusing them of something, which would cause all kinds of trouble. "Especially that skinny weaselly one," she'd said. "She takes offense at a cloudy night. We'd be processing for the rest of our lives."

Certainly Aunt Hermione wouldn't mind if Stoner just kind of casually got Diana's opinion, not in any official way. Not as if she were "consulting a psychic." Diana, knowing Aunt Hermione, might even bring it up herself.

Doubtful. Most of the legitimate psychics she'd met were as tight-lipped as celebrity defense lawyers. Well, she couldn't blame them. They knew things about you that you didn't even know yourself. Say the wrong word, push the wrong button and the Big Bang pales by comparison.

Sometimes it struck her that being a human being, going about your daily business, was an incredibly dangerous undertaking. The streets were full of twisted souls looking for a chance to explode. You never knew what might set them off. Really, she'd rather deal with wild animals than people. At least wild animals were predictable and wouldn't harm you if you read their signals properly. And their signals usually meant, "Stop right there, speak respectfully, and back off."

People, on the other hand, were complicated, convoluted, mixed up, and half the time didn't know why they did what they did. Though if you asked them they'd claim 20/20 insight. In spite of it all, most people went right along living their lives, not giving a second thought to the fact that they were in mortal danger. She thought it must mean they believed in something, God or fate or karma, or at least their own invulnerability.

"Nonsense," Edith Kesselbaum had said once when Stoner had voiced that opinion, "they're all in denial."

So there was plenty of reason to look for the source of their trouble on this plane. They didn't need to go poking around in the metaphysical universe.

Not that she had a problem with the possibility of an unseen world. Most people at least accepted the reality of light bands they couldn't see and wave lengths they couldn't hear. So who was to say there wasn't a whole lot going on that no one knew about? "It's like electricity," Aunt Hermione was fond of saying, "Better to believe, and be prepared, than not to believe and get a nasty shock."

And there was one of their bones of contention. Aunt Hermione was convinced Stoner should be prepared, and being prepared meant working with and honing her natural psychic abilities.

Stoner had no intention of honing her psychic anything. It was like playing with a Ouija board. Open that door, and you never knew what might come through. So, since it was perfectly possible to live a fruitful, productive, and happy life without playing with a Ouija board, don't play with Ouija boards.

The few encounters she'd had with the Unseen had not left her with a jolly feeling about that invisible universe.

Which, of course, was Aunt Hermione's point. Learn how to control what comes through from that place.

Stoner said it worked just as well to keep the door firmly and permanently locked.

Aunt Hermione would counter by pointing out that Stoner had once, without intending to open any doors, become the focus of a particularly nasty haunted house.

Stoner would reply that that had been a coincidence and probably hadn't really happened, anyway. Besides, she'd been drugged and was likely hallucinating.

Aunt Hermione reminded her that Gwen had seen it, too.

Stoner would say they had all been under a lot of stress that night, and then suddenly remember something she'd forgotten to do out in the kitchen.

But, assuming just for the sake of assuming there were unseen forces at work, how would they get to Aunt Hermione? Aunt Hermione's intuition and experience would set off alarms the minute a vampire crossed her path, whether in body or in spirit. She could even spot evil over the phone, on the message machine, and in on-line chat rooms. After all, clairvoyants don't make a living out of being easy to fool. She had her defenses well indexed and firmly in place.

The trouble was, too many people used this psychic phenomenon stuff as a excuse for not confronting the real world. Why assume it was ghosts after Aunt Hermione's soul, when it might just as well be someone who had it in for her and was slipping arsenic into her vitamins?

Because of what Cutter had said? But Cutter was a troubled soul, with a great deal to tell and very little to say. There were memories stored up in him that would probably drive a sane person crazy—the jungles of Vietnam, the war, the drugs, the killing,. He must have seen things—all of the service men and women must have—that she couldn't even imagine, secrets that combatants and the media tacitly agreed could never be spoken of again.

Cutter had his own way of looking at things, that much was obvious, and no doubt his own way of describing them. You couldn't tell if Cutter was speaking of life as he saw it, or in metaphor.

Or if he knew the difference.

At work when she had asked, "Marylou, when Cutter talks to you…" She had tried to think of how to put it delicately, and decided it was impossible. "Is what he says usually real, or does he imagine things?"

"Usually real," Marylou had said. "He doesn't hallucinate, he just can't cope."

"And what he told Aunt Hermione, about someone stealing her soul?"

Marylou had thrown up her hands. "Who knows? I leave that to better and looser minds than mine."

Diana's shop Turquoise always made her think of Aunt Hermione's study back in Boston. It was the incense, the sweet-tangy odor of smoldering herbs that had built up over the years until it was no longer possible to tell the difference between the scent of the room and the scent of Aunt Hermione herself. Aunt Hermione believed that every client's sun sign had its own preferred vibration—allowing for individual differences, of course. Most Scorpios were F-sharps, but some were one F-sharp above middle C, some were one or two below. If a Scorpio were coming for a reading, she'd try to find the fragrance that best matched the F-sharps vibrations of that particular client. It usually turned out to be Hecate, which was no surprise. The Goddess of Vengeance and Scorpions had a lot in common. And F-sharp, while pleasant enough, could turn on you unexpectedly. Stoner suspected that the sound given off by finger nails clawing on a blackboard was F-sharp.

Cancer was G and Circe's Moon. B-flat was the sound of Virgo, with Egyptian Temple as a scent. Aquarians responded to the C major chord and High Joan the Conqueror. Stoner's own sign, Capricorn, called for D and Sandalwood.

Usually Hermione kept the odor light and pleasant, like soft background music. Except for a Taurus. With a Taurus, Stoner could swear her aunt lit one of everything she had in stock, including a few that had gone by. Passing the study door was like going through the horrors of the perfume aisle in a department store.

Once, during one of her more churlish adolescent moments, Stoner had accused her aunt of "sucking up" to her Taurian clients' bad taste. She was looking to pick a fight, and she knew it. Her emotions had been running rampant all day, and by two o'clock in the afternoon she had progressed from "normal adolescent" to "troubled teen." She needed an outlet, and she needed it now.

Aunt Hermione had merely nodded thoughtfully, and explained that Taurians, being of a strongly sensuous nature, enjoyed vibrant tastes, colors, and odors. They were, in fact, made irritable by subtle and bland surroundings. And an irritable Taurus wasn't pleasant to be around, any more than disgruntled bull would be. "So why tempt them," she said, "when they're really quite easy to please if you take the time?"

"By the way, dear," her aunt called after her as she stomped out of the room muttering about 'no fun to fight with,' "that expression you used—something about sucking, wasn't it?—it's quite expressive, and I'm sure it's satisfying to say, but it really is unattractive. I do hope you outgrow it soon."

That had merited a bedroom door slam, but she hadn't used the expression again.

Now she didn't care about Taurians or whether the incense was delicate or cloying. Because some day, she knew, the memories incense brought would be all she had of her aunt.

That is truly grim, she said to herself. You have her dead and buried, and she hasn't even been diagnosed.

But she knew, deep in her gut, that something was terribly, terribly wrong and growing worse. Last night, lying awake, she had heard her aunt pause halfway up the stairs, as if she had to catch her breath. And she looked worse every day, paler and more papery. When she entered a room, it was as if she hadn't come in at all. No energy radiated from her. And nobody knew what to do.

Pull yourself out of this, McTavish, Stoner told herself. You're almost to the point where Edith should give you a label, and a code number for insurance purposes.

It was fairly quiet in Turquoise. Only one other customer, as far as she could tell. It was impossible to predict the rising and falling of the clientele in Diana's store. Some days, like today, it'd be nearly empty. Other days Diana would be so busy she'd have to call in her kid sister to help out. At first, Stoner had thought the busy days were brought on by the *Sale, 20% off* signs in the windows. But, as the year rolled along, she realized that there was always a twenty-percent off sale at Turquoise. Even in the dead of winter, when there was nothing to do but shop in town or go to the Pothole Cinema, or drive over to the Wal-Mart in North Adams and risk sliding off the road to your death on Horseshoe Curve—affectionately known as Truckers' Leap. Once over that embankment, if you didn't end up crashing through the roof of someone's house, you might not be found for months. Nobody from the Mohawk Trail area was ever declared officially "missing" until after the spring thaw.

Anyway, it wasn't the presence or absence of sales that accounted for the up and downs of business at Turquoise. Diana claimed it "just happened," falling back on the midwestern practicality that had been a part of her character before Spirit intruded and put an end to her career as a certified public accountant.

"There I was," she had told Stoner shortly after they first met, "explaining the state tax forms to the new secretary at the Chevy dealer, when I hear myself say, 'Your sister's child's in trouble, but it'll be all right.' It was a real shock, since I didn't even know she had a sister, much less one with a child. And the voice was mine, but not entirely mine, higher and thinner, maybe. Then the whole darn thing came true." She had smiled a little ruefully. "I'll tell you, though, you make a whole lot more money as a CPA than you do as a trance channel."

She'd opened the store on advice of Spirit, who continued to try to tell her what to stock. It wasn't working out terribly well. Spirit had a very different agenda from the tourists who came to Shelburne Falls to see the Bridge of Flowers and the Glacial Potholes.

Diana managed to make ends meet by stocking a few lines of expensive dresses and lingerie, a corner of brightly colored books and toys for children, and some fancy socks and gloves for the tourists. For her regular customers—mostly local pagans, wiccans, herbalists, crystal healers—she carried esoteric and arcane books, smudge sticks and incense, gemstones with various mysterious properties, herbs, pentacles and oils. The two populations met over handmade crystal jewelry.

Stoner liked her. She wore loose-flowing, floor-length dresses that reminded her of Edith Kesselbaum and made her feel calm. Diana's hair was dull blonde shading to brown, and she wore it long and hanging free. Encroaching middle age and two back-to-back pregnancies had given her body just the slightest hint of matronly and maternal solidity.

She was, Stoner thought, a comfortable person.

Diana glanced up, saw Stoner, and raised her eyebrows slightly in a gesture of frustration. The customer was a tourist, and an indecisive one at that. The type was easy to recognize. They took up tremendous amounts of time, asked hundreds of questions, found fault with each item they were shown, and in the end declared it "not exactly what I was looking for," and left without buying.

Which this one did.

Diana came over to where Stoner was looking at a crystal pendant decorated with smaller stones representing the colors of the Chakras. "Are these stones in the right order?" she asked.

Diana leaned against the jewelry case. "Yep. For the dense and the poor of memory."

"Sounds just like me."

"Uh-huh. So what brings you in here on a week day. Worried about your aunt?"

"I hate psychics," Stoner said, studying a tourmaline crystal. "They're always reading your mind."

Diana laughed. "Your aunt looks like death warmed over, and you're as jumpy as a monkey. It doesn't take any special talent to put that together."

"The doctor can't find anything wrong with her."

"So I heard."

Stoner glanced at her. "Where'd you hear that?"

"Mary Scott. She's in the coven."

"I thought they weren't supposed to talk about things that went on in the coven."

"It's a coven, honey. Not an AA meeting."

Stoner studied her hand through a sheer flowered scarf. "Do you know the coven women?"

"Some of them pretty well, some of them a little." Diana noticed something in the jewelry case whose arrangement displeased her and set about fixing it.

"What do you think of them?"

"They seem like a good bunch. None of them shoplift, as far as I know. If they do, they're very good at it." She paused and seemed to be listening. "Wait a minute. I'm getting a message from Spirit." Her eyes widened a little. "It's for you."

"I hope it's about what to have for dinner. It's my week to cook."

Diana shushed her. "They say…they say you're…what in the world?… 'looking for answers in the wrong place.' Yep, that's it, looking for answers in the wrong place."

She didn't need Spirit to tell her that, but it gave her an idea. "Diana, if I can persuade her, could you do a reading for Aunt Hermione? Maybe you can find out what's wrong."

Diana actually blushed a little. "Read for her? That's like blessing the Pope."

"She's tried to do it for herself, but it doesn't get her anywhere." Stoner glanced up. "Her spirits haven't ever refused to talk to her before. To tell you the truth, it scares me. I mean, Aunt Hermione—"

A customer opened the door and set the wind chimes singing. "I'd be honored to do it," Diana said as she started out from behind the counter. She paused and her eyes went blank again for a moment. "Spirit says it'll be all right, as long as everyone does what they're supposed to do. And check what you have in the freezer, left-hand side, third shelf down."

It made absolutely no sense to feel relieved, but she did. More than relieved, optimistic. Because finally Aunt Hermione was going to see someone who spoke her language and maybe could tell what was wrong? Because it was one more chance of stopping this thing before it went any farther? Because it had made Aunt Hermione so happy when she suggested it?

Because of what Cutter had said about her soul?

Or was it because, when she looked into the freezer, she found the pan of frozen lasagna on the left side of the third shelf?

Whatever the reason, she found herself actually smiling as she ripped up the lettuce and waited for the rolls to brown. She felt light, almost bouncy.

Not a very Stoner way to feel, she reminded herself. Could be denial. Even that didn't bring her down.

Something was being done. That was all that mattered. It was being done tonight, and she and Aunt Hermione were doing it together.

The evening was dark and fragrant. Lilacs and grass. Fresh oil from a street they'd repaired a couple of blocks away. The muddy odor of the Deerfield River, swollen with the snow melt from up north. Cutter hunkered down in the shadows by the railroad track and waited. He could see Stoner's outline against the lights in the store windows. They sat in the darkness as if they were together. The two of them, waiting.

Now and then a customer dropped by, and she went into the store for a few minutes and they came out together. Once the customer carried one of the thin pastel bags Diana liked to give out. Another customer didn't seem to have bought anything. A few seconds of conversation, and Stoner went back to her place on the porch.

The old woman—Hermione, she'd insisted he call her, but that didn't seem right. After all, she was as old as his mother, and it wasn't respectful.

No, his mother'd be much older now, wouldn't she? She'd been, what, nearly fifty when he'd left for 'Nam. Sometimes his emotions forgot any time had passed since then. He thought he was still eighteen. Other times he felt as old as forever.

That was thirty years ago. She'd be old now, too. She might even be dead.

He'd thought about going back to see his mother. Not when he first got home. He was too broken up then. But later, when he got out of the VA hospital. The first VA hospital, the one where they'd put his body back together. He planned to go about it real slowly. He couldn't just walk up to the front door like any normal person. She'd get all excited and that would make his head blow up. Or his Dad would answer the door and look right through him as if he didn't exist, they way he always did, and close the door in his face, and when his Mom asked who it was he'd say, "Nobody."

But he could slip into the back yard in the night and watch, the way he did with Marylou and her friends. He could keep anything bad from happening.

Except the other guys, the ones who'd tried to do that, said it wasn't a good thing to do at all. They said it would make your mind shatter.

He was inclined to believe them. They were as crazy as he was, and didn't lie.

Cutter wondered if he'd done the right thing, telling the old woman about the ghosts. Now that he thought about it, he'd taken away their need for secrecy. Now they could just come and do what they wanted to do, and he didn't have time to prepare.

Not even time to study them and guess what to prepare for.

Before 'Nam he wouldn't have had these doubts. But that was what happened to you in the jungle. First it ate your name, and then it ate your body, and finally it ate everything you were sure of.

He'd been sure he could keep his friends safe. Not at first. He wasn't that foolish. But as the months went on and he made all the right calls...when to attack or retreat, which paths were safe and free of land mines, where the VC might be, almost as if he had an instinct for warfare...just when he'd come to trust himself, there'd been that night, and that one wrong decision he'd been so sure was right, and he was the only one who'd survived.

So in the end the jungle took everything. And maybe that was the point of 'Nam after all.

Stoner rested her head on her knees and rubbed the back of her neck. He could tell she was frightened. Not of the dark, but of what was happening in the little room off the store where Diana held her channeling sessions.

He wondered how frightened she'd be if she could see what he could see, scurrying over the railroad ties, hugging the rails.

Without thinking, he groaned a little, just from the enormity of the terror.

Her head went up. She looked around. And listened. Still as a bird listening for a worm.

Cutter stopped breathing. Stopped his heart. Stopped the blood from pumping through his veins.

He'd learned how to die back in that world. To become so still, to pull himself so deep inside himself even the animals couldn't smell life in him. He became a shadow. Then less than a shadow. They could shine a flood light on him, and they wouldn't see him.

He'd learned to slip into the spaces between atoms.

"Cutter?"

No answer.

She held her breath and tried to sense movement or sound. The night was as still and two-dimensional as a photograph.

It must have been her imagination, or an animal, or even a tree branch moaning under the weight of its own leaves.

Why had she thought of Cutter? The last she'd heard from Marylou, the two of them had plans for tonight. She hadn't exactly said what they were, but Stoner doubted it involved creeping around Turquoise and hiding in bushes.

Just the thought of that made her smile. Marylou hiding in bushes was right up there with Marylou passing for homeless in the Big Y World Class Market. Definitely not on the menu.

Then why did she have the feeling Cutter was here?

She tried calling him again, softly.

Still no answer, still that feeling.

She closed her eyes. She could listen better that way.

The feeling faded.

A patch of light fell across her eyelids. Diana had come out of the reading room and turned on the light by the side door. It illuminated the lilacs and alder where she'd thought she'd sensed Cutter. There was no one there.

Diana looked exhausted. Her face was shiny with sweat, her skin seemed tight. There were dark circles under her eyes.

Apprehensive, Stoner got up and went inside. The shell wind chimes clattered in the doorway.

Diana had gone to the kitchenette in the back, and was getting a bottle of spring water from the old refrigerator. She offered one to Stoner.

"Thanks." She unscrewed the cap and took a swallow, trying to appear more casual than she really felt. "Rough session?"

"Your aunt…" Diana shook her head and rolled her eyes. "…has the most demanding collection of spirit guides I've ever met."

"They've been together for a long time," Stoner said.

"Tell me about it. The crowd that lined up to talk to her—if they were corporeal they'd have stretched halfway to Greenfield."

Stoner smiled and wished she'd get on with it.

"I had to limit them to five. I think they held a lottery." She took another swig of her water.

"Uh…how's Aunt Hermione."

"Finishing up her notes," Diana said. "And she wants to meditate."

"But do you have any sense of things?"

"Not much. Most of the time in a reading I go somewhere and don't know what's going on. I might catch a sentence or two, but once things get under way, it's really none of my business."

Scared and frustrated, Stoner put her bottle down too hard. It slopped a little. "Shit," she muttered.

Diana glanced at her. "I know you're worried. I wish I could give you a full report, but I just can't."

"Can't you tell me anything?" She swiped at the spilled water with a paper towel.

Diana scrunched up her face. "I did hear 'soul loss,' so I guess we were right about that. And your name came up."

"Mine."

"Yep. There seemed to be an argument going on."

Oh, great. Aunt Hermione's in trouble and they're arguing about me. "That's it?" she asked.

"Well, it seemed to me the upshot of the discussion—and it got pretty heated from time to time—was that, whatever the problem is, you should solve it."

"That figures."

Diana smiled. "Spirit can be a pain in the neck sometimes, can't it?"

"I wouldn't know," Stoner said. "We're not in the habit of communicating on a daily basis."

"Too bad. You might get along better if you did." She closed her eyes and seemed to listen. "You have an interesting bunch, from what I can tell."

"Yeah," Stoner said wryly, "but they're no good in the kitchen, and they don't do windows." She realized how bitter that sounded, and apologized. "I'm sorry. I have a lot on my mind."

"I know." Diana put her empty glass down. "Well, some day..."

She agreed, to be polite. But the truth was, she neither expected nor wanted to be in everyday communication with Spirit, her own or anyone else's.

"Who's the old Native American woman?" Diana asked.

Her stomach clenched. "Who?"

"An old Native American woman. With some kind of bird on her shoulder." She focused inward. "A crow. She calls you 'green eyes.'"

Stoner caught her breath. "That's Siyamtiwa," She said tightly.

"Siyam-what?"

"In English it means Butterfly-coming-over-the-edge-of-a-flower or something like that. I met her in Arizona. She's a Hopi. I think."

"A very old soul," Diana said. "She's lived hundreds of lifetimes."

"Sometimes she lives several at once," Stoner said.

Diana gave a low whistle. "Just imagine."

"Look, I'm kind of going out of my mind here. Isn't there anything you can tell me?"

"Well..." She was listening again. "She says to remember to do what they tell you."

"And they are?"

"She says you'll know when the time comes, and she hopes you won't make a mess for yourself like you did last time."

Stoner felt herself blushing deeply. "All right," she said quickly.

Diana looked at her. "What's she talking about?"

"Just something…something we had a difference of opinion on." She looked skyward. "You were right, Grandmother. Okay? You were right. Can we forget it?"

"I think she's left," Diana said.

"That figures. She always had to have the last word."

Aunt Hermione was just leaving the reading room when they came back to the front of the store. She looked tired, but it was a normal, everyday kind of tired. She was more alive than she before she went in.

"How are you?" Stoner asked quickly.

"Much better. It's always good to talk to old friends." She handed Diana a sealed envelope.

Diana backed up and raised her hands. "I don't want money. I told you. This was a professional courtesy."

"And this isn't your fee. It's an early Solstice gift." She put it down on the counter. "Take it, if you want. If you don't, leave it here for some tourist to steal." She scribbled something in small writing on the back. "There. A curse. If anyone but you touches it, it'll scare the daylights out of them." She took Stoner's arm. "Come on, niece. I've been in another world for two hours. I need some of your good down-to-earth Capricorn energy."

Chapter 5

"They refused to be more concrete," Aunt Hermione said. They'd reached the middle of the Bridge of Flowers, where a park bench waited beneath a street lamp. "They were quite adamant about it. Let's just sit here for a moment and talk."

Stoner felt her heart tighten. She tried not to let her aunt see how worried she was, but it was clear the older woman was quickly becoming exhausted again.

Aunt Hermione propped one foot up on the bench and hugged her knee. It was a characteristic and very un-old-ladyish gesture that Stoner loved dearly. "I do wish they'd been more specific," she said at last.

"Who are we talking about?"

"The spirits. They're usually much more specific, and certainly less contentious.

"Exactly what did they say?"

"Only that someone really is after my soul—though of course they have their own word for it, and it's a very strange one. I'm not sure I could even pronounce it in body. If they know the motive, they're not telling." She sighed. "Sometimes it's so frustrating, incarnating. If I were in spirit, I'd know everything. But incarnate…well, our knowledge and understanding are spotty."

"If you don't mind," Stoner said, "I prefer you in the flesh and spotty."

"You're very sweet, Stoner. One of the things that makes this time around worth while. Oh, and they said that this is something that you, and only you, can solve." She patted Stoner's knee reassuringly. "Don't worry. I have total and absolute faith in you."

Stoner swallowed heavily. "You always do. I'm not sure it's well-placed."

"You haven't let me down yet. Besides, if they say only you can solve it, they're also saying you can, aren't they?"

"Look," she said, trying to be reasonable even though she really wanted to scream, "how do we know they're telling the truth? Or it could all be a mistake…"

"Spirit doesn't lie. Or make mistakes. We make the mistakes when we misinterpret what they say," her aunt said, and watched a moth circling the street light for a second.

If she tells me that bug is one of her spirit guides, Stoner thought, I'll slit my wrists.

"If we watch very carefully," the older woman said, "we might see a bat harvest this moth."

"Aunt Hermione, the last thing I'm interested in is carnage on the Bridge of Flowers. I want to know what's wrong with you, and what I have to do about it."

"Of course, sometimes there are—well, not to be too critical, but—troubled souls lurking about. Stuck, you know, between this world and the Light. Usually poorly evolved, mired in their base instincts, as it were. They can be dangerous. They're ordinarily quite angry. Or at least greedy. Being poorly evolved…"

"Aunt Hermione…"

"Poltergeists and worse. And then there are the poor ones who don't realize they've passed into transition. But they don't necessarily get in your hair, just go sort of stumbling around wondering where they are and why. And they mean well, poor things. Most hauntings…"

"Aunt Hermione!" She grabbed her aunt's hands. "Stop this. We have a serious problem here."

Her aunt's shoulders drooped. "Yes, I suppose we do."

"Someone 'wants your soul.' Okay. Got it. But what does that mean, exactly? Are they casting spells? Writing nasty letters about you? Screwing up your ads in the West County News? Slipping poison into your food?"

Aunt Hermione looked down at the reflections of town lights in the water, Buckland on one side, Shelburne Falls on the other. "It could mean any or all of those, I suppose."

"And why me? What gives me special skills to solve this? I'm a travel agent, for crying out loud."

"Now, Stoner, you know better than that. Look at the number of people you've helped out of trouble."

Stoner felt frantic. "But it's not my area of expertise. I make it up as I go along."

"And rather successfully, too. Which means you have excellent intuition, wouldn't you say?"

"No, Aunt Hermione, I definitely would not say." She took a deep breath. "I can't do this myself," she said firmly. "We'll find someone who can, but it can't be me." When her aunt didn't answer, she turned to look at her. "I can't," she said again. "It's your life."

"Oh, no, dear," the older woman said, taking her hand and giving it a squeeze. "It's not my life they want."

"Then what?"

"They want my mind."

Sometimes the old house was too quiet. The silence felt lifeless, when the moon was new and the dark like velvet pile. It was better in the winter. Then at least the wood joists creaked and popped as they cooled, as the house released the day's stored up heat. In the stillness of spring, her thoughts were too loud. Even Gwen's soft breathing, beside her in the four-poster bed, wasn't enough to stop the thoughts.

They'd called Edith Kesselbaum first, of course. She said she'd heard of being driven insane by all sorts of things—from chemicals in the brain to life in the army to visiting relatives—but by the loss of one's soul? That was a new one.

Or, rather, an old one. There were stories of persons in primitive societies who went out of their minds because they believed they'd been cursed. But those were peasants, who were ignorant and superstitious.

This got Aunt Hermione into a huff. She believed the Ancient Ones—the people who hadn't been on Planet Earth long enough to develop 'civilizations' and go rampaging around looking for things they didn't really need and ruining it for everyone else—weren't superstitious at all, but knew what the rest of us didn't have the sense to know.

In the interest of avoiding an argument in what was clearly a crisis, Edith suggested they put off that discussion until another time.

Aunt Hermione agreed.

If things turned out all right, Stoner could look forward to that. Edith might have the weight of science, education and history on her side, but Aunt Hermione could be very persuasive when she felt matters of Truth were at stake. Given enough motivation she could, in her own words, "get Jesus to change his mind."

An odd expression, one Stoner'd never heard from anyone else. She wasn't sure what it meant literally, but she certainly knew what it mean in Aunt Hermione's case. When it came to this kind of argument, she was the World Heavyweight Champion.

If she was losing the logic and science rounds—which wasn't the best way to discuss the supernatural, anyway—and referring to her opponent's personal experiences wasn't taking her anywhere, she'd fall back on what she called "tricks" and didn't really have much respect for. Aunt Hermione's ability to manipulate the "laws" of physics was formidable. In fact, she refused to grant them the status of "laws," and referred to them instead as the "suggestions" of physics. She had even survived a Paradox—shifting into a different space/time dimension and running into her pre-travel self with her returning self, then convincing her pre-travel self not to go.

It was widely believed that this would cause the universe to collapse, but it hadn't.

But it wasn't necessary to show off with a Paradox, she had once explained to Stoner, because even the most hard-headed scientific type had a secret desire to be wrong. Deep inside most people there was a tiny spark of hope that God, or Magic, or a Universal Consciousness, or whatever lay behind the struggle and banality of their lives, really existed and would some day explode in front of them in all its Magnificence. Usually, it was enough to make herself invisible or to persuade an animal to perform complex, unusual acts without addressing it directly.

Actually, conversing with animals was the easiest trick of all. You simply did what the animals did themselves, communicate by putting thoughts in their heads. They talked to one another that way. And on more than one occasion a dog lover had suddenly had a wonderful vision of how pleasant it would be to take a walk with her pet. Only to be amazed to find that she'd had this idea at exactly the same moment as every other dog owner in the neighborhood.

Stoner turned on her side and smelled the grassy, damp spring air that drifted in the bedroom window.

Could anyone be putting things in Aunt Hermione's food? That was really hard to imagine. Each of them took a week in the kitchen on a rotating basis, and Aunt Hermione's condition hadn't varied from week to week. No one was taking her glasses of warm milk or red wine at bed time, either. They all used the same jar of vitamins, and the same glasses and plates and flatware. Nobody had "her own" special anything…except for Stoner's coffee mug with the painting of the Tetons that Gwen had had made to remind her of where they'd met.

She felt a hand firm against her back.

"What are you thinking so hard about?" Gwen whispered.

"If there was any way anyone in the house could put chemicals in Aunt Hermione's food."

There was a long silence, then Gwen laughed. "Dearest, do you really think you should say those things out loud?"

She rolled over. "Huh?"

"Someone could take offense, you know."

"But I was including myself, too."

"Well," Gwen said, "that makes all the difference. Do you really believe one of us would harm Aunt Hermione?"

"Maybe. If you'd been hypnotized."

Gwen gave a loud snort of disgust.

Stoner stared up into the near darkness. She could just make out white objects—Gwen's bathrobe hanging from the back of her closet door, the porcelain knobs on the bureau, curtains—and the deeper black of entrances. "I can't afford to overlook anything," she said softly.

"I guess that's true. Stoner, do you really believe you're the only person in the whole world who can stop this?"

"I don't know. Aunt Hermione believes it, so if it's going to happen it'll have to be me who does it. In her mind, anyway. So anything I don't do won't help, will it?"

"Then you think it's psychological."

"No, but I think psychological barriers can defeat anything." She sighed. "I could make a real mess of it, Gwen. Then what?"

They weren't talking about anything approaching love, but Stoner could feel it in Gwen's hand. She cherished that feeling. Even before they were lovers, she'd known she'd feel loved by the touch of Gwen's hand. Before they'd met, really. The minute she'd seen Gwen's photograph, even though Gwen was married and it was pretty tacky to want to feel love through a married woman's hand. And when she'd finally met her—and her sleaze-bucket of a husband who now lay dead and mostly forgotten six feet under—she'd turned as possessive and jealous as an old dog.

"I don't even know where to start," she said.

"If you're trying to figure out which of us has the motive, means and opportunity to kill Aunt Hermione, I'd say you've already started. With a vengeance."

Nobody in the house was sleeping. The lights were out but he could feel the wakefulness. It crackled like electricity. He had to be even more careful now, after what he'd heard at that psychic woman's store. He wished he'd been able to hear more, but when they went out on the Bridge of Flowers he knew the only way to listen without being seen would be to slip into the water and swim under the bridge. But that would make him late to meet Marylou—and wet. He didn't want her to know what he was doing.

He wasn't afraid of what she'd say. He was afraid of what the ghosts'd do if they knew she knew anything. And the only way to prevent that was not to tell her more than he had to. It was hard enough, watching them come after Stoner and her lover and her aunt. He knew he'd go out of control if they went after Marylou.

The clouds broke for an instant. Cutter froze. They were there, clustered around the aunt's window. He forced his hands to move, felt around on the ground for anything to throw. If he couldn't stop or startle them, at least maybe he could get someone's attention inside.

The ground beside him was bare.

Desperate, he watched them. He tried to will them to go away.

One of the ghosts turned and looked in his direction him, its eyes empty as space.

He had the feeling it was laughing.

Then suddenly they were leaving, slipping back out over the window sill like water.

The clouds closed in again.

Hermione stood just inside the bathroom door, her hand on the light switch.

Why had she come in here?

She could recall getting out of bed, moving quietly and not turning on the light so no one would wake up and get nervous about her. So there must have been a purpose. She didn't have to use the toilet. She could still taste her toothpaste, so she hadn't suddenly remember she'd forgotten to brush her teeth. She didn't have any other night time rituals, like face creams—heaven forbid!—or sleeping pills.

So, what? What?

Her mouth was dry. Water, that was it! She wanted a drink.

She closed the door quietly and flipped on the light.

As she waited for the water to run cold, she looked at herself in the mirror, startled at how frail she seemed. Her skin looked like old rags, shapeless and gray with the kind of gray you can never bleach out in the laundry. Tattle-tale gray, they used to call it. Her eyes were fading from blue to the color of slate. Her hair was thin and limp.

I look as if I've been dead for a week.

She hadn't looked this bad this morning. Or when she dressed for bed tonight. As if she were aging a year for every hour that passed.

Like a character in a Stephen King novel.

You look like shit, she told her reflection. It wasn't one of her favorite expressions—falling securely into the category of unoriginal—but it convinced her she was still young enough and alive enough to be gross.

She drank, then slipped back to her room.

Her body felt like dead weight that only wanted to sink into the bed and rest. It was as if a force were pulling her down, through the bed, through the floor, through the earth. Her eyes were heavy, the lids gritty and ponderous as rocks. There was a thickness in her lips. Despite the water, her mouth was dry. Her tongue clung to the roof of her mouth.

Hermione went back to her room and settled herself into bed. It felt delicious to lie down.

Suddenly she remembered that she had invited the coven for a potluck tomorrow evening. Or, as they called it, a "Cauldron Luck." And she'd forgotten to mention it to her housemates. Not that they would mind, or that they had to be there if they didn't want, or that they couldn't be there. It was nothing more than a social gathering, no rituals.

At least, she didn't think it was a ritual occasion. They'd celebrated Beltane weeks ago. There weren't any Sabbats coming up. Not until Solstice.

Was it someone's birthday? Or naming day? Was one of them Croning? Half of them were Crones already, and half of the rest were barely out of Maidenhood. But what about the other four?

She struggled to remember their names, even their Wicca names, but couldn't. She'd seen them just last Sunday. She couldn't have forgotten them all in four days.

There's just too much going on, Hermione thought, and felt a rush of anger. It's too hard keeping up on everything. Not enough time to do anything right.

Tears of frustration leapt to her eyes.

She used to be able to do things right. No matter what it was, whether officiating at a High Holy Day, or sitting down to a cup of coffee with a friend. She always did it easily and smoothly. At least that's how it seemed in retrospect. And she'd certainly worked hard at learning social skills. Through lifetimes too numerous to mention.

Actually, she'd been pretty rough for a long time. It hadn't mattered in the Gypsy life, but then she'd started to take a look at what she was doing. She'd been beaten up on more than one occasion for her smart mouth, and had put her social standing at serious jeopardy among the Dakotas by not acting in the demure manner of an unwed female.

That time she'd been too outspoken for any man to take an interest in her, even the most uncouth. She'd heard the jokes the older women made behind her back. "That Dark Cloud Dancer, maybe she should declare herself a Perpetual Virgin." "The men should teach her to hunt and fight. She'd make a good warrior." Then they'd giggle.

The truth was, she wouldn't have minded being a hunter or a warrior. More than that, she'd wanted to be a holy person, maybe even a ghost dreamer. She already had the power of seeing the shadows of the future. But her mother had laughed and scolded her when she told her what she wanted.

One day, a band of Omahas raided the camp. The Dakotas quickly ran them off, but Dark Cloud Dancing caught the eye of one of the Omaha braves, and he took her with him as his woman.

That entire lifetime was so unpleasant she spent the next three incarnations as a man.

Why was she thinking about that now? And where had she started?

She tried to trace her train of thought, but it was like unsnarling a backlash in a fishing line. She poked and plucked and worried it, and finally gave up.

"It's too much," Hermione whispered to herself in the darkness. "Too much."

She closed her eyes and let the tears come.

Dear God, I'm so tired. I can't do this any more. Can't make appointments with doctors and dentists. Can't remember to save receipts for my tax returns. I'm tired of never having quite enough money to stop worrying. I don't treat my friends well. There's never enough time for them. I don't like to talk on the phone any more. I want to clean the house but don't know where to start. There are piles of things all over my room, and I can't even make out what they are—just stacks of colors and shapes. I started to read a book last week, and now I can't find it, and I can't remember what it was called or even what it was about.

Sometimes I read a paragraph over and over and don't even realize I'm doing it. Last Sunday I didn't understand the comic strips in the Globe.

Memories of old hurts flooded her. An unfaithful lover. Being mocked and called names by the other school children. All the times she'd trusted people and they'd turned on her. The insults her sister showered her with, which she pretended didn't bother her even though they cut like whips. Her parents never came to her rescue. She thought they encouraged it.

She wondered what it would be like to go insane. Sometimes she was tempted to "just do it," as they said in those silly sneaker ads. Just throw herself into it the way you'd throw yourself down a well or over the side of the Empire State Building.

They probably don't let you do that at the Empire State Building, though. It's probably all glassed in and stuffed with security guards and school children. It's not right to hurl yourself off the top of the Empire State Building in front of school children. Not even nasty school children. You probably can't even lean over and take a good look. You probably have to look at the view on a TV screen.

She remembered looking over the side of the Empire State Building. At least, she thought she did. But that might be a past life memory. She might have been one of the Native Americans on the original construction crew. Though she really couldn't remember a past life in which she hadn't been afraid of heights. And as for her present life, well...

Even during the few months she'd spent as a nearly-middle-aged hippie hanging out on Stanyan Street in San Francisco and dropping acid... Even stoned out of her mind, finding meaning in a grain of sand and convinced her physical body could fly, she'd never really been attracted to leaping from high places.

Actually, the glamour of that scene had worn off fast. When you knew the things she knew, getting high was pretty mediocre entertainment. Besides, she made the kids nervous because of her age. They felt as if they were getting stoned with their mother. They were always gracious to her, of course—you did that in the Summer of Love—and even let her join their nude Be-ins. But she could tell they weren't entirely themselves around her. So when autumn came, she changed into "square" clothes and, nearly broke, hopped the train back to Boston, and the family scandal.

The scandal had been the best part.

Her mind went blank.

Hermione rolled onto her side and a pillow slid to the floor. She didn't remember coming back to bed. Wasn't she just in the bathroom? She glanced at the clock. Time had passed. When? How? It'd be dawn in just a couple of hours. She ought to think about what needed to be done for the potluck. But she couldn't make her brain engage.

Damn.

Okay, back to the last thought.

Scandal.

What scandal?

She'd been remembering riding on a train. Crossing prairie, going east. Probably Colorado or Wyoming. She'd spent a lifetime or two in that neighborhood.

But what was she doing in this time? In her mind, she looked down

70

at her lap. She was wearing a skirt and low pumps. The man in the seat ahead was reading a newspaper. Pretending to reach for a dropped magazine, she bent down and pressed the side of her face against the back of the seat, looking for the date on the paper. She'd only caught part of it before he turned and scowled at her. Wednesday, she'd read, and Nineteen Sixty-something.

So there she'd been, on a Wednesday in Nineteen Sixty-something. On a train. She'd been, as Dory Previn once said, on her way to where?

If there was anything like luck in this mess, Stoner thought as she ran a brush through her hair, she was having a bit of it now.

Outside, on the back lawn, the coven was gathering. All of them. All at once, in one place. Perfect for her to check them out without arousing suspicion.

Not that she had the slightest idea what she was looking for, but at least she didn't have to track them down individually to look for it.

Glancing out the window, she saw that they were firing up the grills. A bottle of red wine was making its way around the group.

Please, Aunt Hermione, she thought, be careful what you eat or drink. Her aunt probably hadn't slept last night. Stoner'd heard her get up and go into the bathroom, and was about to go see what was wrong when she heard the water running and the 'thock' of the plastic cup against the sink, then the sound of the doors opening and closing quietly as Aunt Hermione made her way back to her own room.

Okay, no problem.

If she was going to go on like this, alert to every little sound and worried about every move the older woman made, she was going to drive both of them insane.

She slipped into a white shirt and jeans and took one last glance out the window.

She'd met some of the women of the coven before. There was Ruby, an older woman who often gave Aunt Hermione a ride to gatherings. And Dorothy, who was about Stoner's age and whom she'd run into from time to time in the Shelburne Falls market, the non-organic grocery store. She recognized Sabrina, who at twenty was a Maiden and the youngest member of the coven. Her mother, Sylvia, was due to be Croned in another two years. Sabrina had been born when Sylvia was thirty-five—not exactly ancient but older than the usual in those days. There were two older boys in the family, one a professor and one a computer nerd, who were alternately overprotective and disdainful of their baby sister. Probably because of this, Sabrina had a tendency to whine.

The rest were mildly familiar or not at all. She counted. They were still short two. Not counting herself. She wondered if a coven considered fourteen an unlucky number, the way some people thought thirteen at the dinner table was unlucky.

When Gwen got home from school, though, there'd be fifteen. Not knowing—as none of them had—that Aunt Hermione had planned to entertain on a weekday, she'd arranged to meet with parents whose son was barely passing Social Studies. It was to be her last parent conference of the school year, and had been scheduled for weeks. She didn't think she should miss it.

Marylou had stayed at work to cover the office. Later, she had a date with Cutter.

So Stoner was on her own. She didn't mind, really. It was easier to form her own impressions without hearing what her friends thought at the same time.

She took one last look out the window. The charcoal was rebelling. Ruby was on her second book of matches. Sylvia was shaking a rattle and invoking the aid of the Goddess of Fire and Backyard Barbecues. Sabrina looked adolescent and mildly disgusted, but the rest of them seemed to be having a good time.

Giving her hair one final push into place, she shoved her feet into her loafers and trotted down the stairs.

One thing she had learned about witches in the six years Aunt Hermione had been practicing the Craft, they knew how to have a good time. And, contrary to popular belief, they could do it without taking their clothes off. She'd attended a number of open-to-friends-and-family Sabbats. The serious part was solemn and dignified, but there was always feasting and gift-giving and displays of affection afterward. Sometimes the afterward lasted longer than the ceremonies. But then, one of their tenets was that "all acts of joy and pleasure" were the Goddess's rituals.

Stoner had once asked Aunt Hermione if that included popcorn. Her aunt said that popcorn was sacred indeed.

But this wasn't a Sabbat, just a get-together. For no other reason than that they liked one another. The best reason of all.

She looked across the lawn to where her aunt was talking to Sabrina and her mother. For the first time in days her posture was erect, her skin a healthy pink. Her gestures were sure, broad, animated. Even from where she stood at the edge of the back porch, Stoner could see the sparkle in her eyes. Happy to be among friends, among her own kind.

Oh, God, she prayed, or Goddess or Whatever, don't let it be one of these women.

Time to mingle. She crossed the yard to give Ruby a hand with the matches.

It was late by the time they sat down to dinner. The sun was already going down. It was too early for the major influx of mosquitoes, but the black flies were having themselves a rare old time. One of the women, who had spent all of her life in the woodlands of western Massachusetts, had brought a carton of citronella torches and candles. They set them out on and around the tables. It didn't exactly get rid of the insects, but it slowed them down. When the breeze dropped, the sharp pennyroyal-like scent drifted through the evening air.

Stoner found herself a place at the picnic table across from one of the women she hadn't yet met. This was a short, rather nondescript woman of late middle age. Her hair was dark with a scattering of gray. It was cut several inches below shoulder length and hung straight. She wore a pastel print dress with tiny flowers and a round lacy collar, a powder blue cardigan with pearl buttons, and no make-up. Her nails were short, unpolished and filed. Stoner guessed she worked in an office, and sang in the church choir on Sundays. Like a right-wing Christian, in fact. Which was impossible. Born-again Fundamentalists were not the kind of people who joined covens.

Now, that was stereotyping, she told herself roughly. Who's to say what kind of person would choose to follow the Old Religion? Most of the psychics she'd met were the most ordinary, everyday-looking people you'd want to meet. There were pagans who were college professors or librarians or worked in factories.

But probably not a lot of Fundamentalists.

It was a little hard to imagine a witch pledging subservience to her husband.

On the other hand, this woman across from her in the Wal-Mart dress definitely looked like the subservient type. The bitter subservient type.

The woman suddenly looked up, straight into her eyes.

Stoner smiled and introduced herself. A cold chill ran down the middle of her back from the nape of her neck to her legs to the ground and back up. They were the strangest eyes Stoner had ever seen. Black as ink, as if she had no irises at all but only dime-sized pupils resting in pencil thin white outlines. Like the eyes in a home-made doll.

It would be impossible to see what went on behind those eyes.

"Are you all right?" the woman asked.

"Yeah. Yeah, fine." She swung her leg over the bench and settled her plate on the table, glad there were people on either side of her. "I'm Stoner McTavish," she said.

"Hermione's niece. Yes, I know."

Stoner held out her hand but the woman ignored it.

Instead she smiled a quick, wooden smile. "My name is Mogwye."

For some reason, Stoner wanted to say, "I'm sorry about that." It wasn't the name. It was the way the woman said it, as if the very feel of the word were distasteful to her.

"'Mog' as in 'frog', 'wye' as in 'lie'."

"Interesting," Stoner said.

"You wouldn't think so if it was yours."

Stoner poked at her potato salad. "You could change it," she said at last, helpfully.

"Wouldn't make much difference, would it? I'd still know."

"Yes," Stoner said. "I suppose you would." She stared at her plate. There was no way this conversation was going anywhere.

She turned her head to introduce herself to the woman on her left.

Suddenly the day went cold. As if a gust of wind from the Arctic had wrapped itself around her.

It was more than cold. There was something dark and angry and evil in the air. The light seemed to dim as in the shadow of a thunder cloud. She looked around, but no one else looked as if they'd noticed. They should be racing for the house for warmth, or at least putting on sweaters and jackets…

Stoner was filled with a kind of fear she'd seldom known. She felt dizzy. Her stomach churned. The hairs on her arms and the back of her neck stood up stiffly. The back yard turned upside down.

I'm fainting, she thought with amazement, and gripped the edge of the table.

"Stoner." Mogwye was leaning toward her. "Are you all right?"

She swallowed hard. "Did you feel that?"

"I didn't feel anything." The black eyes she couldn't read looked into her. "What was it?"

"Cold. And dark."

Mogwye smiled. This time her smile wasn't just wooden. There was something wrong with it. "No, I didn't. You might be coming down with a virus."

"I might."

"Here." The woman got up and came around the table and took off her sweater and began to put it across Stoner's shoulders.

Panic flooded through her. She didn't want that sweater touching her.

"I have warmer clothes in the house." She got up quickly, nearly knocking Mogwye down. "Excuse me," she said as she brushed past.

That smile again.

Mogwye knew exactly what was happening.

Chapter 6

Mogwye.

A strange name, Hermione thought. A stranger woman. Silent. Withdrawn. Seeming to disapprove of everything and everyone. But a hard worker, who could be counted on to do whatever she said she'd do for the coven, and then go a little bit beyond.

In this day and age, that was a quality Hermione appreciated.

She'd tried to get to know her at first, because of their mutual interests in the paranormal. But if Mogwye really was a practicing psychic, as she said, she wasn't about to assume that as a basis for friendship. Hermione had approached her one evening after the coven meeting and invited her to coffee the next day. Mogwye had replied, pleasantly enough but firmly, that she "didn't socialize."

Hermione took her at her word.

But would she harm anyone? For whatever reason? For what reasons?

She gave her Tarot cards a single shuffle, fanned them, thought of Mogwye and pulled a card that attracted her.

Eight of Cups. Indolence.

She had a good idea of what that felt like. Exhausted and depleted. In the current vernacular, burnout. If this was the way the woman felt, she didn't represent a danger to anyone. She didn't have the energy.

"So what do you think?" Stoner was asking.

"I don't know," Gwen said. "I didn't exactly want to move into her house, but she didn't scare me."

"She scared me."

"I'm telling you, Stoner, she's harmless." Hermione held up the card. "Eight of Cups."

Stoner flung herself out of her chair and came over to stare down at what her aunt was doing.

"See?" Hermione said, offering her the card.

Stoner's face was very red. "This is crazy," she said, her voice trembling a little. "You're in serious trouble and you sit here looking answers in a deck of old cards."

"They've always served me well."

Stoner took the card and looked at it and slammed it down on the table.

"This is peasant stuff," she snapped.

"Thank you," Hermione said in spite of the fact that Stoner's words hurt. "Peasant thinking is very old, and very intuitive."

"I agree," Gwen said. "The cards have always worked for me."

Stoner stomped to the window. The lilacs were blooming. Hermione could tell Stoner hated it. "Everybody in this house has lost their minds."

"Her mind," Gwen corrected gently.

"Don't start. Just don't start." She paced back to the couch and threw herself on it and dug her heels into the coffee table.

"You know," Gwen said, "I'm glad I'm here right now. I've always wondered what you were like as an adolescent."

Hermione caught Gwen's eye and warned her to soft-pedal it.

"Have you eaten?" Marylou asked Stoner.

"I don't remember."

"Well," said Marylou, "there you are." She got up and started for the kitchen. "Do you want breakfast or lunch?"

"It's too early for lunch."

"And too late for breakfast, if we were forced to live by McDonalds' outrageous schedule. If you present yourself as a public service, you should serve breakfast any time. I'll come up with something."

"I'm not hungry."

Marylou rammed her fists on her hips. "And since when does eating have anything to do with hunger? We're talking about nutrition."

"What kind of nutrition?" Gwen asked.

"A bacon sandwich."

"I can't resist that," Gwen said with a laugh. "Make me one, too?"

"Coming up." Marylou turned back to Stoner. "And you'd better get dressed. It's the end of the month. I need you before lunch."

Stoner groaned. "Not the books. Already?"

"Yes, already."

"Do it without me."

"I can't. I need you to find those crumpled receipts you keep stuffed in your clothes and in corners of your desk drawers, and probably in your socks as far as I know."

"Let's do it after work."

"We have softball practice after work."

"I can't do softball today."

"You don't have to," Marylou said. "I can. But we still have to do the books, and there's no way you're going to do them alone. We'll go bankrupt." She flounced from the room.

Hermione thought about her predicament and what she could do about it herself and drew another card.

The Hanged Man. For now, there was nothing she could do.

"Gwen, I really feel stuck," Stoner was saying. "I know there's something about that Mogwye woman, but…"

She decided to pull two cards for Stoner. What she was doing. What she should do.

"I know," Gwen said.

"If there were some way to…well, get a handle on her."

The Devil. Capricorn. Good at taking action in the external environment. That was true enough. She pulled the second card.

"I don't think you should approach her yourself," Gwen said. "From your reaction last night, if she is up to anything, she knows you're onto her."

The Hermit. Turning inward. Seeking answers from one's spirit. That was good. Stoner could always profit from answers from her spirit. "Perhaps you should meditate," she said aloud.

Stoner looked at her as if she were totally deranged. "Sure," she said. "And where were you when your aunt lost her mind? Contemplating my navel."

"Stop it," Gwen said.

She decided to take a chance, and pulled an outcome card. She didn't usually do that in a formal reading. As soon as you did, the clients immediately forgot everything you'd said up to that time. She'd warn them it only hinted at how the future would be if things continued on the path they were on now. But they didn't care. They wanted to know what the future would be, not whether it was set or not. For them, it was always set.

The future. Everyone was afraid of the future.

It was the past they should really be afraid of. When the past came back to haunt you, that was true haunting.

She turned over the card.

The Tower.

A frightening card to the uninitiated. A tower being destroyed by lightning. Fire and chaos all around. Falling bodies. A rain of embers. But the symbolism was deceiving. The Tower was about change. Getting rid of old, calcified beliefs, burning out the unnecessary, clearing the way for new ideas and fresh air. Change inside the psyche.

The question was, to whom did this particular Tower refer? Herself? Or Stoner?

Because she'd had the feeling for a long time now that Stoner's restlessness grew out of a deep hunger, a longing for something that didn't exist. It was tearing her apart, even though she'd denied it many times. You could see it in her eyes. Feel it in her aura.

Maybe that was what the card was saying. Maybe this crisis would bring it to the surface.

If it could do that, Hermione thought, I'd gladly die or go mad.

But I won't go mad for nothing. I'll be damned if I will.

She swept the cards into a pile and wrapped the square of red silk around them.

"I could try to talk to her," Gwen was saying.

Stoner shook her head. "She knows you're part of the household. She'd be on guard against you."

"Well," Gwen said, "I guess that leaves..." She took a deep breath. "Marylou."

"Marylou," Stoner said thoughtfully. "Marylou." She broke into a grin that lit up her whole face. "It's perfect."

"It is?"

"Mogwye's never seen her, so she wouldn't connect her with us. She could just make an appointment. And you know how it is to be around her. She tells you so much about herself that before you know it you're telling her about yourself just to keep up with the conversation." She turned to Hermione. "What do you think?"

"It might work," Hermione said. She reached for her cards but stopped herself.

You didn't need to read the Tarot to know what was going on for Marylou. If she was heading into danger, you could see its gaping mouth with your own two eyes.

Once in the travel agency, Stoner's good mood faded quickly. Marylou had been delighted to be sent on a mission, and had phoned Mogwye immediately to set up an appointment. She claimed it was a dire emergency, and Mogwye put her down for this afternoon.

Good, Stoner thought. The sooner the better. The accounts can wait.

The trouble with that was, it meant Stoner had to handle the softball practice. Which meant she couldn't work on The Problem herself.

But what would she do, anyway, if she had the time? She had no ideas whatsoever.

Nobody had any ideas. That was the frustrating part. Nobody knew where she should start, or how she should go about it. What do you do when one of your loved ones is being driven insane?

She glanced at her watch. An hour and a half to the practice. She had time to drop in on Travis Kolek, M.D.

Jamming her paperwork into the desk drawer, she reached for the phone.

Yes, he certainly remembered Hermione Moore. Anyone who had ever met her probably remembered her. He was delighted to have the opportunity to meet her niece. And he had time free right now.

She liked his office. It was sunny and cluttered and devoid of shiny chrome instruments of torture.

Before he'd discuss her aunt, he said, he had to get her permission. Stoner appreciated that, even though any delay made her as jumpy as a grasshopper. It showed he was careful.

Calling the number he'd written in his file, he connected with Aunt Hermione and said her niece was in his office. What and how much information did he have her permission to share? And would she be willing to sign a release on her next trip in so he wouldn't be defrocked and she couldn't sue him.

They had a laugh together, then he took out a note pad and pen and began to make a list. It was, she assumed, a list of the things Aunt Hermione didn't want her to know.

Stoner was puzzled and a little hurt. She'd never thought Aunt Hermione had secrets from her, or didn't trust her. She wondered how long that had been going on, and what she'd done to raise her distrust. She wondered if it had been that way since she'd first arrived at the brownstone in Boston. She wondered what else she didn't know about Aunt Hermione. She wondered if she really knew her at all. She wondered...

"Would you repeat that?" Travis said into the phone. Then he nodded and wrote some more.

She was beginning to feel foolish. She wished Aunt Hermione had told her she didn't want anything known about her medical condition. But, then, Stoner hadn't asked, had she? It was her responsibility to say what she was about to do and get permission.

But it had been a spur-of-the-moment idea.

And Alexander Graham Bell had never invented the telephone. One simple call would have...

"Okay," Travis said. "I'll tell her."

He tore the page from the note pad.

"Your aunt said…" He handed her the note. "…could you possibly stop by the grocery and pick up these things?"

Stoner wanted to bore through the floor and pull it in after her. "About talking to you," she managed to get out through the clouds of embarrassment, "is it okay?"

"Of course." He leaned back in his chair and made the leather squeak. "She says the two of you have never had secrets between you."

"That's not entirely true," Stoner said.

"Until recently. She attributes that to her current mental distress."

"Distress?" Stoner said in a shrill voice, apprehension reducing her to stupidity.

"Her condition. I'd call it distress. She's certainly distressed."

"We all are," Stoner said.

He smiled a little. "I know, it's an upsetting situation. How can I help?"

She relaxed a little. "Did you find anything wrong with her?"

"Other than the symptoms? Forgetfulness, mental confusion, anxiety? No, I didn't."

"And the blood tests?"

"Completely normal."

"Did you test for drugs? Poisons? Anything like that?"

"Absolutely. Even LSD, MDA, speed, the whole bunch." He rocked in his chair. It sounded like a porch swing. "Though she certainly didn't look like a user to me."

"What about herbal drugs? You know, the kind that don't show up. Like mushrooms and stuff."

"Those are a lot rarer than the mystery writers would have us believe. And most of them do show up eventually, at autopsy if not before."

"Well, that's certainly a comfort," Stoner said wryly.

He noticed her wincing at his squeaking chair and stopped rocking. "I'm sorry," he said. "I do that unconsciously. It makes me feel like a real doctor."

Stoner stared at him. "You're not a real doctor?"

"I am. I just don't feel like one. Do you feel like a real travel agent?"

She shook her head. "But I'm not sure there is such a thing."

"I might have met one once, at least she claimed she was a travel agent, always wanted to be, couldn't imagine any other life" he said. "I'm not certain. She was very bustling and efficient, and seemed to have a packed suitcase behind her desk."

"It couldn't have been anyone at Kesselbaum and McTavish, then. Sometimes Marylou bustles, but she's not efficient. And she wouldn't have a packed suitcase on hand. She hates to travel."

"Interesting vocation, then," he said.

"She likes to think about traveling. And to look at photos and slides. Our customers enjoy that."

"But she could work for a photo processing business. More pictures, less worry."

"Personally, I think what she really likes is telling people where to go and what to do."

"Aha," he said, and lapsed into a brief silence. "Well, where do we go from here?"

"I'm open to suggestions."

"I'd like her to have a neurological work-up. It might be a waste of time, but I'd feel more comfortable if we ruled out every possible medical cause."

"Okay." It would make me more comfortable, too, she thought. No matter what, at this point I just want to find out what's wrong.

"You aunt was reluctant, but she agreed to make a temporary appointment in Worcester for early next week, for your sake. Should I go ahead and confirm it?"

Stoner nodded.

Travis spread his hands. "I'm afraid that's the best I can do." He got to his feet. "It's a helpless feeling, isn't it?"

"You don't know the half of it," Stoner said.

If there was anything she really wasn't up to, it was softball practice. The team was a bunch of hard workers and hard players, but it seemed whenever Stoner was around the practice deteriorated into raucous giggling, pushing one another with hips and hands, overly aggressive base running and guarding, and other show-off performances.

Marylou found this enchanting and referred to it as "baby dyke courtship behavior."

Stoner didn't find it enchanting—though if she thought about it, she knew she'd remember similar activity on the part of her own adolescent self. Mostly she found their hero-worship difficult since it required her to pay a lot of attention to everyone so nobody's feelings would be hurt and nobody would get the idea she was playing favorites. It was exhausting, and sometimes nerve-wracking.

Today she found it nearly impossible to keep herself from shouting, "Will you please grow up and play the damn game?"

Which, of course, she wouldn't do. Not with a pair of mothers lounging on a blanket over by first base. Instead she appointed herself coach/umpire so she had to pay attention to balls and strikes.

She kept them going until they were sweaty and out of breath and no longer in the mood to preen, then called a five-minute break. The mothers had brought an ice chest full of soda and bottled water, which softball mothers were supposed to do. And they had seated themselves in a place where they wouldn't be obvious, but could see every play their daughters made so they could describe it over the dinner table. Which softball mothers were also supposed to do.

Stoner wandered over and got herself a Pepsi, then sat down close enough to the mothers to ward off teenagers. But far enough away not to be thought eavesdropping. She was as hot and tired as the players. She hoped they were impressed.

"...that strange man who loiters around the Buddhist Temple," she heard one of the mothers say.

She took a lazy swallow of soda and lowered her head to her knees as if she were resting.

"But what was he doing here ?" the other asked.

"I don't know, but if they're going to allow that, I really have to think twice about Betsy staying on the team."

The other was silent.

"What could they be thinking of?"

"Well," the other said, "they're new in town. Maybe they don't know better."

"Maybe they don't."

Another silence.

"Someone should tell them."

Another silence.

"Yes," the other mother said, "someone should."

Nobody moved.

Stoner got up, stretched, and ambled over to them. "Excuse me," she said.

The mothers looked embarrassed and smiled hugely. "They look good, don't they?" said one, gesturing toward the field.

"I especially like the tie-dyed tee-shirts," the other said. "It reminds me of my youth."

"I couldn't help overhearing you," Stoner said, and settled herself on the grass beside them. "Who was the man you were talking about?"

"You mean you've never seen him?"

"No, but Marylou, the other coach...I'm Stoner McTavish, by the way...is here a lot more than I am. She might have."

"Well." The mother took a long drink of spring water, undoubtedly priming the gossip pump. "He's an older man, though it's hard to tell his age, really. He looks every age at once, if you know what I mean."

"I'm sure you've seen him around town," the other picked up. "He wanders around in ratty old clothes. They say he lives in a tent out in the woods, by that Buddhist place."

"He probably smells terrible," said the first. "Not that I'd get close enough to find out."

"God only knows where he gets his food. But I have my suspicions."

"Where?" Stoner asked innocently.

"Out of dumpsters, if he doesn't steal it. Oh, I suppose now and then someone gives him a handout."

"Probably Ethel," said the other. She turned to Stoner. "Do you know Ethel? Over at the Trolley Stop?"

Stoner nodded.

"I'm sure I've seen him in there. With the other shell-shocked derelicts."

"And you say he hangs around here?" Stoner asked.

"That's what the girls say. Oh, he never comes down on the field, but they've all seen him lurking at the edge of the woods."

Stoner pretended to be mulling over new information. "Have you heard anything," she asked at last, "to make you think he'd be a danger?"

"Well," second mother said eagerly, "there's nothing that would stand up in a court of law, but there have been rumors."

"What kind of rumors?"

"A few years back, there was a young man down in Adams who killed a girl. Cut her to pieces, from what I hear. He wasn't quite right, had been in the state hospital on and off since he was a child. After the murder, he disappeared into the woods up in the state forest. They looked for him for months. Because he could do it again, don't you know? And they couldn't find a trace."

The other couldn't contain herself any longer. "Months later," she broke in, "some hunters found him dead. Stark naked and hanging from a tree limb by his neck."

"Of course the official word was that he'd committed suicide in a fit or remorse or something. But everyone knows who did it."

84

The police, Stoner thought. Vigilante justice, to save the taxpayers a trial.

"The crazy man," first mother said, in case Stoner had missed the clues.

She couldn't think of anything to say but "Oh."

"I have to give the devil his due, though," said second mother. "He's never lifted a finger to anyone who didn't deserve it."

"Not yet," the other said ominously.

"There've been other incidents?" Stoner asked.

"Vandalism. Tire slashing. Painting words on cars. In the parking lot behind the grocery."

That sounded like adolescent ruffians to her.

"Anyway," first mother said, "better safe than sorry, I always say. It makes me very uneasy, him hanging around where there are young girls in shorts."

"Yes, really," the other said.

The young girls in shorts had rested their sylph-like adolescent bodies and were taking the field. Much to the delight of all the local peeping perverts, no doubt.

Stoner got up. "Thanks for the warning. I'll certainly pass along your concerns to my partner and we'll see what can be done about it."

She went back out onto the field, leaving the mothers very satisfied with themselves.

Marylou was pleased with the way she had handled the Mogwye situation. So pleased, in fact, that she refused to tell them anything until after they'd eaten, then built the tension even more by lingering over her meal. Marylou, who never lingered over anything and certainly not over a meal. There was a good, steady pace about everything she did, especially eating. She claimed to have worked it out so that she had time between bites for both enjoyment and anticipation.

"That's why I'm thin," she often said, although she wasn't. It was her mother who was the thin one. Dr. Edith Kesselbaum, who ate in fast food restaurants whenever possible and was never without a handy Twinkie or Milky Way.

Marylou loved the fact that her mother was a contradiction to everything the dietitians and nutritionists said. "Besides," she'd declare, "look at them. Skinny, skinny, skinny, every single one. So what do they know?"

But tonight Marylou was making them all wait for her to finish, deliberately drawing the energy in the room toward herself.

Stoner didn't blame her. In fact, she liked that about Marylou. Marylou believed that she had nothing to offer to what she called "Stoner's crime-fighting business." So now that she had a chance to contribute, she was going to milk it for all it was worth.

She finally announced that it was time to "retire to the living room for after-dinner coffee and a touch of dessert."

When she had them all seated and arranged to her satisfaction and trying not to giggle, she began. "As you know, I was sent undercover to determine the true nature of the witch Mogwye. I was able to get an appointment immediately, which tells me she is neither retired nor popular. She gave me directions to her house, which I followed to the best of my ability only getting lost on two occasions and having to retrace my steps. The way led far back into the woods, over roads that have yet to see the benefit of the Department of Highways in this lifetime. In a word, dirt. These roads have not been touched since the spring run-off, and are uncomfortable and deeply rutted. Sorry about the mud on the car, Gwen. Just be glad you weren't there to see what almost happened."

Gwen covered her face with her hands and groaned.

"Fortunately," Marylou went on, "I was able to arrive at Mogwye's house nearly on time. It's a small frame house, in a clearing in the forest. Surrounded by about three-quarters of an acre of yard. I say 'yard,' not 'lawn' because this is an unusual kind of yard. She has had it completely cemented over. As she explained to me later, she sees no reason to suffer unnecessarily from insects and weeds.

"She answered the door herself, and ushered me into her 'office,' which is also her living room. In addition to this room, there is a small bedroom and a minuscule bathroom, which I know because I asked to use it. This 'convenient room,' as she calls it, is about the size of a stall in a public rest room. Large enough to remove a tampon but too small to insert one."

Stoner rolled her eyes.

"This does not seem to be a problem for the lady, however, as she appears to be well beyond the change of life."

"Of course she is," Aunt Hermione interrupted. "She's a Crone."

"Her house is furnished with only the most rudimentary necessities of life. Very little furniture, and a single plate, glass, and silverware setting."

"What did you do?" Gwen asked. "Go through her cupboards?"

"I didn't have to. There are no doors on anything. She says mice are less likely to infest when there's no place to hide. Though I suspect it's because of her very large and vicious-looking cat. She calls it a Maine

Coon cat, and has named it Bangor. Which I suppose is better than Boothbay Harbor.

"To anticipate your next question, no, it is not her familiar. Mogwye claims that many practitioners—that's what she calls herself, a practitioner—believe house pets don't make good familiars. Being all too familiar on a daily basis."

She looked to Aunt Hermione for confirmation.

Aunt Hermione nodded.

"For the reading she asked to hold a personal object of mine, something I handle frequently. This was difficult, since I'd dressed for the occasion and wasn't wearing any of my usual clothes or jewelry. We finally settled on my Gold Visa card. The reading was actually amazing. She knew things about me that even you all probably don't know—like falling down and chipping a baby tooth when I was quite young. She knew that my mother was divorced from my father, and that my stepfather is a retired Government worker. She guessed IRS but that's close enough to FBI. She told me the exact nature and quality of my love life, which is none of your business.

"She didn't tell me I had been cursed, or that she could improve my life if I'd give her ten-thousand dollars. In fact, she didn't even urge me to return unless I felt the need. Her rates are in line with what you charge, Aunt Hermione, and she has never been tempted to become a reader on a psychic hot line. From what I can gather, the woman is legitimate and honest."

"But what about Aunt Hermione," Stoner asked. "Could you tell if she might want to hurt her?"

Marylou frowned. "Unfortunately, she had nothing to say about that. I asked her if she'd heard of A.H., being in the same line of work and all. Told her I'd gotten both their names. She was noncommittal. Said she'd heard A.H. was a pretty good clairvoyant, hadn't heard anything bad. She said you had some common acquaintances and interests, but she didn't know you."

Aunt Hermione nodded. "That's just what I'd say about her."

"What was her tone?" Stoner asked. "Did you pick up any undercurrents? Jealousy? Anger?"

"None at all, and I was listening for them. If there's any animosity there, she certainly has it under control. Nothing about you, of course, Stoner. I would have given away too much if I'd brought you up." She took a sip of her coffee, then leaned forward. "I almost forgot. I saw no evidence of herbs or plants, poisonous or otherwise. Of course, that doesn't mean much, since she's surrounded by woods just bursting with plant life."

She gave a little shudder. "Rather creepy, actually. Underbrush."

"Anything else?" Gwen asked.

Marylou shook her head. "That's it. If I'd caught her mixing up some mind-altering potion, or chanting curses in Aunt Hermione's direction, it would have been another matter. But I do think I found out as much as anyone could."

"A. H.," Aunt Hermione said thoughtfully. "You know, I rather like that. Straightforward and to the point, and rather poetic."

"You did a great job," Gwen said. "I can't imagine anyone doing it better." She poked Stoner in the side. "Isn't that right?"

Stoner, who'd been struggling with her feelings of disappointment, said, "Huh?"

"Don't you think Marylou did well?"

"Oh, yeah, sure. I'm sorry. I was just kind of hoping she'd turn out to be guilty or something."

"So was I," Marylou said. "Despite her hospitality, I did find her less than charming. So I guess it's back to the drawing board."

"Well," Stoner said, "it doesn't entirely clear her of suspicion, but it does take her off the short list."

"Who's on the short list?" Marylou asked.

"No one."

Aunt Hermione stood and stretched. "I think I'll go to my room and read for a while. Maybe I'll fall asleep. Thank you, Marylou, this has been one of the most entertaining evenings I've had in a long time." She patted Marylou's head as she went by. "Actually, I believe you should plan to tell us stories at least once a week. You're a natural."

Marylou actually blushed with pleasure. "Thank you."

"A. H.," Aunt Hermione said again. "I have to give that some thought."

"As I recall," Gwen said, "it's my night to do the dishes." She gathered up some of the cups and napkins and dessert dishes.

"Where do we go from here?" Marylou asked after a brief silence.

Stoner shrugged. "I wish I knew. She has an appointment with a neurologist in Worcester the day after tomorrow. If that doesn't turn up anything…"

"You don't put much stock in what her spirits said, do you?"

"I guess not." She hunched down deeper into the sofa. "Someone stealing her soul? Driving her insane? Someone from the Other Side? It's all so…I don't know."

"Makes sense to me," Marylou said.

"I don't even know if there is an 'other side,' much less what goes on there." She looked up at her friend. "Do you?"

"Nobody's ever proved it to me. On the other hand, nobody's ever proved there isn't. I'm keeping an open mind."

"I'm keeping mine shut. I don't want anything else to fall out."

"Your attitude surprises me, actually," Marylou said. She got up and straightened the magazines on the coffee table. "After the experiences you've had."

"I don't want to think about that," Stoner said.

"Well, you know what they say. 'He who refuses to think about the after life is destined to repeat it.'"

Stoner laughed. "It'd be nice, wouldn't it, if we could just whip on over to another plane and get all the answers?"

"Isn't that what Aunt Hermione does in her readings?"

"I'm sure she'd say that. Personally, I think she dips into the other person's collective unconscious or something."

Marylou gave her an indulgent smile. "You don't believe in the other side, but you believe Aunt Hermione is walking around with one foot in everyone else's unconscious. Really, Stoner."

Stoner sighed. "I can't talk about this stuff. It makes me nervous. I wish I could just go away and build bird houses or something."

"I think," Marylou said as she found a bread crumb on her blouse and flicked it away, "you'd better go back to your list making."

"Yeah."

Gwen came in to clear the rest of the coffee cups and a plate of cookies Marylou had nearly polished off.

"If you refuse to deal with ghosts," Marylou said, "you'd better start dealing with people."

Something had been nagging at Stoner since this afternoon at the practice. She decided to say it. "Marylou, I know this is an awkward thing to ask, but...well, how much do you know about Cutter?"

There was a very long, still silence.

Marylou left the room.

"I don't believe this," Gwen said after a while. She was holding the cups balanced precariously on her arm.

"What?"

"What you just did."

"I only asked—"

"You as much as accused Cutter of trying to harm Aunt Hermione.

How could you do that?"

She knew she'd made a terrible mistake. She couldn't think of anything to say.

"Marylou loves him," Gwen went on angrily. "She might even be in love with him."

"But we don't know him."

"Marylou loves him," Gwen repeated. "That's enough to know."

"Not for me," she said stubbornly.

"Cut him some slack, for God's sake. For Marylou's sake."

Stoner stared at the floor. "It's not about Cutter, Gwen. It's about Aunt Hermione."

"It's also about friendship. And loyalty. And trust." She started out. At the doorway she turned. "I'll sleep in with Marylou tonight."

Chapter 7

Two days later it wasn't any better. Marylou still wasn't speaking to her, in spite of her attempts to apologize. And Gwen was forgiving but distant.

Aunt Hermione, who hadn't been there but whom Stoner had told about her bad behavior, couldn't remember what she'd been told. This morning she'd gone to the grocery store and come home without the groceries or her purse.

The only time she seemed to be almost tuned in was when she talked with Grace on the phone. Even then she was so spotty that Grace insisted on coming out to visit next weekend, whether Hermione was better or not. Edith offered to come, but Stoner didn't feel ready for that yet.

Right now she had to do what she could to repair her friendships. She still hadn't come up with the slightest idea of where to begin.

She might as well follow Marylou around. Stalk her. If she could get her to understand, maybe it would fall into place.

Whatever "it" was.

One thing she was certain of, as long as her friends were holding themselves aloof from her, she couldn't even think rationally much less creatively.

So when Marylou left the agency to go to softball practice, Stoner waited a safe five minutes, then locked the door and headed for the field.

She felt pathetic, sitting there on the sidelines looking like a dog whose owners have just driven off for the afternoon without taking it along. Sad-eyed and pitiful. But, unlike the dog, as soon as the owners were out of sight, she wasn't going to go looking for a neighbor's dog to go knock over a few garbage cans with.

Marylou had acknowledged her arrival by simply staring at her and going back to coaching.

That made her angry. Yes, she'd made a mistake. Yes, she'd said something tactless and hurtful. But they'd been friends for more than twenty years. Didn't those years count for anything?

Or was it like the house she'd grown up in and run away from? You could be every mother's ideal, but make one little mistake and the ceiling caves in on you. From saint to scum in a few brief seconds, and years to crawl back up to saint.

Well, damn it, she wasn't going to crawl any more. Not for Marylou, not for Gwen, not even for Aunt Hermione. They could solve their own problems. Mogwye had the right idea. Be a grump and keep the whole world at bay. Hide out in the woods and cement down the lawn. Whatever. She was out of Shelburne Falls and out of their lives.

She got up and walked toward the patch of woods that marked the shortcut home. Striding so if anyone was watching they'd know she was mad. And if nobody was watching, they'd find out when they got home and discovered she'd gone.

She was taking the car, too, by God. Let them figure out how to get by with just one for the three of them. Let dear A. H. conjure up a solution to that problem.

"Stoner."

It was more like a low hiss than a word.

She looked around.

There was nothing there but underbrush, alder bushes with their pine cone-like flowers.

"Stoner."

It made the hair rise on her arms.

He was standing right in front of her and she hadn't seen him. Not until he moved, choosing to be seen.

"Cutter," she said. "You scared me. I wish you wouldn't lurk that way."

His eyes shot back and forth, scanning all the open space around. "They got to you," he said.

"Who?"

"Them. The soul-stealers."

Stoner laughed. "Of course not."

"Yes," he said. "They did. I can feel it."

"This is…" She started to say "crazy," and realized she'd really be in trouble if she did. "…confusing."

"Not if you could see them."

She could feel irritation like acid in her stomach. "Nobody's trying to get me. There's nothing like that going on, and I wish everyone would just shut the hell up about it."

He seemed to smile a little. "That sound like you to you?"

That stopped her. No, it didn't sound like her. She hadn't sounded, or looked, like her for two days now. And while we were on the subject, what she had said to Marylou hadn't sounded like her, either.

And it wasn't like Gwen to give her the ice box treatment.

Or like Marylou to carry a grudge beyond the first flare-up.

"You think something's going on, don't you?" she asked Cutter.

"Nope." He pulled out a vicious-looking Army pocket knife and began opening and closing it rhythmically. "I know it."

She was mesmerized by the knife. "What do you know?"

"I've seen 'em."

"Where?"

"'Nam. Africa. Washington, DC." He gave a crooked grin. Two of his back teeth were missing. "Government's full of them."

She would have laughed, except for the way he was opening and closing the knife. "Would you please put that away," she said. "It makes me nervous."

He folded the knife and slipped it in his pocket. "Afraid I'm going to stick you with it?"

"No."

"Habit of mine. Makes me feel safer. Sometimes I forget where I am."

"I sympathize," Stoner said. "Lately I forget who I am."

Cutter nodded. "They do that."

"There is no they," she said firmly.

"Not where you're lookin'. You're barking up the wrong tree when you should be climbing it." He glanced around. "I gotta go. Been talking too much. When I talk too much, I feel like I'm going to explode."

She put her hand on his arm. "Cutter, I want to apologize. For something I said to Marylou. About you."

"I know what you said." He pulled away, not in a rejecting way but just because the touch made him uncomfortable.

"I'm sorry I was suspicious of you. It was only for a minute. These days I think I'm a little suspicious of everyone."

"Hell," he said, "you better be. It's the only way to stay alive."

He turned away and disappeared.

Marylou and Aunt Hermione insisted that they were driving to Worcester to the Medical Center together, and no one else was invited along.

Stoner had heard a lot of bad ideas in her life, but this one took the cake. "You hate to drive," she pointed out to Marylou.

"Aunt Hermione's driving. I'm going along so there'll be someone to call 911 when she goes into a ditch."

She appealed to her aunt. "You're not well," she said. "You'll get lost. You'll forget to come home."

"Actually," Aunt Hermione said, "I've been feeling a great deal better the past day or so. It'll do me good to accomplish something, even if it's only driving the car."

She was about to argue when she stopped herself. Aunt Hermione really had seemed better. They'd all been feeling better, as if something had lifted from them. Marylou decided that Stoner hadn't meant to hurt anyone, but was merely being her bumbling, inept self when she asked about Cutter. Gwen decided the tension between them was just too awful, and that she realized what Stoner had really been trying to do.

It had all happened since Stoner's conversation with Cutter. But that was only a coincidence.

She hoped.

For herself, Stoner had decided to lighten up and do what Aunt Hermione wanted and see where it led. Not that she had much choice. Absolutely nothing was getting accomplished the way she was going about it.

And she couldn't bear the thought of all of them piling into the car and being crowded and carsick and then piling out at the Medical Center and stepping on one another's heels like ducklings. The living situation was just on the verge of becoming claustrophobic.

"Okay," she said. "Gwen and I'll have a day together."

That seemed to please Gwen, too.

"There are a couple of things I have to do," Stoner explained when they were alone together. "One here and one in Northampton. Do you mind?"

Gwen laughed. "Mind? You must be kidding. Time with my lover and a trip to the big city, all rolled into one."

Northampton wasn't exactly a Big City, not by Boston standards. Compared to Shelburne Falls, though, it was a booming metropolis. In Shelburne Falls, you could eat out at the Railroad restaurant, or get gussied up in your finery and toot on out to the Mohawk Trail for dinner at a quaint and overpriced New England tourist trap. But Northampton had dozens of restaurants of every ethnic influence and level of dress. Although, it being New England, you wouldn't be refused service no matter what you were wearing—unless it was bare feet and no shirt, or you were a dog. You could just about make it through all the restaurants in a month of eating out, and turn around and start all over because a third of them would have closed and reopened as a different kind of ethnic.

There were a lot of small shops offering locally-made art work and pottery for sale, but Shelburne Falls had that in the Salmon Falls Marketplace. And the clothing stores were geared largely toward college students and professionals. What was really interesting about Northampton was that it had once been described in a national supermarket tabloid as 'the home of ten thousands sex-starved lesbians,' or words to that effect.

It always seemed a little strange, to watch the younger lesbians strolling down the street with their arms around one another. They looked so natural, but Stoner could still remember when doing something like that could get you beaten up or worse. She tried to remind herself that these were different times, but the old hesitations lingered. She supposed they always would.

But it was always nice to see lesbians being free, and nice to know, if the mood struck you, you could take your lover's hand in public.

Gwen pulled up in front of the house that their directions had brought them to, and said she'd wait until Stoner was inside, just in case they'd made a mistake. Then she'd be back in about an hour.

Stoner got out and started up the walk.

It was an old, small house set back from the road behind a sprinkling of pine trees. The roof was slate, with a central chimney. A picture window had been installed into the front of the house on one side of the door, and beneath it a flower bed of old fashioned delphinium and stock and salvia. On the other side of the door, there were two paned windows. A large black cat lay on the porch and eyed her sleepily but warily.

She went up the flagstone walk and met her first obstacle. Three doorbells. One was old, a small white button ivoried by age and set into a tarnished metal circle. Beneath it a more up-to-date rectangle with a raised symbol of musical notes. On the door itself was an ancient key-type bell you could ring by giving it a good hard twist. She supposed the new one was what she wanted, but what if there were two residences—one in the back—or a separate office, and she summoned some innocent person needlessly. She could try the key bell, but what if it was an antique and she broke it? Diana had given good directions, but she hadn't mentioned doorbells.

The cat was looking at her as if it were about to distrust her motives. She'd never had any experience with an attack cat, and didn't want to start now. Aunt Hermione's series of cats had been civil but aloof to her, so she figured they didn't see her as the Goddess of Felines.

She rang the bell with the raised musical notes.

It was a late-middle-aged woman who opened the door. Her face tended toward square, and her gray and dark brown hair hung straight and chin-length. Her eyebrows were nearly white below her bangs, her eyes a lively slate blue. She wore a pantsuit of soft, dark, flowered material that looked as if it would be appropriate whether she were doing a few quick yoga exercises, taking a nap, or running out for a last-minute appointment with her tax lawyer.

The cat made a dive for the indoors between their legs.

"Stoner McTavish?"

Stoner nodded and stepped up into the house, which made her a little taller than the older woman. She heard Gwen start the motor, and turned to give her a quick wave.

When she turned back, the woman was holding out her hand. "I'm Elizabeth," she said.

Her handshake was warm and firm.

"Diana recommended you," Stoner said.

"Yes."

Stoner remembered that Diana had set up the appointment, and felt foolish.

"Come in the kitchen," Elizabeth said. "We can talk over coffee."

The cat had taken up residence on the sofa and was doing its best to cover every inch of available space.

"That's a nice cat," Stoner said.

Elizabeth picked up the cat, held it in front of her face and nuzzled it.

The cat licked her nose.

"Actually," she said, "he's a bully and a beast." She nuzzled it again. "Aren't you?"

"What's his name?"

"This week, it's Geddown." The cat leapt from her arms and back onto the sofa. "He doesn't care what you call him, he either answers or he doesn't. Mostly he responds to my voice and my intent."

The kitchen was dark, having few windows but lots of wood. In addition to the conventional appliances, shelves had been built into the walls over old-fashioned free-standing radiators. On one side of the room they were filled with herbs and plates and cups and glasses. On the other side they were filled with books.

Elizabeth motioned her into a chair and placed a plate of sweet rolls on the table. "If you're not hungry," she said, "I am. Help yourself."

"This is a nice kitchen," Stoner said. Now that she was here, she wasn't certain how to begin.

"I'll tell Karen you said so." She put a cup of coffee in front of Stoner. "Karen's my 'significant other,' as they say. We're original, Women's Movement Dinosaurs. That little pot there is sugar. Very hard to find in lesbian households."

Stoner laughed and reached for the sugar bowl. "That's the truth."

Elizabeth brought her coffee to the table and sat. "Thank God I'm old enough to remember condiments."

"I like you already," Stoner said.

"Good. I like you, too. Though I find those green eyes unnervingly attractive, especially with the chestnut hair. Did you come that way originally?"

"Yes, I did."

The woman sighed. "Well, some of us are blessed and some of us are here to learn not to envy." She stirred sugar into her own coffee. "So. Fill me in on your problem."

"It's not really my problem, it's my Aunt Hermione's problem. I mean, it's my problem because I love her and I don't like to see her like this and I don't know what to do. And that's why I'm here, even though I'm not sure I believe... No offense, I hope, but...well, it seems like a lot of mumbo jumbo to me."

If she'd really tried, planned for weeks, she couldn't have said it any worse.

"I will never speak again," she said.

Elizabeth gave her an amused look and took a sweet roll. She tore off a scrap and nibbled on it. "I'm sorry," she said at last. "I was thinking of something and completely missed what you were saying. Could you start over?"

Stoner rubbed her face with her hands. "I'm sorry. Really. That was rude."

"I've heard worse," Elizabeth said. "Although, for sheer incomprehensibility you did pretty well."

"It's just...this thing has me all screwed up." It sounded weak and inadequate and she hated herself for it.

"I understand that. Honestly. And I have heard worse. Shamanism isn't exactly a household word. And many people associate it with hallucinogenic drugs. Imagine the kinds of remarks that generates in this culture." She passed Stoner the plate of rolls. "Now, take a deep breath, relax, and blurt out whatever's on your mind."

Nobody'd told her to do that in years. It threw her back to her early days with Edith Kesselbaum. Sometimes she missed therapy, though it was certainly an uncomfortable experience at the time. But the luxury of an hour of undivided attention and caring from a person who wanted nothing from you but honesty, and who maybe was a little bit wise on top of it…that was pretty hard to come by in the world of every day.

She took a roll and buttered it and thought about where to begin.

"My Aunt Hermione," she said at last. "She's been unwell. I don't mean sick, but it's as if she's wasting away. And she's losing her memory, and sometimes her personality seems to change." She ran out of words.

"And?" Elizabeth prompted.

"She's been to a doctor and there's nothing wrong with her. Nothing they can find, anyway. She's over at the med school in Worcester today having a neurological workup."

"Good. What else?"

Stoner took a bite of the roll and chewed slowly and swallowed. "It started months ago, but I didn't really notice it then. But lately it's been getting worse, and fast." She couldn't think of anything else.

"That's it?"

"I'm afraid so. I'm not very helpful, am I?"

Elizabeth broke off another bit of roll. "You're sure that's all?"

Stoner nodded. "That's all."

"Have you picked up anything on another level? Maybe it strikes you as nonsense, so you don't mention it or think about it."

A thought surfaced briefly. She shoved it back. "Nothing."

Elizabeth smiled at her softly. "I think there is something."

"What makes you think that?"

"The way your eyes shifted to the left, just for a second."

She hesitated. Well, what the hell, she didn't even know this woman and probably wouldn't see her again after today. Probably she'd say she couldn't help, or didn't want to help, or…

"Sometimes I think I can see through her," she said. "Her body. It's as if she's a ghost."

Elizabeth's eyes lit up. "Now we have something to go on. Can you tell me any more?"

"I try not to think about it."

"There's nothing wrong with seeing that, Stoner. Lots of people do. And, like you, they don't want to talk about it."

She liked the way Elizabeth said her name.

The woman was looking at her. "This has been a rough time for you, hasn't it?" Elizabeth asked.

It touched her on a deep and private level and made her want to cry. She shrugged instead, and gave a little laugh. "Psychics make me crazy," she said. "They read your mind."

"I'm not a psychic."

"You're not?"

"Any information I get, I get on a Journey. In Ordinary Reality I'm dense as lead."

"But you understood…"

"That comes from experience. Most people have the same fears you do. And, frankly, if they don't—if they're too eager to do this—I worry they'll enter Non-Ordinary Reality and refuse to come back."

Well, that was spooky enough. For some reason she found it reassuring. Anyone claiming to work at the terminus between reality and fantasy ought to be a little bit spooky. "My aunt's a clairvoyant," she said.

"Good," Elizabeth said. "I have a few issues I need help with. Maybe we can exchange services. Does your aunt know you're coming to see me?"

"No, but she won't mind. In fact, she'll be ecstatic." She realized she sounded a little plaintive.

"This doesn't please you." Elizabeth passed her another roll. She hadn't even realized she'd finished the first.

"Sure, it does. For Aunt Hermione. She's wanted me to get involved with psychic things ever since I came to live with her. She says I have a talent for it. But I'd rather not."

"How come?" Elizabeth brought over the coffee pot and refilled their cups.

She'd never tried to explain this, even to herself. Her reaction had always been sudden and certain, and that was as far as she'd taken it. "I think," she said as the words oozed their way into her mind, "it's always been hard for me to live in…uh…Ordinary Reality." She glanced at Elizabeth to see if she'd gotten the terminology right.

Elizabeth nodded.

"It was hard, growing up different from other people. And my parents hated it, and me."

"For being a lesbian." It wasn't a question, it was a statement, adding her part to the story.

"Right. I ran away from home at sixteen. God, that seems so young now."

"It was."

"Aunt Hermione took me in. I was pretty messed up. Depressed, confused. Hated myself. She got me a therapist and made me finish high school and then college."

"You were lucky to have her."

"I think I'd be dead now if I hadn't. I know I would be." She took a swallow of coffee. "Sometimes, when I look back on it all at once, how hard it was to learn how to live in this world without it taking everything from me... I just feel so tired from it all. The idea of trying to learn how to get along in another world is too much."

Elizabeth drank her coffee and said, "Hmmmm," thoughtfully.

"And who knows what kind of stuff there is over there? Or up there? Or wherever there?"

"Well, there's one thing I can say about Non-Ordinary Reality, it's not homophobic."

"These people, things, spirits that Diana talked to said they wanted me to do it. Help Aunt Hermione. There was something about it that I had to do."

"That must be difficult," Elizabeth said, "feeling the way you do."

Stoner ran her hand through her hair front to back, an old habit from when she was a kid and had a cowlick and her mother would yell if it stuck up. "I just want to run away. But there's Aunt Hermione, I can't run out on her. And if I'm the only one who can help..."

"Sort of like being a child and forced to go to the dentist."

She felt an enormous rush of fear and sadness. "Yeah, pretty much like that."

Elizabeth leaned back in her chair. "Okay. If your aunt wants to do this, and if it seems like the right way to go, and if it's necessary for you to be a part of it...that's a lot of 'if's...there are things you can do to protect yourself. I'll show you how. And there will be people with you every inch of the way."

"Will you be there? Wherever there is?"

"If that's what you want, of course. But you have guardian spirits, too, Stoner. It's just a matter of meeting them."

"Well," Gwen said. "Elizabeth sounds like a truly wonderful woman. Should I be jealous?"

Stoner shifted onto her side. The sun was hot, and filtering softly through the trees that arched over the park. "Gwen, you should never be jealous. Like it or not, you're stuck with me."

"Life is good," Gwen said. She stretched out beside her.

Stoner fingered a strand of Gwen's hair, counting the few grays. She had just enough silver to lighten the already light brown. It had been like that when Stoner first met her, and it hadn't changed in the years since. It probably wouldn't until one day—maybe when she was about eighty-five or something—she'd wake up one morning completely gray.

The thought that they might still be together then was so overwhelming it scared her. The thought that they might not scared her even more.

She fondled short strands of Gwen's hair. "Elizabeth says this stuff works whether you believe it or not."

"Thank God. If it doesn't, you won't have to feel guilty for the rest of your life, thinking you ruined it by not believing."

"Yeah." She was silent for a while, feeling the sun, feeling the softness of Gwen's hair.

"What'll she do for her?" Gwen asked.

"Take a journey into Non-Ordinary Reality."

"Sounds like fun."

"Not much," Stoner said.

Gwen smiled. "Not for you, maybe. When she gets into this Non-Ordinary place, what happens?"

"Try to find out what's wrong. She thinks maybe it's power loss. Or an intrusion. Or soul loss."

"I know all about power loss," Gwen said. "I used to have a car that kept losing power on the Turnpike. It turned out to be the alternator."

Stoner smiled. "I don't think it's that kind of power. See, there are these Power Animals, spirit animals that help us through things, and when they get lost we have power loss."

"That's what I said," Gwen said. "I lost horsepower."

Stoner swatted her lightly. "Pay attention. And an intrusion is something black and ugly that gets in you and makes you sick."

"Sort of like your first lover."

"Yes, sort of. Do you want to hear this, or not?"

"I want to, but my head won't behave."

Stoner tilted Gwen's head up to look her in the eye. "Where did you go while I was talking to Elizabeth?"

Gwen looked guilty. "Nowhere."

"Come on. I know a chocolate high when I see one."

"Bart's," Gwen mumbled.

"I knew it. I'll bet it was a brownie sundae with chocolate sauce."

"I had to. I'm premenstrual."

"Uh-huh."

"Honest." She snuggled closer. "Tell me about intrusions? Please?"

"Okay." She lay down with Gwen's head on her arm and looked up at the trees. "Intrusions make you sick. They start as thought forms. Maybe you're a really negative kind of person. Or sometimes someone wills them into you."

"Someone like our friend Mogwye?"

"Maybe. People in cities get them a lot."

"Air pollution?"

"Negativity. People put out negative energy at random, and then you come along and suck it up."

She stroked Gwen's shoulder. "Soul loss is caused by trauma. You send a part of your soul away and it gets lost. Or someone takes it."

"That's what Cutter said."

"I know."

Gwen was silent for a moment, and then she said, "Stoner, are you sure you're all right?"

"I'm fine. What?"

"You're talking about this stuff as if it's second nature to you. If I did, it wouldn't mean much, but when you do it's cause for deep concern."

"I know. But when Elizabeth talks about it, it just sounds so…well, so ordinary."

"Not to me. Not coming from you."

Stoner didn't know what to say. Gwen was right, of course. But thinking like this felt almost comfortable—for the moment. Letting herself go with it, not trying to make sense. It was like the feeling she got when she studied a beach stone or a blade of grass. A feeling of amazement at the complexity and perfectness of it.

Not corn, though. Corn was too scary. Corn took one little seed and a little dirt and water and turned itself into a six-foot plant with hundreds of copies of itself all tucked into corn condominiums. One little seed. That was power. If corn ever decided to run amok, they were all done for. It wasn't a good idea to antagonize corn.

And how about Cutter? Is it a good idea to antagonize Cutter?

The thought popped into her mind and startled her and made her heart race.

But Cutter had warned them. Cutter had been helpful. Cutter seemed to understand.

Cutter showed up in exactly the right place at exactly the right time.

If she could translate his more cryptic comments correctly, Cutter knew a lot about what was going on.

As much as she did. Maybe more.

How?

Gwen had drifted off to sleep, no doubt dreaming of chocolate. Stoner started to wake her, then held herself back. Gwen hadn't been pleased with her for questioning Marylou about him. Maybe she should wait a bit and see what she could find out for herself.

And keep an eye on Cutter.

But he appeared like mist, and disappeared like mist.

How do you keep an eye on mist?

Chapter 8

Finally, Hermione thought as Elizabeth gave her a hand up from the rug, we're doing something that makes sense.

It hadn't been a long session, but neither of them had expected it to be. All they had to do was keep their intent in mind, and before the drums had even started the Power Animals and Spirit Guides—and a few curious on-lookers—were gathering in the Lower World.

Hermione's Power Animal of the moment, a small brown spider who intended to teach her how to use the wind to travel from place to place, led her down the hole in a hollow tree and into the piercing light of Non-Ordinary Reality. She hadn't done this kind of Shamanic Journeying before, at least not in this lifetime. But it seemed both natural and right. She supposed she'd gotten her training at another time and place, and Elizabeth's refresher course had been exact and brief.

She and Elizabeth had greeted one another like kindred souls. There was an instant empathy between them—as that old Hopi woman of Stoner's would say, they 'made good medicine' together. Even though neither had any memory of having met the other before, they found to their delight that their minds ran along the same tracks.

"Well," Elizabeth said after she had rolled up the rug they'd been lying on and made them each a glass of iced tea and written in her journal while Hermione took a few moments to rest and acclimate herself to Ordinary Reality. "It's a soul loss problem, all right."

Hermione wasn't at all surprised. "But what in the world is it about?"

"They wouldn't—or couldn't—tell me. My Guide gave me very explicit instructions. Or, rather, she gave them to my Power Animal. Did you find a Power Animal."

"I did." Hermione stirred her tea and hesitated. "Is it all right to tell you about it?"

"Of course, if that's your inclination."

"I haven't been in this particular neighborhood before," she said. "At least as far as I recall. You will let me know if I break any rules?"

"There aren't many," Elizabeth said. "Everything you need to know you should get from your Guide and your Power Animal. Pay attention to them. Did you meet a Guide?"

"Several. Fortunately, none of the old crowd. They'd have wanted to gossip and give me advice all day and into the night." She took a sip of the tea, which was herbal and quite refreshing. "The animal that led me to the Lower World was a spider."

"Oh?" Elizabeth seemed as delighted as a child.

"A small brown spider. It said its name was Rusty." She filled in what else she could recall about webs and breezes.

"That's perfect, isn't it?" Elizabeth's eyes glittered. She started a fresh page in her notebook and scribbled madly. "Navigating your way through a troubled wind, and using it to your advantage. Exactly what you need."

This time she couldn't help smiling at the Shaman's excitement. "It's wonderful to meet someone who's excited by her work."

Elizabeth looked a little embarrassed. "I've been doing this for years, and it always surprises me. I think there's a part of me that doesn't expect it to work. Or at least not in such elegant ways."

"Spirit's full of surprises," Hermione said.

"More than we could ever imagine," Elizabeth agreed. "There's one thing here that concerns me, though."

She knew exactly what her Shaman meant. "My niece."

"My Guide told me it's absolutely essential that she be involved."

Hermione nodded. "I've had that message, too."

"And yet…from talking to her… I hope I'm not betraying any confidences, but I get the feeling she's not comfortable with this."

"She's not."

"It puzzles me. Especially growing up with you."

"It puzzles me, too," Hermione said. "Maybe something in a past life. We've lived quite a few together, but there are always a few dark corners from other times." She looked around the little room where they sat. The candles were still lit and glowing softly. The bowl of water for the Water Spirits was calm and smooth as glass. No unwanted vibrations in this room. The walls were hung with medicine shields made from skins and tiny bones and dried plants and colorful bits of string. Crystals lay everywhere. On the floor, the shelves, the low tables. Even between them on the couch. It was a restful room, with a healing atmosphere.

Geddown came to the French doors that led to the living room beyond and glared at them malevolently.

"Are we in his spot?" Hermione asked.

"We're keeping him from his favorite sunbeam." Elizabeth turned and stuck her tongue out at the cat, which walked away with a look of disdain. "It's only his favorite because we're keeping him from it."

Hermione laughed. "Cats are all alike," she said. "But you don't dare tell them that. You'd think," she went on after they had silently contemplated the joy and mystery of cats, "she'd take the psychic world in stride. Stoner, that is. Not your cat. She's not exactly a stranger to it. Certainly she believes it works for me, and I've never heard her be critical or mocking. But when it comes to her personally…she's never been taken with it. There's always a little fear."

"There is with me, too," Elizabeth said. "Don't you feel it?"

Hermione thought. "A little. Not exactly fear, more like apprehension. You never know what they're going to want from you next."

"Exactly."

"And, frankly," Hermione said, leaning forward confidentially, "I've had to ignore them on more than one occasion."

"Me, too. And times I wish I had. Not that what they ask is that bad, it's the getting to it that can be hellish."

"I suppose that's because it's left to us to work out the details." Hermione chuckled. "And their sense of time…"

"Don't even talk about it," Elizabeth said. "They think we can take a minute and stretch it into a year. Just because they can."

"A skill we lose when we incarnate. And you can spend an entire incarnation getting it back."

"And then you pass into transition, where you don't need it."

"Does it ever occur to you we might be a little bit nuts, doing this plane over and over?"

"Absolutely," Elizabeth said. "Earth is the mental hospital of the universe." She stretched her arms over her head. "You know, it's a real luxury to talk with someone like this. When we both know what we're talking about."

"Or flatter ourselves that we do," Hermione said.

Elizabeth laughed.

How many lifetimes did I go through and never meet this woman? Hermione wondered. And why did we wait so long?

"Well," Elizabeth said, "I suppose we should think about getting your soul pieces back. I saw at least four, myself, but I'm sure there are more lurking here and there."

"No wonder my fuel tank's approaching empty."

"Now, here's what we'll do." She took a sheet of paper from her notebook and started a list. "It would help if you can round up as many of your close friends as possible for the ceremony. It's good to have loved ones to welcome you back."

"All right." That meant Grace and Gwen and Marylou and Stoner... Stoner.

She had a gnawing feeling she didn't like. As much as she felt it would be good for her niece to learn a little about psychic matters in a participatory way, now that she was actually faced with it, she was hesitant. Stoner's reluctance could be based on very real dangers.

"What is it?" Elizabeth asked.

"I was thinking about Stoner. I don't know what to do about this."

"Yes, it's a judgment call."

The trouble was, Hermione trusted intuition. Even the intuition of people who didn't believe in intuition. Maybe even more so, since it had to be a strong message to cut through all that disbelief.

She stared into a candle flame. If it would just come clear. Or even only a little clearer. "I don't know what to do," she said.

"Well, let's schedule the retrieval for a week from now. It'll give you time to make up your mind. And maybe you can go a little deeper into what's bothering Stoner about it."

Hermione nodded. "Elizabeth, in my place, what would you do?"

The Shaman thought. "I think I would dance."

"Dance? "

"Dancing can be very powerful. Dance your Power Animal until you feel at one with it, then ask what you should do."

She couldn't help smiling a little. "And how does one dance a spider."

"Simple," Elizabeth said. "Dance the way a spider would dance."

"Hang a rope from the rafters and swing from it? At my age?" Hermione chuckled. "I'm afraid that would be too much even for Shelburne Falls."

"You haven't lived there very long, have you?" Elizabeth said. "Oh, and by the way, to draw in real power, dance naked."

"Now, that," Hermione said, "is going too far. I may be New Age, but I'm not young. It's important to set an example of dignity and restraint for the young."

"From what I can sense," Elizabeth said as she got up, "you already have a model of dignity and restraint in your household. You need to set an example of risk and play."

Stoner wanted to run. Anywhere. And keep on running. Somewhere there were no problems, and nobody needing her and no occult mumbo jumbo. Where there was nothing to be afraid of and no one to be afraid for. Where she didn't care about anyone.

She looked up at the moon, pale against the daytime sky—a crescent moon, its horns pointing north. Waxing or waning? Coming or going? She could never remember which.

Aunt Hermione always knew what the moon was doing. Witches were like that. Some of them really got into it, basing haircuts and house cleanings and bill paying on the lunar phases. Aunt Hermione had pared it down to a simple principle. The lunar month was divided into comings and goings. If you want to start something, do it at the waxing moon. If you want to end it, do it while the moon is waning.

And to catch a soul-taker? Is that a coming thing or a going thing?

She had a hunch Mogwye would know the answer to that. And a lot of other things besides. Like when and how to cast a spell. And how to heal, and how to catch a soul.

Mogwye wouldn't pursue the soul, Stoner thought. Mogwye would spin a web or set a trap, put out a little bait and let it come to her.

Maybe she was doing that now. Arousing Stoner's interest and concern at the potluck, then sitting back to see what she'd do with it.

Well, two could play at that game.

Assuming both of them knew how the game was played, which Stoner definitely did not.

There was nothing she could do about Mogwye, anyway. That was for Marylou to handle

She sighed. Life had certainly decided to throw a lot of challenges her way. Foremost being its habit of constantly putting her in situations where she had to think deviously, something she'd never been able to do. If there was a lesson in this, she wished someone would give her a few hints as to what it was. The only one that came immediately to mind was, "Learn to approach life as though you have a criminal mind."

She hardly thought the cosmos would put that out as a good thing.

Challenges and lessons. Those were the buzzwords these days. There weren't any tragedies or disasters any more, just challenges and lessons. Good old American Happy-Think.

Well, thank you very much, but what she was looking at now was an aunt who was unwell and losing her soul or her mind or both. Who could only be saved by Stoner doing something the nature of which she didn't understand for beans. And, incidentally, which she really, really didn't want to understand. That was one big hairy challenge.

She felt a rush of anger and picked up a stone and hurled it out into the street.

"Damn it, what do you want from me?"

Did anyone hear? She glanced around quickly. Nothing moving. Except maybe Cutter's soul takers.

Sometimes these days she felt as if they were taking a little of her soul, too. Nothing pleased her. Nothing excited her. There were times over the past week when she'd looked up at Gwen unexpectedly and felt nothing. No flutters, no tingles, no rushes of warmth. One morning she'd stayed in bed pretending sleep and watched as Gwen went through the little morning rituals—finding her reading glasses, sitting on the edge of the bed while she checked her schedule, slipping her feet into her shoes, a last-minute run of comb through hair, touching Stoner's face lightly and lovingly as she left the room—that used to reassure her that everything was right with the world. But on that particular morning she'd merely watched her coldly and wondered if she was falling out of love.

Or maybe they were only reaching a new stage in their relationship, the one in which passion deepened into love, the one in which they'd be friends as well as lovers, and family, and...

Stoner had to admit it, she was starting to know how it felt to be Aunt Hermione. Depressed was how it felt. She was beginning to be forgetful, too, because she couldn't interest herself in anything long enough to remember it. Couldn't focus on it, really. She'd try to read, and her eyes would dutifully travel across the page, and suddenly she'd realize she was reading the last sentence in the paragraph and had no idea what was in the middle.

Maybe someone was trying to steal bits of her soul, too. She didn't feel as if there were much there worth stealing.

"Stoner?"

She looked up.

Gwen stood at the bottom of the porch steps, her arms filled with books and papers. Her shirt was half out of her skirt. There was a dark smudge on one cheek. Her hair looked as if she'd been attacked by cats.

Stoner felt a hard knot of fear in her stomach. "Are you all right? What happened?"

"Nothing. I got a ride home with a junior with a convertible. Always memorable but predictable." Gwen shifted the books. "Help me with these, will you?"

She jumped up and caught the books just as they began to cascade to the ground. "Productive day?"

Gwen grunted. "Mayhem. If I make it through to the end of the week, it'll be a miracle." She dropped onto the porch steps and dug a crumpled envelope from her pocket. "Perfect day to get this."

Stoner set the books aside and peered into the envelope. "Pink-slipped again."

"No surprise, of course, and it probably doesn't mean much. It's just something they like to do so we can't enjoy the summer."

"You'll be rehired," Stoner said as she handed back the envelope. "No way they're going to let you go."

"Unless the one I'm replacing decides to come back. I'm the new kid on the block, you know." She blew her hair out of her eyes. "Not that I begrudge her. It's just hard going from seniority to juniority. Is that a word?"

"I don't think so."

Gwen leaned back on her elbows. "God, by this time of the year, I sometimes wish they'd dump me. I could spend the rest of my life supporting myself returning bottles and cans."

"You'd be stir-crazy in a minute." She took Gwen's hand. "Besides, think of the winters."

"We could move to Florida for the winter. Would you?"

"Never. Florida's full of rich people and bugs."

"Which do you hate more?"

"I don't hate either of them. Bugs disgust me, and rich people scare me. I'm always afraid I'm invisible to them, and they'll step on me or run me down."

Gwen squeezed her hand. "And what's new with that topic we are carefully avoiding?"

"Aunt Hermione?"

"Uh-huh."

"She's still at Elizabeth's."

"So you don't know what Elizabeth recommends."

"Sure, I do. She told me when I saw her. That's not going to change." She tried to focus on the touch of Gwen's hand, so she wouldn't feel her own anxiety. "I'm going to have to do something I really, really don't want to do and make a mess of it."

"You don't have to do it, Stoner. Everyone was clear that it's your choice."

Stoner grimaced. "Is it? This is about Aunt Hermione. Where's the choice in that?"

Gwen stroked the back of Stoner's hand with her thumb, absent-mindedly and frowned. "What are you afraid of?" she asked softly.

"I don't know." She glanced over. "I really don't know. The whole thing ties me in knots. I guess I'm more comfortable in Ordinary Reality."

"Really? Have you taken a good look around lately?"

Stoner laughed a little humorlessly. "Anyway, it's all probably a lot of nonsense—ghosts and soul-stealing and all that. I'll bet we'll find out it's some nasty person doing some nasty, very clever breaking and entering."

"It would have to be very clever indeed," Gwen said. "Unless you're still thinking about an inside job."

"Not here. But I can't get the coven out of my mind. She goes there every week. They serve food. It wouldn't be hard…"

"No, it wouldn't."

"But how do I get close to that? If someone really is doing this."

"Someone like Mogwye?" Gwen suggested.

"Yeah, someone like that. The only person she doesn't know in the household is Marylou. And she's talking to her again right now. If she seeks her out too many times, Mogwye will be suspicious for sure."

"What we need," Gwen said, "is someone who can watch Mogwye and Aunt Hermione in the same place together."

Mogwye was pleased with herself, the way she could appear calm and unconcerned, maybe even a little stupid. Should have been an actress, or even a poker player. A riverboat gambler. She wondered if she'd ever been that. In the past, maybe, or maybe in the future. It all went around and around, anyway. Yesterday was tomorrow's future, they said.

The woman was in the bathroom. Checking to see if anything in the house had changed since last time, she imagined. Well, it hadn't, so she might as well not waste their time. She hadn't found an excuse that would take her into the sleeping loft yet, but she was working on it, you could tell. It amused and annoyed her, the way they assumed she was stupid enough to fall for this charade. If she was stupid, they were more than stupid, that was how she saw it.

She wasn't sure why she was supposed to do this, but she'd had a dream. She always did what her dreams told her, and so far everything had come out just the way she wanted.

Her sister-in-law, the Born-again, said her dreams came from the Devil. She'd say that, of course. The bitch thought everything that was fun or even interesting was from the Devil. A great compliment to His Nibs, admirers like that.

Mogwye didn't believe in the Devil. She didn't believe in God, either. She only believed in dreams. It was because of dreams that she'd become a witch. After she'd seen the movie "Rosemary's Baby," she'd dreamed of witches for months. That was how she knew what she was supposed to be.

The toilet flushed. Mogwye focused her attention on her facial muscles, making sure everything was in placid order. She couldn't help but smile a little, eager to go on with the pitiful lies she was telling the Kesselbaum woman.

"Inside the coven," Stoner said. "That'd be the best place." She frowned. "But there's no way we could infiltrate the coven. And we don't know where they meet. Even Aunt Hermione wouldn't divulge that."

"Yeah." Gwen pulled a blade of crabgrass and made a whistle of it between her hands. She blew a couple of times. "I guess we're stuck, unless..."

Suddenly she looked over at Stoner.

Stoner had the same thought at the same moment.

"Cutter," they said.

Marylou couldn't wait until after dinner to begin her story this time. "I arrived promptly," she started in before they were all seated at the table, "bearing flowers. Mogwye mentioned last time that the only thing she missed from having paved over the yard was flowers. A bright and fragrant bouquet of old-fashioned snapdragons and larkspur."

She stopped long enough to fill her plate with meat loaf and mashed potatoes and winter squash with a river of gravy over it all. Aunt Hermione passed her the hard rolls and she took one and broke it and dipped it in the gravy.

"I told her," she said as she munched happily away on a morsel of roll, "that I was terribly grateful to her for seeing me again so soon. An emergency had arisen."

She looked around at her audience.

"And?" Gwen said eagerly.

"And...now this is the clever part." Marylou broke a shred of meat loaf from the slab on her plate, dipped it in potatoes and then gravy.

Stoner felt like grabbing the entire bowl of potatoes and building Devil's Tower National Monument.

"I told her," Marylou went on, "that there'd been a sudden serious illness in my family. I think I said it was my father." She paused for a moment, thoughtfully. "I hope I said it was my father. I mean, I hope I was consistent. Not saying 'father' one minute and 'mother' the next. You know."

"I'm sure you were fine," Stoner said through clenched teeth.

Marylou glanced at her. "Are you all right?"

"Sure. I just wish you'd...well, do you think you could speed things up a bit?" That sounded harsh. "Your dinner's getting cold," she added quickly.

"Gosh, so it is. Okay. So. I was testing her to assess her reaction to illness. Would she offer suggestions? Give me a spell to cast or something? Ask whether he...or she... God, I hope I didn't screw that up. Whether the victim had enemies. See what I'm getting at?"

They all saw and nodded.

"Well," said Marylou, "she didn't bat an eye. Just asked if the person were hospitalized, was I satisfied with the kind of care he/she was getting? What was the prognosis?" She spread her hands and shrugged. "Not a word about alternative methods of healing. What do you think of that? I think it proves she's innocent."

"I think," Stoner said, "she's pulling a fast one." Any witch of sincerity, or even a decent healer/clairvoyant would have suggested a white candle at the very least. And a prayer or two to the Goddess. Aunt Hermione would have suggested they offer one together right on the spot. "Visualize the person's name," she'd have said, "in great shining white letters. Concentrate. Pray that wholeness and harmony may be restored in their lives." Then she'd have sat silently for a little while until the prayers had gone wherever prayers went.

Marylou looked at her as if she were ungrateful.

"Time will tell," Aunt Hermione said.

"All right, this is the important part," Marylou moved on. "She completely opened up to me about herself. How her family had abused her as a baby. How she'd run away from home, taken up with a young man...just a child, really, like herself. Had a baby, which was taken from her by nuns in the home for unwed mothers she'd found refuge in."

"I believe the part about the nuns," Gwen said hopefully.

"Me, too," Aunt Hermione agreed. "And look around this table. Gwen, you were mistreated as a child, and Stoner ran away from home. Marylou has taken up with a whole series of unsavory characters—present boyfriend excepted, of course. Each element of the story is believable."

Stoner couldn't tell if her aunt meant it, or if she was being ironic. She nodded in agreement.

"I think," Aunt Hermione said, "until we know more, we should give her the benefit of the doubt. She hasn't done anything except be an unpleasant person, and she probably has good reason for that." She took a swallow of coffee. "And I still keep coming back to the fact that I haven't sensed any strange energy coming from her toward me."

"But what about me?" Stoner broke in. "At the potluck. I know she was sending bad vibrations in my direction."

"That may well be," her aunt said, "but we don't have a clue as to why, do we? Maybe you offended her in some way."

"Those were heavy vibes. There aren't too many people I've offended that badly."

"Actually," Gwen said, "there are quite a few. My ex-husband, for one, then there was that psychologist Millicent Tunes, and…"

"Okay, okay," Stoner said. "I've made some enemies. But not without doing something. I'd never even met her before that night."

"There's the matter of past…," Aunt Hermione began.

Stoner's temper flared. "Please. Don't start in on past lives. I can't bear it." She wanted something nice and concrete, with only three dimensions and easily visible on this very Earth plane.

"You're right," Aunt Hermione said. "I don't know everything." She gave Stoner an apologetic smile. "Even though I sometimes act as if I do." She pushed her chair back from the table. "If you'll excuse me, I want to listen to a new meditation tape Cecilia, one of the clairvoyants at P.A.R.A., gave me last night. She made it herself. And I need to start pulling together the plans for the soul retrieval. If you have nothing to add, Marylou?"

"Only one thing. I thought it was kind of curious. She asked me if anyone had ever put a curse on me, because of all the jewelry I was wearing."

"Why would anyone curse you for your jewelry?" Gwen asked. "I could see cursing someone for their perfume, especially in a public place, but why jewelry?"

"She said it's commonplace—that was the word she used, 'commonplace'—to wear jewelry to counteract a curse. Did you ever hear of that, Aunt Hermione?"

The older woman thought for a moment. "I don't believe I have. Unless she was referring to crystals. People often wear crystals to ward off negative energy. Tourmaline is supposed to be especially effective."

"I'm not wearing crystals, only silver, and she was definitely referring to me."

"In that case I have no idea what she meant. Was she wearing any?"

"Not that I could tell."

"It certainly is curious," Aunt Hermione said. "Call me when you're ready for the dishes to be washed."

Stoner was about to tell her it wasn't necessary, she'd be happy to do them. But the last time she'd done that Aunt Hermione had just about taken her head off, snapping that she was "still good for some things."

At the entrance to the living room, Hermione turned. "Marylou, I think it would be a good idea if you didn't consult Mogwye again for a while. We don't want to arouse her suspicion. Just in case."

"Fine," Marylou said. "Though she still hasn't really told me what to do about my sick father."

Aunt Hermione laughed. "Light a white candle."

"This is really confusing," Marylou said at last. "One minute she says she doesn't believe Mogwye means any harm, and the next she tells us to be on our guard. What does she really believe?"

"Everything," Gwen said.

There was a brief silence around the table, the unspoken question in the air, "What do we do next?"

Gwen yawned and stretched a little. "Are you thinking what I'm thinking?" she asked Stoner.

Stoner nodded. "Time for plan B."

Marylou looked at them questioningly.

"Ask Cutter for help."

"Well!" said Marylou. "It's about time."

"We need someone to observe Aunt Hermione and Mogwye at the Esbat," Gwen explained, "and there's no one we can think of who's better at making himself invisible than Cutter."

"Obviously," Marylou said, "you haven't met some of my friends from the Big Y World Class Market."

"I didn't know you'd made friends there," Stoner said.

"That just shows you how clever they are."

Gwen laughed. "Or you are."

"But we know Cutter," Stoner went on. "And he has a way of…" she grimaced, hating to even acknowledge this part of it, "…seeing things the rest of us can't."

"Stoner," Marylou said seriously, "are you feeling all right?"

"I'm fine. I just—these things happen."

"Not to you."

"Look," she said with a flash of irritation, "I'm not saying I believe anything. But we don't have much time. There'll be a full moon on Monday night, and that's when the soul retrieval's coming down. I'd like to see what we're dealing with before then, Mogwye-wise."

What she didn't say was that what she really hoped was that it could be avoided if she could prove someone—all right, admit it, Mogwye—was behind this. She was, after all, their most logical, and only, suspect. She had motive—professional jealousy or something they hadn't thought of. Means—access to various healing and not-so-healing herbs as well as knowledge of how to use them. Most witches had that, or access to it. And opportunity, lots of opportunity. Opportunity this weekend, as a matter of fact, since the coven had its weekly meetings on Sundays.

It would be cutting it close, but there might be time to gather enough evidence to call for a postponement…she almost called it a "stay of execution"…of the Journey.

She still didn't understand her reluctance, only that it was growing by the day. In fact, she had passed from simple reluctance to genuine fear. All she knew was that something terrible was going to happen if she went on that Journey, something that would change her life. Her life might not be quite perfection as it was, but it was satisfactory. She had no desire to change it.

Or did she? Satisfactory was one thing, but satisfied was another. There was something definitely unsatisfied. But maybe everyone's life was like that. Not quite perfect. It was probably the human condition. It was just ridiculous American corporate advertising that made people think life should and could be perfect. That kind of thinking opened the door to all sorts of nonsense, from household cleaners that wrecked the environment to nursery schools where children were expected to choose a career track before the age of five. Big bucks for the fitness industry and the guys who made a fortune peddling self-improvement tapes over late-night television.

She didn't expect life to be perfect. She never had. The trouble was, no one could give you a good description of what it was supposed to be like. Nothing to compare it to, so you could sort of assess how you were doing every now and then. If you were making a mess, you could look around for what you were doing wrong, and if you were doing it okay, you could relax and get used to being unsatisfied because it didn't mean anything, it was just a part of normal living.

"You're not happy," Gwen said suddenly.

"What?" Startled, she looked around. Marylou had left the room at some point. She hadn't noticed. "No, I… I mean, everything's fine."

"I don't mean about us. You're not happy in your life."

"Yeah, well, I am worried about Aunt Hermione." She felt completely flustered, and knew she was hiding the truth and couldn't stop herself.

"No," Gwen said, and leaned across the table toward her. "In your life. Something's missing, isn't it?"

"I… I don't know. I mean, what…?"

"You haven't really been right in months."

She hated and loved the way Gwen always saw through her. "Yeah, I guess… I don't know. I feel as if I don't know what to do with my life. I mean, it's okay and all but…well, is this what I'm here for, to be a travel agent?"

Gwen smiled. "I doubt it."

"But I don't know what I want. I want something. I want to do something, to give something." It embarrassed her to say that. "But I don't know what."

"Yes," Gwen said. "As my students would say, 'bummer.'"

Stoner had to smile at that. "I'm afraid it's a little more serious than 'bummer.'"

"So is 'bummer.' It really means they're so miserable they could die, but they want to appear cool." She looked Stoner hard in the eye. "Sound familiar?"

Stoner nodded.

"Please, Stoner, when things like that are bothering you, talk to me. I know it without you telling me, and it makes me crazy when you don't talk."

She smiled. "I'm like Aunt Hermione that way. It's probably genetic."

"It's worse than that," Gwen said. "It's Yankee."

"I know. But everyone else has things on their minds, too. Aunt Hermione, and your teaching, and Marylou with Cutter…"

Gwen reached across the table and trapped Stoner's hands beneath her own. "But this is you, love. You. My Stoner. I don't care if it's nothing more than a hangnail. I want you to share it with me. I want us to be 'us.' Do you understand?"

Stoner nodded, feeling ashamed but loved at the same time.

"Say it out loud."

She glanced up. "I understand, Miss Owens."

Gwen slapped her hand lightly. "Okay. Now let's see what Cutter can do for us."

Chapter 9

At last, a little time alone. Hermione breathed a sigh of relief that was—blessedly—audible in the empty house. Stoner and Marylou were at work, Marylou having convinced a group of tourists to let her plan a sight-seeing trip around the area ending with a night at Tanglewood. Not only was it a boost to their business, but it required a lot of arranging.

Gwen had gone down to Greenfield to a teachers' workshop on computers in the classroom.

There'd been a good deal of secretive buzzing and a sudden stoppage of conversation when she entered the kitchen this morning. But there was no way to guess what they were up to. Besides, she really didn't have the energy to question them or even talk to them beyond the amenities. She'd taken her coffee and some cold macaroni and cheese from Tuesday's dinner, and gone into her sanctuary. Stoner didn't even try to follow, which confirmed that they were plotting something.

Whatever it was, she hoped it wouldn't require much activity on her part. But no one said anything about it, and she heard them leave—first Gwen, then Stoner and Marylou together—for their various activities.

At last she could dance her Spider.

She'd done a little tentative dancing right after the journey, but the house was always occupied, and she frankly felt a little self-conscious waving her arms around and scuttling back and forth across the bedroom floor.

Naked was out of the question, of course, and so were hanging ropes. But she was willing to try to dance like a Spider. She only hoped Travis wouldn't decide to drop around to see how she was doing. He'd done it last week, just to report that there was no bad news, only good, from the neurologicals and other lab tests. She'd been about to slip into the tub, and had to open the door dressed only in her bathrobe. She could have just let him stand there, of course, but curiosity had gotten the better of her.

"Everything's normal," he'd said cheerily. "All the tests came back negative."

Hermione had felt a bit negative, herself. Pulling her robe together where it threatened to slip and expose breasts, she had politely informed him that he could have called in that information. And that "good" news is not necessarily good when you know there's something wrong with you but you don't know what it is. She was tempted to tell him in addition not to contact her again until he had a diagnosis in mind, but he looked pitiful. Like a puppy that bounds up to greet you, and all you do is complain about its muddy feet.

To make up for her lack of appreciation, she offered him a glass of iced tea. He accepted. Then she realized they were out of iced tea, and had to make some from scratch and then drink it and chat with him, and by the time he left, her one precious hour of silent alone time was gone.

Maybe she should spend a lifetime or two working on her problem of spinelessness, Hermione thought as she combed through their collections of CD's and tapes looking for music to dance a Spider by. But the thought of the trials she'd have to put herself through on the way to learning were daunting. Of course, that was from her current perspective. Somehow, when you got to the Between, everything seemed easy.

That was because you weren't lugging around a human body and coarse human emotions and a perspective on life that ended at the tip of your nose.

Ah, a tarantella! Perfect. She slipped it into the player, locked the front door, pulled the shades, and stood in the center of the room, eyes closed, as she let the music take her.

At first she didn't move at all. Then she found herself spinning slowly, toward each corner of the room and back to the table that marked the center. Out and back, out and back, each time returning to the center, spinning threads of light. The music invited her to link the arms of the cobweb and she began to circle the table, each circle a little wider, circling, circling until the whole room shimmered with threads of silver light and droplets of stars.

Hermione stood and gazed at it, her heart pounding with the beauty of it, her lungs swelling with pride. A slight breeze came up and shook the web, setting the star drops to winking.

"Swinging breeze!" she heard herself shout, and let the wind take her. She soared high over the room, her web a net to support her if she fell. Higher, higher until she was through the ceiling, through the roof, over the town. The river below, sepia with runoff from the snow states to the north, threaded its way between hills of springtime green, beneath a sky of thin, pale blue.

"Glorious," she whispered to the wind.

"Yes," the wind answered.

Other creatures were afloat. A red-tailed hawk circling for its dinner. Insects as small as atoms. Dust from comets and meteors. An eagle. Pollen. A single snow flake, a raindrop holding a tiny rainbow.

She wondered where the smoke was, the polluting exhale of factories. Looking down, she saw nothing of people and their industry.

We've flown outside of time, she thought.

And then she was back, sliding to earth on a thin silver thread, trailing behind her a golden rope that glistened in the sunlight. Down through clouds and treetops and finally into her home, where her net caught her and eased her to the ground and back to herself.

"Thank you," she said to Spider, invisible but there in spirit. "It must be very wonderful to be you."

Cutter raised his head and froze, a snake caught in a sudden flash of light or movement, testing the air with only the tip of its tongue. Something was wrong. Or at least changed. Different. Not necessarily danger, he reminded himself. Changed didn't always mean danger. He could remember when it didn't, before he went to war. Before he went crazy. He remembered what it felt like to be sane. He wished he didn't. It hurt.

It hurt to remember when he was younger, when he could walk into a grocery store simply because he needed or wanted something, or because he was bored. When he didn't have to wait for a day when he felt strong enough that he was pretty sure he wouldn't suddenly start screaming. He remembered when he could greet people on the street, even folks he barely knew, and shoot the breeze for a while. And wouldn't have to go home afterward to change his clothes because the ones he wore were drenched with fear-sweat. He remembered when he could eat a meal without holding each bite in his mouth for minutes while his tongue probed for tiny splinters of bamboo or glass and tasted for poison.

He hoped the day would come soon when he didn't remember any more. Because he knew he'd never be sane again.

The docs at the VA didn't like him to talk that way. They accused him of "defeatism," and lectured him about "self-fulfilling prophesies"—which was the one thing that could really make him laugh, it was so ridiculous and superstitious—and claimed he was only making himself sicker with that kind of attitude. Attitude, as if it was a jacket he could put on or take off. They didn't understand that insanity had attached itself to him and bored its way into every organ and cell and nerve in his body. Insanity steered the ribbons of blood through his veins. Insanity filtered what he heard and didn't hear, and made up dreams for him to dream. Insanity kept him alive. He knew they meant well, but they hadn't seen the Beast.

Where had he gone? She was certain she'd seen him, kneeling by a garden of rocks, dressed in his robes and plucking bits of fallen leaf from between the stones. Close enough so she knew it was Cutter. And now he'd disappeared. She glanced toward the woods. Maybe he'd ducked in there. But nothing was moving. When she glanced back, he was there again, kneeling among the white stones.

All right, she thought, Cutter has his ways, and laughed to herself a little hysterically. She walked up to him.

He sat back on his heels, a bit of dead grass between his fingers.

"Hi," Stoner said.

Cutter nodded, his face unreadable. Was he angry? Glad to see her? Impatient at her interruption? Afraid she was going to criticize him?

"I… uh…wanted to ask a favor of you," she said.

He only nodded again and waited.

"Don't you want to stand up?" she asked. "It looks uncomfortable, kneeling on those stones."

"I been uncomfortable before," he said.

"Well, sure, I can imagine. But why be if you don't have to?"

He merely shrugged. The truth was, he wanted his head to stay lower than hers, so she wouldn't be afraid. Women were a little bit afraid of men all the time, anyway, or should be. He didn't want to add to it by being tall.

Stoner folded her legs under her and sat beside him, on the grass. She didn't want to make him nervous by towering over him.

Cutter's mouth cracked in a little smile. Women were like that, too. Didn't want anyone to feel left out or put down.

She noticed the smile but decided to ignore it, afraid that to ask him about it would make him feel he was being scrutinized. Marylou had specifically warned her against making Cutter feel scrutinized. "Whatever you do," she'd said, "don't scrutinize."

They glanced at each other and looked at the ground and watched a couple of ants navigate the mountainous terrain of the rock garden.

"I have a problem," Stoner said when she couldn't bear the silence any more.

"Didn't figure this was a date," Cutter said. "Marylou'd kill me."

She let herself laugh, which produced a tiny, visible grin from him. "I was hoping you'd be willing to help."

"Do what I can." He wished she'd hurry up and get to the point. His anxiety was rising like fire ants around a plundered mound.

"It's Aunt Hermione. You know she's not well."

He nodded. Of course he knew. He'd warned her about the ghosts.

"And we can't find out what's wrong."

He knew that, too. And nodded again.

"I think someone might be doing something to her. Putting things in her food or something."

Or something? He knew exactly what that "something" was. Did she? Did she know about "somethings" like hungry ghosts?

"And there's someone I'm a little suspicious of."

Good God, woman, will you get to the point?

Stoner took a deep breath. "There's a woman in her coven named Mogwye. I think she might be behind it. I mean, I have my suspicions. I know we don't have any proof, and it's not fair to accuse her…well, anyway, I just have a hunch."

Of course! A witch! Usually witches turned their backs on ghosts—the kind of ghosts that tormented him. They wanted nothing to do with things that trailed darkness, didn't want to give them energy. There was no way you'd find a decent witch working with them, or using them. Uh-uh. The only thing he'd ever seen a real witch do with a hungry ghost was politely invite it to move along. Naturally, there were people who liked to muck around with that kind of thing—thrill-seekers, assholes, and plain old loonies. They generally learned it was a bad idea. Learned the hard way.

But witches, good or bad, had the skills. To evoke and conjure and use. And sometimes they lost control of the situation. It all got away from them and there was hell to pay. That was why the ones with half a brain thought it was better not to mess around in the first place.

If they wanted to, though, they could. He felt excitement surge within him, pushing aside his anxiety.

"Yeah," he said, almost looking Stoner in the eye before he stopped himself. "It could be a witch. It sure could."

"The thing is, we need someone to…well, frankly, to spy on her. At the Esbat this Sunday. And she knows all of us, and anyway we couldn't go because it's not open to outsiders and besides I don't even know where they hold them."

He started to say, "I do," but she was rushing on.

"See, we need to know if she's slipping something in Aunt Hermione's food or anything like that."

Or anything like cursing or casting spells, he added to himself.

Stoner took another deep breath. "So what I was wondering, since you're pretty good at sneaking around and hiding..." She realized what she'd just said and blushed deeply. "I don't mean that in a negative way, like you're a dishonest person or anything, but you have...well, certain skills."

"Uh-huh," he said.

"So, will you help us out? I mean, what do you think?"

He was silent for a moment. Stoner waited, her stomach in knots. "I think," he said at last, "it takes you a God-awful long time to get to the point."

She lit up. "You'll do it?"

"Yep."

Stoner let all of her breath out at once. "Thank you. This Sunday. Around six in the evening. Can you find the place? Marylou said you might have been there...you know...out of curiosity or something."

"Yep."

"I owe you. Forever."

He brushed away the idea with a flick of his wrist. "One thing. Better not let your aunt know about this. She'd give herself away, peeking around to see if she can see me. It's human nature."

"Okay," Stoner said.

"Anything else?"

"No. Thanks."

He got to his feet. His knees felt like glass where the stones had dug into them. "Meet me Sunday night. After dark. Your back yard."

"How will I know when you're there?" she asked.

"You'll know." He turned and walked away.

She was better than he expected. He'd been certain he'd know her by the way she greeted the old woman. Certain there'd be a telltale spark of energy between them that would point out that this one was the soul taker. But, even though he watched as hard as he could, he couldn't pick her out.

At first he thought maybe she hadn't arrived yet, but now there were thirteen of them and they were dressing for the ceremony, slipping into their black robes with the coarse red belts of rope. Once they got busy with the doings, there wouldn't be anything to give her away until they were finished.

Concentrating his attention to a laser beam, he swept the gathering, probing, willing his intuition to tell him something. Nothing.

They were forming the circle. Quickly, he scanned one more time. One of the women froze, shook her head slightly, and looked around, not at the other women, but at the woods just beyond the clearing.

Bingo, he thought as he sucked his energy back into himself. She had sensed him. And she didn't seem to have located him. Now he had to stay very still and quiet.

He could feel her searching for him, tiny waves of electricity bouncing off the auras of the trees that surrounded and hid him. The leaves moving ever so slightly. Too slightly to be seen, only sensed as tiny drafts of cool charged air.

The waves passed him. Slowed. Stopped. Began to return...

"Mogwye," one of the women said. "We're closing the circle."

Confirmation.

She scurried to her place and the priestess began the ceremonies. By the time the circle was closed and protected, he couldn't have gotten in no matter how hard he tried. But he wouldn't have tried, anyway. This was private stuff. Religious stuff. He wasn't about to mess with religious stuff.

He didn't mind. He could have a nap now. Even the subtlest change in the atmosphere would waken him. It was a skill that had saved his life more than once in 'Nam. Trouble was, even after years—decades, really—back in the States, those sensors were always on. He wondered if he had ever slept through an entire night.

Cutter stretched out on his tree limb and stared up into the darkening twilight. From below he could hear the murmur of women's voices. He knew the rituals by heart. Not the exact words, he figured it could be hazardous to his health to hear the exact words, but the rise and fall of tempo and feeling told him what was happening. It comforted and lulled him.

He didn't know if he'd been dreaming. If he had, it wasn't one of those screamers he usually had. It wouldn't have mattered, anyway. They wouldn't have heard him. Nobody ever heard him when he screamed.

But something had wakened him, and wakened him with his adrenaline already flowing, his heart pounding, his muscles clenched. The ceremony was still going on. The voices hadn't changed. They were about half way through now. They'd flattered the Goddess and placated all the nature Gods, and had reached the wishing and singing part. It all sounded okay.

Beneath all that praising and rejoicing and glorifying, without speaking aloud, someone was placing a curse. And he knew exactly who it was and what they were saying.

He wondered what he should do. His orders had been to observe and identify, that was all. Besides, he didn't know what he could do. Witches' curses were way outside his area of expertise. Leave that to someone who knew more. Hermione, for instance. She'd know what to do if she knew what was happening. But maybe he should intervene, anyway, stop it before...

Suddenly he found himself back in the jungle in 'Nam, with the night sounds all around that were maybe only animals but maybe Cong or even friendlies. The lieutenant was dead, and that left him in charge. His orders had been to "observe, and if necessary engage." Observe, when he couldn't see anything through the darkness. Listen, when it was impossible to tell one sound from another. Sit tight and they might pass you by, or mow you down like ducks in the three-for-a-dollar shooting booth at the county fair. Move and they might...

Cutter pinched his leg hard to get rid of the memory. This wasn't Southeast Asia, and those weren't the enemy down there. It was just the indecision, the damned indecision. Every time it came on him, the memories flooded back. And it always ended the same way, with the screams and the blood and the heavy, acrid smell of gunpowder. And then the silence. The hours and hours of silence.

The way it really had.

They were opening the circle now. Cutter lowered his eyelids briefly with relief, glad the hypnotic chanting was over, and that unspoken chanting underneath. Now they'd eat and drink and laugh and gossip, and he could watch to see if Mogwye put anything—anything real, anything solid, anything with form and substance—into Hermione's food or wine.

Mogwye was startled when Hermione entered the Esbat. She'd expected her to be at least as pale and weak and dotty as the last time she'd seen her. But she looked better. Not as good as she had before this started, but clearly improved, healthier, with more color in her face and spring in her step.

What had gone wrong? Was she losing her power? Had Hermione found someone whose strength of will was even greater than Mogwye's own? Was it possible? And what should she do about it?

The answer came to her during the ceremony. She needed something concrete, something that belonged to Hermione, that only Hermione would touch. It would help her to focus her energies, keep the channels clear. Somewhere along the line she had let herself get sloppy, had let her intention weaken, and static had crept in.

They were slipping out of their robes now, relieved to be rid of the heavy cloth in the June evening heat. The torches were lit, the wine and food passed. Someone had brought along an article an idiot reporter had written for the *Greenfield Recorder*, explaining the significance of the Summer Solstice. It was a miracle he'd gotten the date right. They passed it around and read it and laughed. It gave Mogwye an idea.

It was late. Aunt Hermione had come home two hours ago, and had gone straight to bed. She wasn't even going to read tonight, she said. The evening had worn her out. And she looked worn out, more so than she'd looked in days.

Stoner wanted to question her. What had she eaten? Who brought it? Was she careful? Were the wine bottles open or closed before the ritual started? How about after? Did anyone act in a suspicious…?

Her aunt brushed her questions aside with a gesture of irritation. She was tired, that was all there was to it. It'd been a long day and an active ceremony, to say nothing of the time spent planning for the upcoming Solstice, one of the year's High Holy Days. She was seventy-five years old and hadn't found the fountain of youth, so could she please be excused and allowed to get a little rest?

Stoner apologized and kissed Aunt Hermione's dry, parchment-like cheek. "Good night," she said, her heart clenching. "I'll see you in the morning."

Aunt Hermione merely nodded and trudged up the stairs.

Now where was Cutter? Where the hell was Cutter?

Marylou and Gwen came in from the movies down in Greenfield. They asked if there was any news, got one whiff of Stoner's mood, and decided Aunt Hermione had the right idea about retiring for the night.

Alone downstairs in the silent house, Stoner tried to interest herself in a book, a magazine, a game of solitaire. Nothing worked. An occasional snap or rustle from outside made her look up and listen, but it wasn't Cutter. She toured the downstairs, from the front door to the back to the front, then started over again. Once she even unlocked the basement door and whispered into the darkness, "Cutter?" There was no answer.

Another hour passed. The clock on the mantel got on her nerves. She went into the kitchen and browsed through the refrigerator, but nothing appealed to her. Three times she decided he wasn't coming, and started up the stairs to bed. Three times she decided to wait just a few more minutes, in case.

She threw herself down on the couch and counted the ticks of the clock, which made as much sense as anything. She drifted off to sleep.

"Don't be afraid. It's me."

It could have been a dream. She opened her eyes.

Cutter stood in the entrance to the living room.

"You could have told me you were going to sneak in like this," she said angrily.

"Sorry," he said. "I'm accustomed to getting around that way."

"And where've you been? I'd about given up."

"They weren't asleep."

"What difference would that make?"

"You didn't say to tell them."

Of course. He wanted to do exactly as he was told. Literally. Like an anxious little boy. It must be horrible to be so insecure. "You're right," she said. "Sit down."

"I'd rather stand this time," he said.

"Okay." She waited. He didn't say anything. "So. Did you see her?"

"Yep."

"Find out anything?"

"Yep. She's puttin' a curse on your aunt."

"A curse? Like—"

"Like a curse," Cutter said. "Black magic. Voodoo."

"Her food?" Stoner began.

"Nothin' in her food. A curse."

Stoner found herself speechless.

"Your aunt doesn't know?"

She shook her head. "I don't think so."

"Better tell her."

"Maybe you should. You know the details."

"Tried to tell her before. She won't listen to me. Probably thinks I'm crazy." He grinned awkwardly. "I am, kinda. But not that way."

"What do you think we should do?"

Cutter shrugged. "Your aunt ought to know. She's the witch."

"I don't think anyone's ever put a curse on her before."

"Well, if she figures out how to get it off, tell her to get the one off me, too. Gotta go."

And he went.

Cutter must have made a mistake, Hermione thought. She gazed out over the tops of the lilacs toward the hills behind the house. Mogwye couldn't do this. She doesn't have the power. Enough for some minor mischief, maybe, or even to conjure a poltergeist. But not this.

She rested her head against the back of the sofa. Her body felt as heavy as wet clay. Her mind floated, thoughts sliding away before she could even note them. Her uneaten breakfast lay on the table in front of her. She wasn't hungry, and it was tasteless. Tasteless. Leftover cherry pie, her favorite breakfast, was tasteless.

Her eyelids were too heavy to keep open. She let them drift shut. Just a few minutes, she granted herself. A few minutes to rest and then I'll be able to…whatever it was I came in here to do.

Look something up. That was it, find the notebook on spells and curses.

But she couldn't find it, and then she couldn't find her reading glasses. She looked over every corner of the living room, her reading room, the kitchen. She asked the others, no one had seen them. No one recalled her wearing them since yesterday afternoon. Started upstairs but remembered she hadn't read in bed last night, too tired. She had worn them at the Esbat, to read that newspaper article. She checked the pockets of her cloak. Not there.

She'd lost them. She never lost her glasses. She was known for not losing things, and now she'd lost her glasses.

Slipping away. That was what it was, slipping away. Away and away and away…

That was when she sat down to rest.

How long could she go on this way? Useless as a bag of sand in a drought. Never been useless before. Didn't like it. Made her feel like garbage, garbage too worthless to even collect flies.

Suddenly she wanted Grace. If she was dying, at least let her die with the face of her lover in her mind.

She tried to get up to reach the telephone, but she was too tired, too heavy to move. Later, when she'd had a little nap. Just a little nap.

It was two in the afternoon by the time she awoke, a dampness at the corners of her eyes and mouth. Leaking tears in her sleep, drooling. Senile and brain-dead, she thought with disgust at her own body.

How had it happened so fast? In weeks, she'd fallen completely apart. Women didn't do that. Men did, they suddenly let go, everything at once, overnight practically. But women eased into old age gracefully, gradually, able to savor each change, to know it and wonder at it if they were so inclined.

Hermione was inclined, or had been. Now they'd taken that opportunity away from her.

Tears of self-pity rose in her eyes and made her hate herself even more.

She'd been on the verge of hanging up the phone when Grace answered. "Grace."

"Angel," Grace said when she heard Hermione's voice. "How are you? I've been worried sick. I've dropped in on you, astrally, a dozen times in the last week, but you're always asleep."

"That's what I am, most of the time. I'm sorry I haven't returned your visits. It seems I just don't have the energy."

"Tell me what's going on. All of it."

Hermione described the new tiredness and the new confusion and the depression and the Esbat and Mogwye and Cutter and the tasteless pie and her missing glasses...

"Run that last one by me again," Grace said.

"I've lost my reading glasses."

"And you last had them where?"

"The last time I remember was at the..." She broke off.

Grace waited.

"At the Esbat," Hermione finished, hope sparking a little. "Mogwye has them."

"Which is why she could get the drop on you," her lover said. "She has your possession in her possession. It's the only way a left-hand-path two-bit, poor excuse for a witch could possibly out-hex you."

"I'm not hexing her, Grace."

"Well, maybe you should."

Hermione smiled. Grace was like the Goddess Demeter, soft as summer when everyone behaved. But she could winter all over you if you harmed someone she loved. "I'm not going to hex her," she said.

"Of course you're not." Grace sighed lovingly. "But that says nothing about what I might do."

"Grace..."

"What are the chances of you getting a wee snippet of something of hers?"

"Slim, I'm afraid. I'm not very good at breaking and entering."

"But your friend Cutter is." When Hermione, disapproving of using a third party in Magic business, didn't answer, she went on. "For the love of the Goddess, Angel, it's only for two days. Until the Soul Retrieval. And it's not to hurt her, it's to protect yourself. Now, how much can that hurt Cutter's karma? And what if it is his karma to do this sort of thing? Do you really want to interfere with that?"

"You're always turning things upside down," Hermione said in exasperation. "Why do you always confuse me?"

"It's a Leo thing," Grace said. "You wouldn't understand."

"Are you sure it's not an Italian thing?"

"That, too. You wouldn't understand that, either."

"I miss you, Grace."

"I miss you, too. But I'll be there tomorrow, unless you want me to come tonight."

"Tomorrow's fine. I feel better." She really did feel better. But Grace always made her feel better. Something told her it wouldn't last.

"How's that niece of yours? Making any progress?"

"I'm afraid not," Hermione said. "She still doesn't want to touch anything psychic."

"Slow and stubborn as a mule," Grace said. "Is she coming to the Journey?"

"To it, but maybe not on it. I don't know if she'll participate."

"She has to move at her own pace, I suppose. Can't make a plant grow by stretching it. Well," she said with finality, "I'm going to put away my groceries. You save enough energy for a good romp between the sheets."

Hermione grinned. "Will do. Who with?"

"With the Goddess, of course. All acts of love and pleasure are her sacraments. Mine, too."

Mogwye didn't like the looks of this one. For one thing, she was tall. Tall and Spanish-looking. Mogwye didn't trust tall, Spanish-looking women. Never had. She didn't know why, probably something the dreams had warned her about.

She had a cold, aloof, expressionless face, and it was hard to tell if she was looking down her nose, or just tall. The face of a tax collector, or one of those licensing people from the state who were always sniffing around. Mogwye tried to pick up something psychically but couldn't, which felt like tax collector for sure.

The woman said she was from New York City, and rattled off a list of names of people who'd recommended Mogwye's services. Most of them she'd never heard of. A few were "celebrity psychics" who got themselves interviewed on television. When Mogwye wondered aloud how they could have come by her name, Señora said someone knew someone who'd been to her, and had told friends she was good at her work.

Mogwye wished she kept better records so she could trace it back. But if she wanted to spend her life that way, she'd have been a bookkeeper.

Señora claimed someone was stealing from her. She needed to know who it was and what to do about it.

What was she doing in this part of Massachusetts? Mogwye wanted to know. She busied herself with lighting candles and getting out her cards, to make it appear like a casual, conversation-making question.

The tall woman settled herself gracefully in a chair and placed her handbag on her lap. She was on her way to the Colrain Conference Center, she said.

The Clean Living Center, Mogwye always called it to herself. A bunch of Earth-worshipping, weed-eating, non-smoking makers of prayer wheels pretending to be Indians. Who made their "guests" wash the dishes and charged a pretty penny for the privilege. Self-righteous, self-proclaimed New Age types who chanted over their dinners—holding hands, of course—and told themselves they were Healing the Earth. All this a half mile down the road from the defunct, rotting nuclear power plant.

It was a little hard to visualize Two Spanish Eyes in that place, but you never knew. All sorts of people showed up there.

Meanwhile, La Dama was quietly waiting for her to speak. For pearls of wisdom to cascade from her lips.

Mogwye closed her eyes. "I think this question is not for the cards," she said. No question was ever for the cards. She didn't use the cards. They were too confusing, what with their spreads and reversals and Major Arcana and Court Cards and God knows what. If she used the cards, she'd be looking things up every three seconds. "Is there something I could hold? Something you usually wear or frequently handle?"

The woman searched through her purse and pulled out a fresh lace-embroidered handkerchief and offered it to her.

"It would be better with something you use," Mogwye said.

Doña Española smiled in a modest way. "But I always carry this with me. Always. It's handmade, you see. By a relative, now deceased. It's very dear to me."

Well, that was no surprise. This one's nose probably never dripped. It wouldn't be seemly.

Nodding solemnly, Mogwye took the handkerchief and held it between her hands. Picking up vibrations. Again, there was nothing. Was the woman dead? A zombie? She frowned. "It's someone close to you," she fudged. "No, someone who is no longer close to you. Someone angry. A woman."

That was safe enough. There was probably not a woman alive who hadn't had a falling out with another woman at some time in the past.

"It isn't your money that she wants," Mogwye went on. "She wants…she wants to get your attention. She wants you to notice her so she can apologize. She wants to be your friend again."

She opened her eyes. "Does that sound like anyone you know?"

"Yes, as a matter of fact, it does."

"Reach out to her," Mogwye said. "Let her know you also want to be friends. Or don't you?"

"I do. Very much."

The woman stood up and retrieved her handkerchief. "Thank you so much. This has been very helpful." She dropped money in the bowl by the door and left.

Jesus H. Christ, where do they come from?

Mogwye was exhausted. It was as if she'd been reading non-stop for days. Muchita Bonita was a real energy sucker.

For the first time in years, Mogwye wished she had a television set, so she could just vegetate.

"There you go," Grace said as she handed Hermione her glasses and began stripping off her formal clothes. "Let's get sacramental."

Chapter 10

"All right," Elizabeth said, "before we start is there anything anyone needs to say or ask?"

Marylou raised her hand. "Do you make a lot of enemies in this work?"

Elizabeth frowned, puzzled by the question. "Enemies? Not that I know of. People come to me for help. If the spirits can help them, they're usually grateful. If not, they accept it." She contemplated for a moment. "I'm curious. What makes you ask that?"

"Your jewelry."

The shaman looked down at her necklace of turquoise and her bracelets of silver and tourmaline and rough wooden beads. "I don't understand."

"You wear so much jewelry. A witch told me that meant you were try-ing to ward off a lot of curses."

"Oh, Marylou," Aunt Hermione said in a sadly exasperated tone.

Elizabeth didn't even smile. "That could work, if you believe it."

"It's hogwash," Aunt Hermione said roughly.

Stoner'd never heard her aunt talk like this before. She felt a wave of sick despair.

Grace tugged at Aunt Hermione's sleeve. "What's the matter with you? Are you possessed?"

Aunt Hermione blinked and seemed to come to herself. "I'm sorry. I'd never discount someone else's beliefs. Marylou, Elizabeth, my apologies."

"Forget it," Marylou said.

Elizabeth turned to the rest of them. "This is what we frequently see in cases of soul loss. Changes of personality, impulsivity. As if the shadow/unconscious had taken control of the rest of the psyche."

"Good God," Aunt Hermione muttered. "A Freudian shaman."

"I think we'd better start as soon as possible," Elizabeth said. "But,

133

Marylou, to address your question, my Power Animal protects me from curses and spells. The jewelry is a reminder of past Journeys of power or significance, or suggestions from my guides."

Marylou nodded.

"The tourmaline, for instance, was recommended by a guide who calls himself Hebrew Prophet. It takes incoming negative energy, focuses it, and directs it back to the sender."

"Clever," Marylou said. "I wonder if it would work against airline ticket agents."

Elizabeth smiled. "Try it." She looked around. "Now, if there are no other questions, I suggest we take a bathroom break. Once we get going, we don't want to have to stop. Then we can collect our items for the altar."

She set about preparing the room, shading the windows, setting up candles, clearing space for them all amid the hundreds of rocks and crystals and feathers that were scattered—but probably not really scattered—about on the floor, on the couch, on chairs. She brought in bowls of water and laid out two colorful blankets side by side. Placed small pillows at one end of the blankets, and topped them off with bandannas folded for eye shades.

Stoner watched her for a while in silence. "Elizabeth," she said after a while.

"Yes?"

"I don't think I want to do this."

"Still have reservations?"

"I'm afraid so."

Elizabeth stopped what she was doing and sat beside her on the couch. "It's perfectly safe," she said. "The spirits won't come near you unless you ask them to, and they certainly won't come near you if you ask them not to."

"I know." It still felt wrong.

"You don't even have to be in the room. You're only here to welcome Hermione's soul parts home. That happens after the Journey. Gwen and Marylou and Grace will be here with you. They're not going on the Journey, either."

She looked up. "I can do that? It's not cheating?"

Elizabeth smiled. "It's not cheating."

"I feel like such a baby, not wanting to do this."

Elizabeth touched her hand. "It's not your time, Stoner. Maybe it's not even your lifetime for this. If something's holding you back, you should

134

trust that feeling."

Stoner wrapped her fingers through Elizabeth's. "You must think I'm really silly."

"No," Elizabeth said, "I think you're very wise. You just don't know how much you know." She gave Stoner's hand a little squeeze. "Okay, let's get this show on the road."

She could see what they were doing through the French doors that led from the living room into Elizabeth's Journey room. Aunt Hermione lying on one of the blankets, her eyes covered. Marylou and Grace and Gwen lounged at the back of the room. Elizabeth shook her rattle as she circled Aunt Hermione. Now and then she'd whistle, or do a kind of wordless singing.

Stoner stroked the cat, whose name this week was a sharply-spoken "In!" The table in front of her was decorated with crystals Grace had provided, silver jewelry from Marylou, a deer hide medicine bag Gwen had made for the occasion, photographs of Aunt Hermione at all ages, and food. Small sandwiches and candies (in case the soul piece that returned was a child), licorice, cookies, and cherry pie. Lots of cherry pie. That had been Marylou's idea. In case Aunt Hermione decided to stay wherever it was she went, she said, they'd have something to lure her back.

There was Aunt Hermione's favorite casserole, a marvelous concoction from the '50s made of wide noodles, tuna, onions, and Velveeta. Crab Rangoon and egg rolls and a mountain of Dragon and Phoenix from the Chinese take-out. Beans and potato salad from Bub's Bar-B-Que. Collard greens and corn bread from Dot and Mel's Soul Food Heaven.

Marylou had claimed she was going to lose her lunch right on the spot. The nameless casserole was bad enough, but boiled collard greens were the icing on the cake.

Gwen pointed out that Marylou relished canned smoked oysters, and you couldn't get any more vile than that, they stank right through the can.

Marylou had fumbled for a response, failed, and decided she had to oversee the iced tea.

Elizabeth had stopped circling and rattling and chanting and had turned on the shamanic drumming CD. She stretched out on the other blanket, hip to hip with Aunt Hermione, and covered her eyes.

Stoner leaned back against the pillows and offered up a prayer of thanksgiving that she hadn't had to be in there. Nothing much was happening except the drumming. At least nothing she could see. But it felt much safer out here with "In!" She resisted the temptation to snitch a Crab Rangoon, and let her eyes drift shut.

Rapid drumming brought her awake. She felt rested, more rested than she had in weeks...had it only been weeks? It felt like months. As if she had slept without dreams, without fear, without worry. Deep, luxuriant, safe sleep.

Yet, now that she was awake, something nagged at her. There was something she had to do, something she had forgotten. She tried to track it down, but it wouldn't come.

Elizabeth was helping Aunt Hermione into a sitting position, placing her own cupped hands over the top of her head. Then she began to circle her again, rattle in hand.

Bills all paid? She thought so.

Maybe the car. Was I supposed to bring the car in for an oil change or inspection? About that funny squeaking sound when you step on the accelerator? Did I leave something in the trunk that's melting or rotting or getting ready to blow up?

She didn't think so.

The others were clustered around Aunt Hermione, laughing, and patting and kissing her.

Elizabeth slipped through the door and came to sit on the edge of the table in front of Stoner.

"How'd it go?" Stoner asked.

"Good. And not so good," Elizabeth said. She was obviously troubled. "We did retrieve some soul parts, but I don't think they were all that significant. I wanted to talk to you before the rest come out. Hermione needs to rest and incorporate what we've done. I don't want to worry her at this point."

Stoner felt enough worry for both of them. "What can we do?"

"Several things. I'll outline them along with the others." Elizabeth glanced toward the Journey room. "The problem is, I couldn't find out what happened to this missing piece. Usually, whether they choose to return or not, I can find out where they are. But there's no trace. Now, I could do another Journey, or try an extraction in case it's not a loss we're looking at, but an excess of negativity that's built up. But I really don't think that's it."

"Neither do I," Stoner said. "It feels as if something's missing in her."

The others were standing now. Elizabeth went on quickly. "It's possible that she's voluntarily given away a part of her soul. She denied it at our initial interview, but she might not even be aware of it on this plane. I have to ask you this: despite your apprehension, if it becomes necessary for you to participate in this, will you?"

"Yes," Stoner said without thinking, and felt a surge of light-headedness. "Do you think it would make a difference?"

"I think...no, I know it would."

"But I don't understand..."

The French doors opened. Elizabeth stood and went toward them with a smile. Stoner got up and opened her arms to embrace her aunt.

They were all hungry, even Marylou, who refused to eat anything but Dragon and Phoenix and cherry pie, but ate enough of that to sink a battleship.

Aunt Hermione seemed a little better, though really not much. Distracted, maybe, and expending some effort to appear less troubled than she was. She chattered on about what a wonderful experience it had all been, and how colorful the Lower World was, describing the animals and the scenery and the people she'd met, and how Spider had approached each. She must have thought she was getting away with it, fooling them.

From the I-won't-commit-myself-at-this-point looks on all their faces, she wasn't fooling them one bit.

Elizabeth described her Journey to the Upper World, her meetings with her Spirit Guides. She told amusing stories, like the brief consultation with the ancient Native American chief who presented himself to her as a healer and diagnostician of pet problems. He informed her that her cat was entering middle age—which would last a very long time, no need for alarm—but would really prefer to be called by only one name, thank you very much. It was more consistent, but especially more dignified. He requested that he be addressed as "Charles."

"Charles?" Marylou said, and pointed to where he lay in the middle of the sofa while they hugged the ends to give him room. "That animal thinks he's a Charles? As in the Prince of Wales, no doubt. If you ask me, he's a Charlie if anything."

Charles got up from his sleeping spot and crawled into Marylou's lap and promptly went back to sleep.

"Hey," Gwen said, "he likes you. You two must be on the same wavelength."

"It's hearing that name that he likes," Marylou said. "Trust me, there is no special affinity between Charlie and me."

Charles woke, climbed up Marylou's chest, giving her cheek a sniff and a lick as he went by, and draped himself across her shoulder.

"Somehow," Elizabeth said with a laugh, "I have the feeling we should stick with 'Geddown.'"

She was avoiding the real issue, Stoner thought, and wondered if she should intervene. She decided it would be safer to trust in Elizabeth's sense of timing and discretion.

"The problem is," Elizabeth began over coffee, "I really can't feel that this retrieval is complete." She cleared her throat and looked uncomfortable, then covered it over. "There are a number of things that aren't cleared up yet. I'm not concerned. Soul parts return at their own pace, and sometimes the change is quite subtle. So, Hermione, I suggest you try to stay tuned in to your spirit. I'm sure that's not hard for you...and let me know right away if you feel anything. For better or worse."

Aunt Hermione merely smiled agreeably.

"The rest of you, if you notice any change in her, bring it to her attention."

They all nodded like obedient school children. Even Grace, who would usually have more than a few suggestions to make at a time like this.

She's really worried, Stoner thought. Well, guess what, Grace. You have never been less alone in your life.

"Meanwhile," Elizabeth went on, "we might be thinking about other things we can do, on the remote chance that we need to do more." She was trying to sound casual and matter-of-fact, like a dentist saying if you don't like the taste of Colgate, try Crest. "I'll check with my Guides again, to see if they have suggestions. If any of you were visited by Power Animals during the retrieval, see if you can connect with them—for your own benefit, of course—but ask if they have any thoughts for us."

Stoner sat upright. She suddenly remembered a bit of dream, from just now. The old, wild burro who had met her in the Southwest, during a trip into what Elizabeth could probably call Non-Ordinary Reality. For herself, Stoner preferred to think of it as a hallucination superimposed on some rather peculiar doings.

She hadn't thought of the burro in a couple of years. Funny that it would show up now. But, of course, there was all this talk of Power Animals, and this sort of spooky setting...not too surprising she'd warp back to that other strange place.

Sure, that was it.

Elizabeth was looking at her in a waiting kind of way.

"Sorry," Stoner said. "I was thinking of something irrelevant."

"Okay," Elizabeth addressed them all but gave Stoner a penetrating look, "if anything does occur to you—if anything occurs at all—please let me know right away." She sat down, and it was clear the session had ended.

"I want to add one thing," Aunt Hermione said, getting to her feet with barely-disguised effort. "I appreciate all of you being here, caring about me." Her eyes filled. "It's very touching to have such good friends." Her voice dropped in tone and volume. "Very, very touching." She stared at the floor for a moment. "Now," she said briskly, "let's see what we want to do with all this leftover food. Elizabeth gets first choice, then Grace, then the rest of us. Marylou, you get to pick last."

Marylou snorted, and everything was apparently back to normal.

He forced himself to wait for them out in the open, on their front porch, like a normal person. At least there were no ghosts here, not in the middle of the day. But his tee-shirt stuck to him like damp skin, fear sweat had seeped out of every pore. Back in 'Nam, the Cong would have smelled him in an instant. They were real good at smelling fear.

All day he'd been edgy, even before he'd decided to try to act sane. Edgy the way the maples get edgy before a storm, turning their leaves upside down. Beaten down edgy, like animals going flat and silent except for their twitching ears. And, like the trees and the animals, he didn't know if the storm would be good or bad for him, just that it was coming.

He'd spent last night outside the Mogwye's house. If anything was going to attack his friends, he thought it would come from there. It had tried. He could see its effort, a kind of shimmer surrounding the house. But it couldn't get out. There must be something very powerful around, to keep the shimmer all tied up like that.

Cutter put the brakes on his thoughts and backed up a little. "His friends," he'd called them. Friends. The word made a funny taste in his mouth, a little like sand, a little like honey. He got down from the porch and found a patch of bare dirt and a twig and wrote it in the ground. Friends.

Seeing it written out like that, right there on Mother Earth, made it real. Friends. He had friends. Several friends. Not just people who were kind to him because he was crazy and pathetic, but friends who asked him for help. Who thought he could help. Who knew he would try to help.

He knelt down in front of the word and just looked at it. And looked at it. And looked at it.

Then, glancing around to be sure no one was watching, he added in very, very small letters, "+ me."

That was too much. Quickly, he rubbed out the words, before anyone could see and get angry.

But that couldn't change the fact that he'd seen them. He could rub them out of the dirt, but he couldn't rub them out of his mind. He let his thoughts drift over to them. "Friends + me."

He couldn't remember the last time he'd felt those words. Long before he went away to war and didn't quite come back. Tentatively, he let a thread of Now go back and touch a thread of Then.

Fear and joy filled him, so big and so alive he had to cry.

By the time the car pulled up he had taken himself in hand. That was what his father used to call it, taking yourself in hand. "Take yourself in hand, boy," his father used to say. Still, he had to grab the edge of the porch with one hand to keep from running.

It was only the old lady and the new one and Stoner. He'd expected Marylou to be with them. Marylou would be like a flak jacket, might not save your life but it would soften the blow.

His fear jacked itself up to terror.

Stoner got to him first. He was glad of that. "She'll be along in a minute," she said quickly. "They stopped at the grocery store."

"I ought to go. I'm not real clean." It was the only thing he could think of.

"You're fine by me," Stoner said. She turned to her aunt and Grace. "This is Aunt Hermione's friend, Grace D'Addario."

He couldn't run now if he wanted to. He'd turned to stone. Legs, arms, and tongue. All stone. Looked on the face of Medusa, he thought. But she wasn't deadly like Medusa. She was beautiful, and the energy that flowed around her was all the colors of the rainbow.

Stoner had turned to the woman. "And this is our friend Cutter."

She'd used the word.

He stopped breathing.

Grace was looking at him, her eyes soft and reassuring. "Well, Cutter."

He ought to shake hands. But he couldn't. It would make everything so big it'd kill him.

He only nodded. "Ma'am."

"They fucked you up quite royally, didn't they?" Grace asked. She knew the problem. He felt himself relax a little. "Yes, Ma'am," he said. He liked the way she said "fucked up." She knew what it meant, not like the docs at the VA who only said it because they heard the guys saying it and wanted to sound like they were one of them. They meant well, most of them, but they didn't know shit from sunbeams.

"I don't suppose there's anything anyone can do," Grace said.

"No, Ma'am."

Grace studied him, pulling on her lower lip, deep in thought. "Well, then," she said at last, "I imagine you're waiting to find out what you're supposed to do with it."

"Yes, I am."

"Nothing yet?"

He shook his head.

"It'll come." She turned to the others. "Nothing is ever wasted in Spirit. There's a reason for the things Cutter has endured. He's being prepared."

"That's right," Cutter said, hearing what he'd always suspected himself. Which was why he hadn't hung himself years ago.

"Have you seen the Beast?" Grace asked him.

"Yes, Ma'am." A long-remembered feeling filled his chest. A feeling of safety and awe, and something like humor.

"Once you've seen the Beast," Grace explained, "you have to go insane or die. The Buddha recognized that, and I suspect the Christ did, too." She gave a little impatient-at-herself snort. "Listen to me, pontificating like the Pope, the old bastard."

Cutter found he could move and speak. "How'd it go?" he asked.

Stoner's eyes shifted to the ground. Aunt Hermione's eyes shifted inward. "We really don't know yet," Grace said.

"I'm sorry," he said. He was too filled with emotion to stay, emotions of every size and color, all in motion, overwhelming.

"Marylou can fill you in if you like," Stoner said. She'd noticed his paleness and guessed claustrophobia had set in. "We have to get this stuff in the fridge. Want to come in with us, or should I tell her to meet you later?"

"Later," he said with a sigh of gratitude, and moved to go.

As he passed her, Grace leaned down and kissed his forehead. "Blessed be, Cutter."

"Same to you, Ma'am."

Hermione was glad they'd eaten so much at Elizabeth's. She didn't think she could stay awake long enough for dinner.

Grace offered to stay over a couple of days, but Hermione told her she had things to do for the Solstice. Besides, Grace was High Priestess of her own coven, and shouldn't disappoint them on one of the highest Holy Days of the year. There was no way Grace could argue with that. She knew things hadn't gone particularly well at the soul retrieval. But they still had hope that something might come along in a few days, the way Elizabeth had said.

"Do you really believe that?" Hermione asked her, a little sarcastically.

"No."

"Grace, what am I going to do?"

Her friend and lover looked at her gently. "I don't know. There's something behind all this, there always is. But it's being kept veiled. It has to do with you, of course, since you're the target. And you must have entered into the contract Between."

"I must have," Hermione agreed.

"If it's one of those puzzle games you're so fond of, you certainly picked a doozie."

"I certainly did," Hermione said with a wry smile. "I don't need the whole answer right now, I just wish I could figure out the next move."

Grace stuffed the rest of her clothing into her overnight bag. "You know Spirit never lets you go over the edge."

"True. But sometimes Spirit has a really uncomfortable idea of what constitutes the edge."

"Well," Grace said as she closed her suitcase and glanced around the room. "I guess that's it. You know I've forgotten something, but I'll get it next time out. What time's your Sabbat?"

"Eight."

"Good. Mine's at nine. I'll go O.O.B., as the young ones say, and drop in on yours."

"And I'll astral travel, as we old ones say, to yours at ten." She stood at the entrance to the guest room and felt helpless.

Grace put one hand behind her neck and drew her forward and kissed her for a long time. "It's going to be fine, Angel. I know it. Blessed be."

With Grace gone, the emptiness was sudden and nearly tangible. She almost wished she'd never come.

She ought to go to bed now, even though it was still light. If she just stretched out for a while, maybe she'd feel better. But her clothes were uncomfortable and she didn't have the strength to undress. She stared at her bookshelf. Nothing interested her.

They were all so optimistic, those writers. Or maybe you couldn't get a book published if it wasn't optimistic. Maybe the public wouldn't read anything downbeat. Nobody wanted to hear bad news. Nobody wanted to hear about reality.

If it was true, what they were implying, that the key to this lay with Stoner, then she was sunk. Because she could not, would not involve her where she didn't want to be involved. It wasn't right, and it wasn't fair. And that, friends, was what reality was all about.

The people who loved you most dearly couldn't always save you. It wasn't their fault, it was just how it was. Being human meant being limited, period. If you wanted everything to be possible, go incarnate as Wonder Woman.

It was stifling, this humanness. Old legs couldn't run, very young legs couldn't support. The loving old lost their loved ones, the loving young couldn't contain it. Over and over and over, lifetime after lifetime until there just wasn't any magic left any more.

The thing that saved you from complete despair was the return ticket, the stub you carried for the day you'd had enough. Many people thought terrible things would happen to you if you used it before your "time." That was wrong. What happened was that you woke up and wondered just what had been all that terrible, and jumped right in to do it all again.

Still, maybe it was time to get up and leave this particular movie.

The possibility perked her up a little. A little. Not enough to take the return ticket out of her pocket. Only enough to start to think about how she could cash it in.

A soft tap at the door. "Aunt Hermione."

Hermione groaned to herself. Not now. "Come on in," she said.

Stoner looked pale and sheepish. "Did Grace leave?"

"About an hour ago." Hermione sat up. "I was taking a little rest."

"I'm sorry." She started to go.

"Wait, Stoner." Hermione patted the bed beside her. "Come sit with me." She took her niece's hand. "We haven't had much time together lately."

"I know," Stoner said, stroking the back of her aunt's hand. "I've been preoccupied."

"So have I."

"I've missed you."

"Me, too. Cherry pie is not an adequate substitute for you."

Stoner smiled a little. "I want you to know, I'm not jealous of Grace any more."

"I'm glad," Hermione said. "It's such a painful emotion."

"You really love each other, don't you?"

"Yes, we do."

Stoner thought silently for a moment. "Aunt Hermione, who is she?"

"A very old soul," her aunt said. She looked a little sad. "I suspect this may be her final incarnation on this plane."

"I'm sorry. That must be hard."

"I try to reassure myself that some day I'll get where she's going, and we'll be together again. Meanwhile, it's bittersweet. But I'm glad I had the chance to meet her." She got up and began folding her laundry and putting it in her bureau drawers.

Stoner went to the window. Marylou and Cutter sat at the edge of the trees, watching the sun set. "I almost envy Cutter," she said. "He may be insane, but he knows he's insane. He accepts himself as insane. He doesn't torture himself trying to figure it out."

"And Marylou," her aunt added. "She's sane and knows it, and doesn't waste her time wondering." She went to stand beside Stoner. "They make kind of a nice couple, don't they?"

"Yeah. They do."

She slipped an arm around her niece's shoulders. "So do we."

"Not quite the same way." Stoner took Aunt Hermione's hand and rested her head against her neck.

"We have. Many, many times. I think we've been just about every kind of nice couple two people can be. This time, we're a family couple."

"Do you think we were ever lovers?" Stoner murmured.

"I know we were. I'd give you details, but you'd be...perturbed."

Stoner pulled away a little to glance at her. "I would?"

"Only because you couldn't keep the lifetimes separated. And you're so very proper."

"Someday I might shock you."

"Surprise me, maybe. But not shock me."

Stoner perched on the window sill and folded her arms. "Aunt Hermione," she began.

"Yes, dear?"

"What's going on?"

"You know," the older woman said, looking hard at her, "I really can't figure it out."

"Are you scared?"

"A little. Are you?"

Stoner nodded. "It all comes down to me, doesn't it?"

There was a very long silence. "I think it does," Aunt Hermione said in a low, apologetic voice.

"Damn."

"Damn, indeed."

"I want to do the right thing."

"I know you do. Whatever you decide will be the right thing."

It was growing dark outside. "It must be around eight, eight-thirty, don't you think?"

"Around that."

Stoner looked up at her. "I think I'd better call Elizabeth."

Hermione looked down into the younger woman's honest face and troubled eyes and thought how very lucky she was to know her.

The return ticket would have to wait for a while.

Chapter 11

The cat was sunning himself on the front step, taking up every available inch of passing room, even though he really wasn't all that large.

She wondered how he managed it. But cats were like that. She remembered that from her sometimes-traumatic years with Aunt Hermione's cat, Diablo. He could be light as a feather, or sound like a herd of elephants stampeding through the living room. As small as a mouse when you tried to hide something away in a tiny nook. No crack or hole was tight enough to keep him out. Or space-taking as a Great Dane. He could cross the room so delicately even the dust wasn't disturbed, and two seconds later bump his tail against the TV dial so hard it turned the TV off.

Shape shifters. Enigmas. With that look of seeing through you and into you and beyond you with an expression that said they were listening very hard to someone you couldn't see. Cats always seemed to know something, and they weren't about to tell.

Stoner reached across him to ring the bell just as Elizabeth opened the door.

"What are you doing?" she asked. "Talking to him?"

"Trying to figure him out."

Elizabeth threw up her hands and said, "Uhh," in a way that clearly said, "Don't even bother." She turned her attention to the cat. "Come on, Charles, move it. Let the woman in."

Stoner smiled. "'Charles' is it? I see he won."

"Don't they always?" She scooped up the cat and held him. "In," she said to Stoner. "Hurry."

She returned Charles to his step and closed the door.

It sounded to Stoner a little like the slamming of a cell door. No getting out now. Kind of like the moment they lock you into the House of Horrors ride, and you suddenly realize it was the last ride in the world you'd ever intended to get on but it was too late, the car was moving and no one could hear you and even if they could they'd think your screams for help were all part of the entertainment and you were having a great time.

"Okay," Elizabeth said, and led her into the Journey room. "You might try breathing," she added with a little smile.

"Right," Stoner said, and gulped air.

"Now, we've already established that you're afraid of this but don't know why." She sat on the floor and motioned for Stoner to sit beside her. "Suppose I run through what we'll do and what you can expect, and you stop me at any point that makes you feel anxious."

Stop, Stoner thought.

There was a soft thud from outside the room, someone else in the house, moving around upstairs. Stoner glanced up.

"That's Karen. She won't bother us."

"Is she a Shaman, too?"

"Yep. You're surrounded. You might as well surrender."

Stoner felt herself blush. "It's not that bad."

"I know." Elizabeth grinned. "A little Shamanic humor. Bad Shamanic humor. Actually, most Shamanic humor is pretty bad. But you are surrounded, you know, by beings of light. Every minute of every day and night, wherever you go, spirits are there to help you. All you have to do is call on them."

Sounded claustrophobic to her. "And if I don't, they'll stay away?"

"Well…" Elizabeth hesitated. "Not always, actually. Sometimes they have to intervene, if you're in real danger. But it's always for your own good."

Just like all the wonderful things people do to one another "for your own good," Stoner thought. People like mothers and doctors and dentists and fathers and fundamentalist Christians.

Elizabeth had noticed her dropping out of the conversation and waited for her to come back.

"Sorry," Stoner said. "My mind wandered."

"Anything I should know?"

She shook her head. "Just that 'for your own good' stuff."

"Ah." She thought for a moment. "What the spirits are most interested in is helping you find your true path. It's completely different from that other 'own good' razz-ma-tazz."

Stoner laughed. "Well, since I haven't the slightest idea what my true path is, it must be pretty confusing for my spirits."

"Not for them. They already know. Maybe they can give you a hand with that, sort of a reward for courageous behavior."

Stoner grimaced.

"Which brings up a good point," Elizabeth went on. "The most important thing when you're Journeying is to form a definite intention and hold to it. Unless you're just going on a Journey to look around—kind of sight-seeing in Non-Ordinary Reality—in which case 'looking around' would be your intention."

"Uh-huh," Stoner said, and felt a headache begin.

"Our intention for this Journey is to see what you can do for your aunt. Do I have that right?"

"I guess so."

"So, as we begin, just say to yourself, 'This is a Journey to find out how to help Aunt Hermione.' Or however you'd put it. Keep that focus and relax, and let the spirits do the rest."

Oh, sure. Perfect trust, relax, nothing to worry about. Just like handing over your luggage to an airline.

"Here's what'll happen. You'll lie down and cover your eyes. Find a place, real or made up, that feels safe to you and can provide an entrance to the Upper World or Lower World. It can be a staircase, or a tree trunk, or a cave, anything you like. Hold your intention steady. I'll rattle and whistle and sing a little to invite the spirits to join us. When I feel them here, I'll put on the drumming tape and we're off."

Stoner could feel her anxiety fighting to break through, like the bubbles in a shaken Champagne bottle. "This is a little scary," she said.

"Because it's your first time." Elizabeth gave her a reassuring glance. "Once you've done it, it won't be so frightening. Remember, your Power Animal is there to protect and guide you."

"What if I don't have a Power Animal?"

"I think one will come forward for you. If it doesn't, don't worry. Sometimes they take a while to show themselves. If you meet a certain animal on your Journey that seems familiar, or you have an affinity for—or one that appears to you three times—it's probably your Power Animal. Simply welcome it, and follow its direction."

"What if it's a liar, or a trick?"

"Spirit isn't like that. They have more important things to do." Elizabeth took a sip of water from the glass beside her. "There's only one word of caution…"

Here it comes, Stoner thought. The hitch.

"If you meet an animal with fangs, who shows them in a threatening manner, turn around and go the other way."

"Turn my back on it? That doesn't sound wise."

"It won't hurt you. It's simply warning you not to go in that particular direction."

Yeah? Well, how come nobody's showing up to warn me not to go in this particular direction?

"Okay?" Elizabeth asked.

Stoner nodded. "Okay. Let's get it over with."

"Need a bathroom break?"

"No, thanks." God, it was like going to the dentist, or the first day of school, or—

Elizabeth touched her arm. "Remember, Stoner, I'm right here with you. If anything goes wrong, I'll pull you out."

"Right," Stoner said. "Now you tell me. At the last minute. Something can go wrong."

"Nothing can go wrong. I'm trying to reassure that part of you that doesn't believe that. Some people like to carry a life jacket even on dry land." She got up. "Come on. Stretch out on that rug, make yourself comfortable, and cover your eyes."

Stoner lay down and put the bandanna over her eyes. "Happy trails," she said.

Above the hiss of the rattles, she could hear Elizabeth's silver bracelets singing against one another. The sound reminded her of Marylou and was comforting. Marylou was so solid, so everyday, so Just There. A little surprising for a Scorpio, but Aunt Hermione said it was because she was evolved. Evolved Scorpios could change and transform themselves as easily as a snake sheds its skin. They could even soar like eagles, leaving behind the stinging, secretive parts of their natures. An unevolved Scorpio, on the other hand, could be a very nasty thing indeed.

Mind wandering.

She yanked it back.

Elizabeth began to whistle, a windy kind of sound. It reminded Stoner of a night breeze blowing down a long canyon. She could almost smell the sage, opening its pores to the evening in hopes of capturing a drop of dew.

She was suddenly homesick for Arizona, even though she'd only been there for a couple of weeks. But there had been something about the place that had felt easy and right. Past life stuff, Aunt Hermione would say. Maybe, maybe.

Drifting again. She grabbed the reins of her thoughts and gave them a good, hard tug.

Hold the intention. To learn how to help Aunt Hermione.

Now Elizabeth was singing, or chanting. She couldn't make out words. It sounded strong and deep and old. Very old. She was tempted to uncover her eyes for a second, but was afraid she'd see, not Elizabeth, but some old medicine man. And it wouldn't be this Northampton, Massachusetts, room they were in, but a dark place where a fire crackled and roared, and sparks flew up to join their star cousins in the night sky.

Hold the intention.

She could see the sparks and the stars and the raging bonfire and felt her feet trying to leave the ground. She didn't fight it this time, but let herself float skyward with the sparks.

A moment of silence, and then the drums began. Softly at first, like running footsteps. The volume rose rapidly until it filled her head and blocked out all the sound around her. Her heart gave a little lurch, then joined the tempo of the drums.

Whoa, she thought, a person could have a coronary doing this. Concentrating, she slowed her heart to every second beat, then every third, and every fourth. It felt smooth, like gliding.

A slight pressure against her hip as Elizabeth lay down beside her. Okay, she said to herself silently, for Aunt Hermione.

A large, old tree rose in front of her as she rode the drums. So large she could fit inside. So old it had rotted to form an entrance door. She slipped inside the door and found herself in darkness, engulfed in the silence and the odor of decaying wood. The pleasant, damp odor of cool, rich soil.

Elizabeth had said she could go up or down from here. Which should she do? The trunk opened to the sky, and down into the earth.

"Hey," she called, her voice resonant in the hollow wood, "which way am I supposed to go?"

From below she heard a snorting, snuffling sound.

"Are you talking to me?"

More snorting.

"Okay," she said, "I'm coming." She took a step toward what looked like stairs made from roots, and found herself falling.

No, not falling exactly, floating downward like a feather on a breeze.

The tree trunk became a tunnel with walls of earth, then stone. Black stones, roughly squared but not sharp. It was pleasantly cool in here, and quiet. She realized it had been several minutes since she'd heard the drums, but when she focused her hearing she could make them out, very, very far away.

Like falling asleep, she thought.

Hold the intention.

The tunnel leveled off and widened and she was standing. She reached out to touch the wall. The coal-like stones were cool and wet, but not slimy. Bits of moss and fern grew in the interstices. Beyond lay the entrance to the tunnel, and beyond that the sight of brown sand and blue water.

The snorting sound came again. It was almost like a chuckle. Tentatively, she approached the entrance.

A large, soft pillow-like nose, then a pair of tawny pointed ears appeared.

Stoner laughed. "Burro," she said.

"So, Green Eyes, you haven't forgotten your old friends," said a familiar, rough voice with an undertone of gentleness.

She couldn't believe it. "Siyamtiwa?"

"Who'd you think? Shirley MacLaine?"

The old Hopi woman showed herself from behind a palm tree. Or maybe not, maybe she just showed herself. Siyamtiwa was like that.

It brought tears to Stoner's eyes. "It's so good to see you."

The old woman grunted. "Not always."

"Well, you gave me some hard times." She wanted to reach out and embrace her, but was afraid she'd disappear.

"You gave yourself hard times," Siyamtiwa said. "Could have stopped any time. Didn't that old gypsy tell you that?"

"Old gypsy?" Stoner frowned in puzzlement. "I don't know who you're talking about."

The Hopi stamped her foot impatiently. "You live most of your life with her, don't even know who she is? I oughta turn you into a crow."

"Aunt Hermione? A Gypsy? Oh, you mean in a past life."

Siyamtiwa grunted again. "You're some quick learner. Quick like Tortoise."

"Thank you," Stoner said.

The other woman rolled her eyes.

"You're really here?" She was so glad to see her she could barely keep from laughing.

Siyamtiwa looked down at herself, then turned and looked behind her. "Yep, I'm here."

"I thought you were dead."

"I look dead? Gotta get more sun."

"No, but you could be my imagination."

"Maybe I was then, too."

"They said you'd died. They buried you."

Siyamtiwa nodded. "That's what they say."

"You were dead, officially."

"When the spring comes and the snow melts, do you call the snow dead?"

"Well, no," Stoner said, "we call it melted."

Siyamtiwa shrugged poetically.

"Is Raven here, too?"

Siyamtiwa became Raven, then herself again, so quickly Stoner wasn't sure she'd seen it.

"You're the same...whatever."

"Stuck with each other," Siyamtiwa said. "You listening to your aunt these days?"

"She's why I'm here. She's having trouble."

"I think maybe you're the trouble she's having."

"What do you mean?"

Siyamtiwa shrugged. "I don't know. Idea just settled on me. Like a butterfly."

"Here's another of our old friends." Stoner stroked the burro's ears. He nudged her with his nose.

"You treat that one with respect," Siyamtiwa said. "That's your Animal of Power."

"This little donkey?"

"Burro. You call him Burro. Capital B. Perfect Power Animal for you. Slow, plodding, but gets there."

"No offense, Burro," Stoner said, "but wouldn't I need someone faster and more...well, fierce?"

"Animal Spirits know, you don't," Siyamtiwa said. "So shut up, listen, learn."

"Yes, Ma'am," Stoner said, humbled.

"And don't say that 'Ma'am' at me. Makes me feel white. What'd you bring me?"

Stoner showed her empty hands. "I didn't know I'd meet you."

"What'd you bring me?" Siyamtiwa asked.

"I'm sorry, nothing. I didn't know I'd run into you."

Siyamtiwa grunted. "When I was young, we didn't go nowhere without taking a gift. Couple beads. Little bit of tobacco. Something sweet. Never know who you're going to run into."

"I'll remember next time. I will see you again, won't I?"

"You oughta wait until I leave to say that. Makes me feel unwelcome."

"I'm sorry," Stoner said.

"Maybe sometimes you see me now, any old day, just don't recognize me." She chuckled. "Maybe the boy that pumps your gas, maybe that's me."

Stoner thought of the skinny, dark-haired, acne-ravaged adolescent in baggy pants and sweat shirt who worked evenings in the local Mobil station. "I doubt it."

Siyamtiwa folded her arms. "Well, next time you bring me something."

"Anything. What would you like?"

"Twelve virgins."

She was stunned. "Where would I get twelve virgins?"

"You figure that one out." The old woman shook her head. "Why they always give me the hard ones?" she muttered to herself.

"Because you're so good at what you do," Stoner said.

Siyamtiwa nearly smiled, but her self-control defeated her facial muscles. "Good," she said. "Placate. Good thing to do with Elders. What you want from me?"

"I guess I'm here to...well, to help Aunt Hermione. What do you think I should do next?"

"Questions," Siyamtiwa said. "You ever stop to think maybe you have some answers?"

Stoner was embarrassed with herself. Helpless dependence had never been an attractive quality to her, especially when she was the helpless one, and now here she was...

She forced herself to think.

Assuming her intention had been to find a way to help Aunt Hermione, and she had ended up here, then this must be the way to help Aunt Hermione.

"You gotta make a Journey," Siyamtiwa said impatiently. "Find her soul. Bring it back."

"Find her soul?"

"Not the whole thing. Part that got lost, went away."

"Why would her soul do that?"

"What'a you ask me for? None of my business."

"I don't know how to do that," Stoner said.

Siyamtiwa shook her head. "You wear me down. Make me old before my time."

Despite her anxiety, she really had to laugh at that one. Here was the oldest person she'd ever met in her life, or probably ever would. The time for "old before my time" had long passed. She said as much.

"Yep, I'm pretty old, I guess. Too old for this, that's for sure."

"What I mean is...well, you've probably picked up a lot of wisdom over the years."

"You bet," Siyamtiwa said.

"So you should be doing something more, more elevated than this."

"Like what?"

"Like solving the big problems of life or something."

"Uh-huh." The old woman plucked a bit of straw from beside the path and chewed on it. "I did that kinda thing for a while. Nobody wanted to hear. And when they did hear, they ignored. Not much of an 'elevated' thing to do."

"But I want to hear," Stoner said eagerly. "I have a problem and I don't know what I'm doing, and I can use all the advice I can get."

"Gonna be a long day," Siyamtiwa said, shaking her head. She looked tired.

"Would you like to sit down?"

The old woman raised one eyebrow. "It's okay for you to sit? I thought maybe you had somethin' wrong with your behind."

Non-Ordinary Reality or not, Stoner blushed a very Ordinary blush.

Siyamtiwa made a stern face. "You call me here, you say I'm old, you don't offer me a seat. Good manners you got."

"For Pete's sake, just sit down!"

The old woman folded her legs under her and dropped to the ground. Stoner sat beside her.

"I didn't call you," she said peevishly.

"You called me."

"I didn't."

"Sometimes you call, you don't even know it. How many times you go out and there's the one person you needed to see, and maybe you didn't even know it until that moment. How'd that person know to be there if you didn't call?"

"You're right," Stoner said. "It's going to be a long day."

Siyamtiwa produced three brightly-colored stones from somewhere in her clothes and tossed them on the ground. She frowned and picked them up and tossed them again. With a nod of satisfaction, she looked up. "What you wanta know?"

Stoner felt that helplessness again. "I don't even know what I need to know," she said.

"Okay." Siyamtiwa tossed the stones. "We start with big picture. You Whites like the Big Picture, but you always gotta have it explained."

"Yes, we do. It's a genetic defect."

"First thing you gotta understand," Siyamtiwa went on, "is about the old guys, the Grandparents. Grandmother Earth, she's in charge of all the little hard things, the stuff you call atoms, stuff like that."

Stoner nodded.

"Now, Grandfather Sky, he's in charge of the spaces between the hard stuff. When Grandmother Earth and Grandfather Sky get together, they make what you call 'things.' You still with me?"

"Still with you."

"'Course, this is only my opinion. Someone else might tell you somethin' else."

"It works for me," Stoner said.

"But you know what's missing? Something that makes everythin' move around and come together and fall apart, all that."

"I know. Physics."

Siyamtiwa just looked at her.

"God?" she asked in a smaller voice.

"Great Spirit," Siyamtiwa said. "Bigger than Physics God, bigger than White God, bigger than The Grandparents. Knows everythin'. Does everythin'. Without Great Spirit, nothin' lives, nothin' changes, nothin'. You want an orange?"

"Sure." She didn't, really, but this time she was determined to see where Siyamtiwa got it.

The orange appeared in Siyamtiwa's hand. She passed it to Stoner. "This is Non-Ordinary Reality," she said. "You gotta stop lookin' for Ordinary stuff." She produced a second orange and peeled it, thrusting her chin in Stoner's direction. "Eat."

Stoner tried a bite. It was delicious. "We don't get fruit like this back in Ordinary Reality," she said.

"You bet. That place, everything kinda washed out. Like someone sprayed gray paint on it. Doesn't seem real. How do you like my story about the Gods?"

"I like it," Stoner said.

"Pretty, huh?"

"Very pretty."

Siyamtiwa nodded soberly. "That's what matters. Nobody knows anythin' for sure, so you see somethin' pretty, makes you happy, might as well believe that."

Stoner nodded her agreement.

"What good's walking around with a long face, nothin' means anything, Other World one big joke, only one way to look at it? Believe everythin', then you never wrong and never right and you have a good time."

They finished their oranges at leisure, in silence. Siyamtiwa licked the last of the juice from her fingers, then tossed the peels to Burro. By the time he grabbed them from the air, they'd turned into an apple.

Stoner laughed with surprise and delight.

"Magic. Small stuff. That trick done by a professional," Siyamtiwa said. "Don't attempt at home." She produced a pipe and lit it. "Grandparents," she puffed out a few small clouds of smoke. It smelled of a thousand things: burning wood and incense and flowers and hay and rain and orchards in bloom and freshly mowed grass and… "You get in trouble, you go to their children for advice."

"Their children?"

Siyamtiwa waved her arm. "All around you. Everywhere. Great Spirit's in all the kids of the Grandparents. Even the bad ones. In rocks and plants and animals. Especially animals. They know a lot. Rocks only know maybe one thing. They're real slow. Don't have energy for a lot of ideas, but the one thing they know is very, very old. Stood the test of time."

"What's the one thing?"

"Different for each one. So, you wanta know somethin' old, you ask that question, see who answers."

"How will I know that?"

"They'll get your attention. Maybe make a big color so you can't miss 'em. Maybe trip you up or climb in your shoe. Maybe fall on your head. You'd notice that, I bet." She blew out another cloud of fragrant smoke. "But you be careful not to waste rock's energy, takes 'em a long time to get it back. Couple hundred years, sometimes."

Stoner thought of all the people she knew who were always asking questions of crystals. She mentioned it.

"Crystals are different. Long time ago, they figured out how to take energy from your question, use it to send back the answer. That's why they make themselves sparkly. So you'll take them home and feed them your energy."

Stoner was appalled. "You mean all these crystals we have around are actually draining our energy?"

"Don't need much. You get it back in first five seconds of sleep. That too much to pay for truth? Or you just wanta go around all filled up all the time knowing nothing? White man's way?"

"Of course not."

"So you pay out a little of that spirit energy you got too much of, anyway. Good investment."

"All right." But she was still disappointed. She'd hoped for more specific help.

Siyamtiwa sensed her frustration. "I'll tell you somethin'. Get you started."

Stoner looked at her eagerly.

"You gotta find a piece of the old gypsy's soul. Teeny little chunk that got chopped off, 'cause whatever was goin' on, it didn't want no part of it. So it went away. You gotta walk around, call to it. When you find it, you bring it home."

"That's all? It's that easy?"

Siyamtiwa blew smoke in four directions before she answered. "Well, sometimes it don't wanta come. And sometimes someone took it and they don't wanta give it back. Then you have to work things out."

"And how do I do that?"

"Convince 'em. Or trade somethin' for it. Sometimes you gotta fight."

Stoner buried her face in her hands. "I can't do this. I really can't." She choked back tears.

The old woman blew fragrant, comforting smoke around her.

"I don't know how to find lost pieces of people. I don't know how to argue and fight with...with...whatever..." She glanced up helplessly.

Siyamtiwa's look was gentle. "That's okay, Green Eyes. You'll do all right."

It was the nicest thing the old woman had ever said to her. It frightened her. She probably thought Stoner was doomed, and was being kind to her out of compassion.

Her companion gave an impatient grunt.

"You're reading my mind, aren't you?"

"Kinda hard not to. It's pretty loud."

Stoner poked the ground impatiently with one finger. "I hate that. It's so, so rude. "

"Well, you gotta be careful how you use it," Siyamtiwa said placidly, obviously not giving a damn about the moral and social implications of eavesdropping on personal thoughts. "You ought to try it. Get that old Gypsy to teach you."

"No, thanks. I have enough trouble with her poking around in my thoughts."

"Then get her to show you how to keep them to yourself."

Stoner looked at her. "I can do that? Block them so no one can read them?"

"Yep. Anything you can do, you can not do." The old woman frowned musingly. "Or is it other way around?"

Burro made a snuffling, attention-getting sound.

She reached out and wrapped her hand around his ear. It was very soft.

He blew breath toward her, then shook his head and took a step backward.

"Don't you like that?" she asked him.

Burro nodded deeply, tossing his mane. He took another step and turned his head toward the water.

"Do you want a drink?"

He pawed the dirt with one foot, then walked deliberately away from her. He looked around, stared at her, and put the thought in her head to follow.

Follow.

"Time to go," Siyamtiwa said.

She got up and took a few steps and waited for Siyamtiwa to catch up. The Hopi woman just stood looking after her.

"Aren't you coming?"

Siyamtiwa shook her head. "This not my Journey. I only came to say hello."

Stoner felt a sinking in her stomach. For a minute there, with her old friend along for a guide, it seemed almost possible. But now...

"I'm not your only old friend," Siyamtiwa said.

Stoner glanced toward Burro, who hung his head and looked hurt and sad.

She felt a pang of guilt and pity, and went to put her arm around his neck. "I'm sorry," she murmured into his ear "I didn't mean it that way."

"You better learn how to hear him," Siyamtiwa said. "You do what he says. That animal volunteered for this." She dropped her voice and muttered, "Musta been drunk."

"I'm sorry," Stoner said again, half to Burro and half to Siyamtiwa.

Burro made a sound like chuckling.

"He's a good Burro and he knows you," Siyamtiwa said. "A good Power Animal even if he's not very pretty."

"He's pretty enough," Stoner said defensively, and squeezed Burro's neck tighter. "As pretty as that bunch you hang out with."

"Crow?" Siyamtiwa laughed. "That's one funny-looking animal, all right. Works pretty good, though, when you gotta see a long way." She looked as if she was beginning to fade. "I gotta go now. You wore me out. Next time you come, don't forget those twelve virgins."

"But where am I going to get twelve—"

Siyamtiwa was gone.

When the drums called her back, that was all she remembered. That and a few flashes of landscape—a wide desert with dim violet mountains in the distance, a river through a jungle, a dim and icy place where glacial floes punctured a black sky, the streets of a strange but familiar town. She knew there was more, but it stayed out of reach.

"I guess I just had the scenic tour," she said to Elizabeth, a little apologetically, when she had finished telling her about the Journey.

"You met your Power Animal and a spirit who taught you how to listen to Spirit. Sounds like a good day's work to me." She smiled. "Especially for a non-believer Journeying under protest."

Yes, when she thought about it, it wasn't bad at that. Against her better judgment, she felt proud of herself. "What do you think of Siyamtiwa's explanation of the universe. Pretty wild, huh?"

"I think," Elizabeth said, "your spirit guide wouldn't tell you something you're not capable of believing for yourself."

"I still don't know what I'm doing."

"You know as much as you need to know. The spirits can tell you the rest." She reviewed the notes she'd made of her own Journey. "My guide did have one suggestion for you. Eat lightly in the morning, and get yourself a bracelet of wooden beads and rawhide."

"I don't know if I can. Tomorrow's the last day of the full moon. Aunt Hermione thinks we should go then."

"I know. Well, do your best. That's all anybody expects. We'll be all set for you here, a little after noon. I've put aside the afternoon, in case this takes a while."

Takes a while? She couldn't imagine doing what needed to be done, and doing it well, in a dozen years. "I don't suppose you know where I can get twelve virgins."

"Any particular kind of virgins?"

"Virgin virgins."

The Shaman laughed. "I couldn't even find twelve Virgos, but I think I can come up with a partridge in a pear tree for you."

"Thank you very much," Stoner said wryly.

Elizabeth put her pen and notebook aside and stood up. "I hate to rush you, but I have to take another trip today."

"You really do a lot of Journeying in a day, don't you?"

"Yeah," Elizabeth said. "This one's all the way to the supermarket."

Hermione decided she had maybe twenty-four hours left in her. She hoped it'd be enough. The moon would soon begin to wane. Already she could feel herself waning.

She lay on her bed, unable to move, falling asleep for a few seconds here and there. But she couldn't stay asleep. Her muscles quivered as if they'd been touched by electricity. She could feel it building up, the tension, the need to release it. But shaking her legs, or stretching them, even trying to startle her own body didn't help. There was nothing she could do but lie there until it became unbearable. Then her whole being would jerk like a puppet, and there'd be quiet in her body for a few minutes.

It didn't even help to walk around. Not that she could. She'd think about it, and think about it, all the time knowing she didn't have the energy to move. Sooner or later the compulsion to use the bathroom would override her lethargy, but as soon as she lay back down on the bed the electricity would start to build again.

How long will it be before I go completely out of my mind? she wondered. She was tempted to let go now. To let her mind spin out, just to make it stop.

Cutter linked his mind to hers and felt that tension in his own body. He knew it like a first cousin. It came from days of crouching in a water-filled foxhole with the rain pouring down and the explosions so loud and so near that you got in the habit of checking to see if you were alive every few minutes.

Sometimes, even listening for your heart or touching your skin looking for warmth, you couldn't really tell whether you were alive or dead. A few of the guys would take out their knives and cut themselves, just to see the blood. You wouldn't see blood if you were dead.

Sometimes you'd just think back through your life, remembering everything you'd ever done until you were pretty sure you'd never done anything horrible enough to send you here. But then you couldn't be certain you remembered everything.

Sticking yourself with a knife was better.

He didn't do much of that, though. Only when he really had to, when he couldn't convince himself any other way. And only when it mattered. Most of the time it didn't matter. Dead or alive, it was all about the same. He was here, and the jungle was here, and the Beast was here. Death was all around, whether it was in you or not.

And it was in all of them, even the ones who survived, even the ones who came home with whole bodies. For the rest of their lives, they'd carry Death inside them like a cancer.

So his name wasn't Cutter because of cutting. Not like some of the guys, who gave themselves nicknames like talismans, who thought they could keep themselves safe by taking what was inside and carrying it out in the open. If that had been the case, he'd have called himself 'Death.'

His name was Cutter because that was his name. He'd had a first name, too, at one time, but he couldn't remember it. It had scared him, the first time he tried to remember his name but couldn't. But it didn't scare him any more. It didn't matter. Now he was just Cutter.

Something touched her hand and she opened her eyes. Stoner sat beside her on the bed, looking down at her.

Hermione felt tears well up from somewhere deep inside her. Not tears of sadness or fear, but the tears that always came when she thought of her niece's sweet face and loving eyes. Tears of gratitude for the time with her. She knew there'd been other lifetimes with her, and would be again, but this one was so very special. Tears of longing for it to be forever, this moment of seeing her and feeling her and loving her. Hermione let them flow.

"Grace is here," Stoner said softly. She stroked Hermione's hand.

"So early?"

"It's after eight. She's been here since six. We had dinner. We didn't want to wake you."

I ought to get up, she thought. I'm being a terrible hostess.

She couldn't find the energy to move.

"You must be hungry," Stoner said. Her eyes were puffy and sore-looking.

"Have you been crying?"

Stoner nodded in an ashamed way. "I couldn't help it. I'm scared, Aunt Hermione."

Hermione forced herself to smile. "You're going to be fine."

"But what if I'm not? What if I make a mess of it? If something happens to you, it'll be all my fault, and I can't bear that."

"Whatever's going to happen has already happened, don't you know that?" she said reassuringly. "This is only a shadow of the future. And you're going to do just fine. Spirit wouldn't have picked you for this unless you were the right one."

Stoner was silent for a moment, then blurted out, "What if you die?"

"If I die, I'll see you later, Alligator." She had said that to Stoner a hundred times when she was a child. Every time she visited her sister, as she was leaving, the terror would engulf the child. Hermione understood. There wasn't much love for little Stoner in that house, with both her parents absorbed in their own self-interests and what they wanted her to be for them. Hermione loved the child for the singular, extraordinary little soul she was. Partings were wrenching for them both.

She made a gesture with her hand. "Come here," she said. "Lie down beside me for a minute, then we'll go act like adults."

She smiled as Stoner snuggled up against her, head on Hermione's arm, the way she used to as a child. "Do you remember, when you were very little, I promised you I'd never lie to you?"

She felt Stoner nod.

"Well, I've never broken that promise, and the rules are still in effect."

"Okay," Stoner said.

"Now, I want you to listen to me, I'm telling you the absolute truth. I am not going to die. Not now. I'd know it if I were. I always know. It just doesn't feel right for dying." She held Stoner tighter so she wouldn't interrupt. "But I want you to know, in case I'm too addled to tell you when the time comes, it's been an absolute joy and privilege to have been loved by you."

Stoner was silent for a long time. Hermione could tell she was either crying or trying not to cry. She let her do whatever she needed to do, kissing her lightly on the top of her head. After a while, she said, "We'd better go, dear. Before they come looking for us. You know Marylou, she'll decide we should all cuddle here and have a picnic."

Stoner sat up and scrubbed at her eyes with the heels of her hands. She looked about nineteen.

"How can I do this?" she asked miserably. "Siyamtiwa wants twelve virgins. I don't even know twelve virgins."

Hermione laughed. "Of course you do. Your entire softball team."

Stoner stared at her. "That's what she meant?"

"No doubt. She's an old fox, that one."

Stoner ran her hand through her hair. "God, I feel so stupid." She thought for a moment. "Wait a minute, there are fourteen women on the team."

Hermione smiled and raised one eyebrow. "I don't think that's any of our business, dear."

He'd never seen so many hungry ghosts all at one time. They surrounded the house, clinging to the walls, covering the ground floor with darkness like old ivy. But they didn't move, only sat and waited. The power of the High Priestess bound them.

Mogwye hung her black dress in her makeshift closet and slid the old bedspread across the rope to close it off. Almost over now. Tomorrow would be hard, but she'd tackled harder things than this. The girl was a pushover. She'd already drained her with nothing more than a look. As for Hermione Moore…well, that witch had about as much power as a double-A flashlight battery.

She slipped into bed and reached for her new romantic novel. Her cat jumped up and stood on her chest and stared down at her, trying to get her attention. Trying to remind her there might be something she'd over-looked.

Mogwye laughed and shoved him aside.

Grace lit the candles and incense. "If you feel you're up to it," she said to Hermione, "I think we should call on the Goddess for help."

From her bed, Hermione nodded. She didn't feel up to it, but she knew Grace was right. Drawing all of her energy to her, she got up and went to stand beside her lover. She could feel the strength of Grace's aura, and drew on that force as they went through the ritual of blessing.

Twelve Blue Shirts could hardly sleep. Coach had ordered them to a special 'field trip.' When she'd explained it first as a 'kind of religious thing' they'd grumbled, and rebellion was in the wings. But Coach had explained that the whole thing was being managed by an ancient Indian woman who'd specifically asked for twelve virgins. That had made them giggle and nudge one another with their elbows. Until Coach had explained that Virgins originally meant women who weren't dependent on men. That excited them even more.

Two of the Blue Shirts had skipped practice to go out with their boyfriends. They hadn't heard Coach's order. They slept soundly.

Stoner didn't sleep. Fear and premonitions of doom played a game of badminton in her head. Gwen sensed her restlessness and took her hand.

In the still darkness of Hermione's room, Grace said a silent prayer for Cutter's soul.

The full moon began to die, turning soft, rotting at its waning edge.

Chapter 12

Such a fuss over one person, Hermione thought. They were all there, Grace and Marylou and Stoner and Gwen and Elizabeth and Karen her partner. And the twelve virgins in their freshly washed and ironed uniforms. Even Cutter, though he couldn't bring himself to come in. Diana had given her sets of crystals for everyone, quartz points for clarity and tourmaline to dispel negativity. Cecilia from PARA had gathered all the psychics—legitimate psychics, of course, Cecilia was adamant about having nothing to do with "Gypsies" as she called them—she could find into her living room and asked them to send healing energy. At one time, Hermione might have taken personal offense at the slur against Gypsies. But that was lifetimes ago and, besides, Cecilia was Italian. Italians, like everyone else, had their prejudices and superstitions.

There was nothing from the coven. She and Stoner had discussed it, and agreed that the less chance there was of Mogwye finding out what was going on, the better. Even though they'd uncovered nothing that pointed to Mogwye in all of this, Stoner still felt uneasy about her. Hermione'd avoided the Full Moon ceremony, claiming she felt too ill to attend, which was the truth. If Mogwye thought anything about that, it would be that her spells were working. She'd be satisfied, and wouldn't have any reason to take further action.

Travis had sent flowers and good wishes. Hermione smiled as she recalled the afternoon last week when he'd stopped by to see how she was doing. She had decided to enter a trance, thinking perhaps she could get a broader view of the situation if she went out of body. Just as she was slipping loose from her earth bonds, she had heard a loud, angry male voice. She had concentrated as hard as she could, to hold onto the trance, but the anger intruded. It had really been annoying. She hadn't been pulled out of a trance in the past twelve lifetimes, and the time before that it had taken a total eclipse of the sun to do it.

But the voice was going on and on, growing louder and more angry.

She had let herself slip back to her body just a little, to see if she could make out what was happening. She couldn't hear the words, but she heard the emotions under them.

The man hadn't been angry, he'd been terrified. What if it was Cutter, finally gone over the edge? Taking a deep breath, she dove back into the everyday world. The man was shaking her by the shoulders and shouting, "Come back to me, God damn it! Don't you dare die on me, old lady!"

It had been Travis. He'd seen her in trance, and had thought she was dying. He was using every ounce of his CPR training on her. She thought she was going to split something trying to hold her laughter inside. If he didn't break her ribs first, what with all his pounding and shaking and forcing her to breathe at a pace that wasn't natural to her at all. It really was unpleasant. She decided to teach him a lesson. "So that's how you speak to poor dying souls," she said in a haughty voice popping her eyes open suddenly. "How very nice. The last thing they hear on this side is you swearing like a drunken sailor. Your mother must be so proud."

Travis had jumped back as if he'd seen a ghost, which he probably believed he had. "I thought…" he stammered. "I was trying to bring you back."

"And what business is it of yours if I come back?" Hermione huffed. "If I want to come back I'm perfectly capable of making that decision for myself. I don't need some juvenile delinquent yelling at me."

He'd looked as if he might sink into a puddle of Silly Putty on the floor, so she relented a little and thanked him—stiffly—for his concern.

Hermione had suggested he get a grip on himself and sent him home to read Deepak Chopra.

"Finally," Grace said into her ear, "a smile from you."

Hermione leaned against her lover's arm. "This is a little overwhelming."

"I know. It means you're loved. That's never easy to take."

Grace was her usual calm, reassuring self, as if there were not a single doubt in her mind that this would work.

Hermione wondered if she really believed that, or had privileged information from the Goddess, or was just a very good actor.

Grace started to lead her into the Journey room, but Elizabeth stopped her.

"We have to meet out here," she explained. "We'd never fit in there." She peered at Hermione and gave a low grunt. "It's pretty bad, isn't it?"

"To tell you the truth," Hermione said in a low voice so the others couldn't hear, "I think we'd better get under way as soon as possible."

Her aunt had gone down hill even in the past five minutes. She seemed barely alive. Stoner felt pale, and cold all over. This was it, she knew. If the soul retrieval didn't work, there wouldn't be time left to try anything else.

Gwen squeezed her hand. Stoner barely felt it.

"Whatever happens," Gwen said, "I'll be right here."

Stoner knew what she meant. Even if she failed, Gwen would be there to comfort her, to support her, to love her and help her put the pieces of her life back together.

"Okay," she said aloud, hoping she sounded more self-assured than she felt, diving into the deep end before she had a chance to find out how cold the water was. "Let's get moving."

She lay down and covered her eyes. Elizabeth invoked the Spirits, singing and rattling an invitation to join them, asking for their help, circling the blanket where Stoner lay, rattling protection.

Stoner's curiosity got the better of her. She let her eyes drift open a slit.

Elizabeth's face was changing, growing wider and shorter. Her skin darkened. Her hair and eyes were black. Her forehead protruded a little. She bent forward slightly from the waist, legs rising and falling as if she were running. Her clothes were ragged, and decorated with faded colors. Except she wasn't a 'she' any more. She was a man, an old man. Her voice was deeper, louder, harsher. There was a look of determination on her face. An angry look, as if she were trying to frighten away demons.

Instead of scaring her, Elizabeth's transformation was comforting.

The Shaman fell silent, the drums began.

Stoner let herself be taken by the rhythm.

This time she knew where to go, and sent herself into the black rock tunnel to the Lower World. Burro was there, as she knew he would be. There was no sign of Siyamtiwa, twelve virgins or no twelve virgins. But that didn't mean anything. She could be a tree or a stone or a drop of water in the river, or just herself, present but invisible.

So far, so good, Stoner thought. Now what?

Burro turned and looked at her, then seemed to gesture with his head toward a patch of grass a little distance away.

She got the point. These Spirit Guides, or whatever they were, liked you to hustle a little for them. She brought him a carefully chosen handful of the grass.

He nodded deeply and chewed the treat slowly and methodically.

Stoner waited.

Burro belched softly and began moving back toward the tunnel entrance. She followed him.

It was dark in there. She couldn't see, but she could feel Burro beside her. She reached out and touched his firm, silky shoulder.

Immediately they were going up, slowly at first, then faster and faster. Her body felt as light as helium. Then she realized it wasn't her body at all, not her physical body. There was no physical body, but all the sensations and emotions were still there.

Burro was leaving, she felt him say, but only for a little while. Another Power Animal was taking over. There would be someone to greet her at the other end, and he would see her when she got back.

She wanted to ask him why. Was he limited to the Lower World? But he was gone.

Something was still pulling her upward. She looked up and saw a little pink bird. A hummingbird. In its tiny beak it held a silver thread. The thread was attached to her solar plexus.

Still rising. Past tree branches, through clouds. Into a rosy mist.

There was no feeling of height, or fear of falling. The rising was as natural as breathing.

Suddenly she felt a break, a change of atmosphere, like breaking through from the bottom of a lake into dry air. She was standing now, on a flat, arid plain with violet mountains in the distance.

A figure came toward her. Human. It came closer. A Native American, an old man. Not old by Siyamtiwa's standards, but old by the standards of his time and place. He strode toward her, carrying his feathered walking stick, moving with ease and authority.

She knew his name. Old Man of a Hundred Crows.

She hadn't heard it. It had simply appeared in her mind.

"Are you here to help me?" she asked.

He nodded. But you're not ready yet, he said without saying it. We have to get the worries out of your mind.

Old Man waved his arm in a circle, and the air was filled with the beating of wings. The hundred crows and hovered near them.

Stoner tried not to think of Hitchcock's "The Birds."

Old Man heard her thoughts, and smiled. Lie down, he said. I'll turn your worries into ants, and my crows will eat them.

Well, that struck her as particularly gruesome.

This isn't Ordinary Reality, Old Man said. Think of it as symbolic, if it makes you feel better.

Okay. Symbolically, she lay down and closed her eyes. She could see the crows poke their beaks into the crevices of her brain, pulling up the ants, pecking at them as they tried to burrow deeper or run away.

It felt good, like someone softly tapping her head. Gentle. Cleansing. Her mind relaxed.

This is highly strange, she thought.

Old Man smiled at her again. Okay, now we go, he said.

He heard the drums begin inside the house. No one would come out to check on him now. Silently, he eased himself off the lounge chair. He'd thought about going in with them, when they first arrived, but as soon as he got out of Marylou's car his hands began to sweat and perspiration dripped down his arms and a terrible buzzing began in his ears and pain rasped his brain like thorns. Marylou had told him, gently, to go into the back yard.

It was the people. The place was filled with people. He knew most of them, a little, but that made it worse. They knew something about him, which meant they could grab bits of him if they wanted to. Strangers weren't interested. And people he was close to...well, that would be Marylou, and Marylou just didn't take pieces of you.

Karen, the Shaman's lady friend, had come out to see if he needed anything. He liked how she looked, high cheek-boned and calm, with a glitter in her eye as if she might have to play a practical joke on you any minute. Someone you could talk to.

That made him want to crawl inside himself and hide. He forced himself to say he was fine.

She wouldn't be satisfied until she'd put up the lounge chair for him. He made himself sit in it, and to smile as if he really was grateful, but he only wished she'd go away. The chair was too high from the ground. He felt conspicuous. Anyone, anything could see him. They'd get to him before he even knew they were there.

It was kind of the Shaman and her lady to think of him. He knew that. But kindness made him feel things. It was dangerous to feel things.

He found an overgrown bush. There was a break in the branches, an entrance of sorts. Cutter crawled inside. It was cool here, and safe. He was alone. No one could find him until he showed himself.

Cutter took a deep breath and closed his eyes. He had places to go.

Far in the distance she could just make out the shapes of buildings.

"Is that where we're going?" she asked.

Old Man nodded and lengthened his stride.

Stoner trotted to catch up with him. "Do you think you could slow down a little?" she pleaded, gasping for breath, her lungs burning.

He stopped and looked down at her. *You're tired? You don't have a body here, how can it be tired?*

"I don't?" She looked down at herself. Seemed pretty solid to her.

Jump, he ordered.

Startled by the unexpected command, she jumped. Her feet hit the hard-packed ground with a jolt.

Higher.

She jumped a little higher.

Old Man waved his arm. *See that bird up there?*

It was one of his crows, of course. It circled about fifty feet above their heads.

Get me that crow.

Stoner said, "Huh?"

Jump up there and get me that crow.

He waited.

Stoner stood there like the idiot she felt like.

Put your thought on the crow, then follow your thought. Don't forget to come back down.

She looked up at the crow and willed herself to it.

The crow was in her hands. It hopped onto her shoulder. It must have decided to come to her.

She could feel Old Man laughing.

Something made her look down. She was floating, five stories above the ground. Old Man was no bigger than a cat.

Hey, she thought, call me Peter Pan, I'm flying. It felt good, not frightening or dizzying. She would have expected a touch of vertigo—back home she could get dizzy pruning a tree. But she only felt clear-headed and confident.

Let's try a barrel roll. She concentrated.

There was sky above her, then earth above her. The mountains, hugging the horizon, appeared as she turned.

Mountaintops. Snowcaps.

Treading air, she contemplated them. For some reason, she wanted to go closer.

She turned a few mid-air somersaults and called down to Old Man, "Okay if I check out the mountains?"

With a laugh, he waved her forward.

She willed herself to go, and she was there.

Bare sharp rock, deep crevasses filled with captured snow. Wind and cold. Bitter cold. She felt it, but it didn't wound her. It was like a sensation from a distance. And she felt the timelessness of the place, a place that never changed, where the wind and snow blew forever.

This is what it's like to be a rock up here, she thought. Patiently waiting, waiting for something to happen billions of years from now.

It felt so calm, so peaceful to wait like this. She was lulled by it, let herself sink into it.

Old Man's thoughts reached her. You can come back to this place another time, he said. But now you have a job to do.

Oh, God, Aunt Hermione! Guilt flooded through her. She raced back to her Guide.

"I'm sorry," she said breathlessly.

That's okay. He seemed amused by her, as if she were a child seeing the world for the first time.

"But Aunt Hermione. She's dying."

She's okay for now. We have her.

"What do you mean?"

We slowed time for her. Since you got here, maybe—he looked at the sky—maybe one minute has passed. We can slow it, but we can't stop it. Ready to go now?

"Ready."

He stepped out ahead of her. She hesitated, then threw her thoughts forward toward him.

She came even with him. Hah! She tossed her attention to a large rock about twenty-five feet away.

Laughing, she turned back to see him walking toward her. "Beat you," she called.

Old Man caught up with her instantly. Okay, let's have a race. To that town over there.

"Good," she said, full of herself. "I'll give you a quarter-mile lead."

Fair enough, considering my age. She knew he was mocking her, but she didn't care. Last one there's a rotten egg.

Naturally, they landed at the same moment. The crow was still on her shoulder. Can I go now, boss? it asked Old Man.

Old Man nodded and the crow flew off. They don't like cities, he explained. Too many people want to eat them.

"I understand that," Stoner said. "I've had to eat a little crow myself in my time."

He laughed. 'Eat a little crow.' I forgot about that one. Have to tell my friends about it.

"You speak our language so well," Stoner said. "And yet you seem to be…well, not of our time. When did you live, and where?"

Everywhere, every time, he replied. He gestured toward the town. Enough questions.

It was an ancient-looking place. A high adobe wall with raised platform towers at the corners. The platforms were deserted. A huge wooden door was set in the wall.

"Should we knock?" Stoner asked.

They know we're here.

Then they were standing inside the walls, in the courtyard of a palace. The palace was built of heavy rock, with a domed roof, ornate in its simplicity. A pathway of mosaics led to the palace door, the tiles forming pictures of palm trees and oases and leopards and deer-like animals. A man driving a chariot fought with a lion in one scene. In another, men on horseback charged futilely at the walls while others atop the platforms hurled spears down on them.

Market stalls, little more than lean-tos with roofs of cloth, lay scattered about. It seemed deserted.

"Where are the people?" Stoner asked.

The sun's very hot now, Old Man explained. Noon your time. They'll be back when the air cools.

Now that he mentioned it, she was aware of the heat, sharp and blistering. As hot as it had been cold in the mountains, and with the same distant feeling.

"You said they know we're here. Can they see us?"

Some can. Some can't. It depends on their degree of evolution. Those who can see us know why we're here. We won't disturb them and they won't disturb us.

"It looks sort of familiar. Like a picture from my college Ancient History class. Like Babylon, maybe, only different."

This isn't Babylon. Babylon's a much, much bigger city. This is a minor principality. Not exactly small potatoes, but not big time. Your pictures are based on what someone thought about the ruins they found. Suggestive but not accurate. This is the real thing.

"Real."

He smiled at her indulgently and shrugged. That time business again. So hard for white people to understand. There is no time. Everything is happening all at once and all the time. He looked at her, and could tell she didn't get it. He smiled again. Go ahead and explore.

The palace stood in the center of the walled compound. Around the edges were small adobe homes, some standing alone, some in clusters. A few had gardens, tiny but lush. What looked like a community field lay between the houses and the palace. It took up several acres, and was filled with blossoming and blooming and fruiting plants. She didn't recognize most of them.

About an acre was devoted to wheat. Another to fruit trees. She could smell the tart odor of lemons, the sweetness of orange blossoms. Avocados hung from branches like orioles' nests. Toward the periphery, date palms squatted on sandy ground. Bees hummed, the sound of a jet engine coming to life.

"Guess we'd better not disturb those bees," she said.

Speak to them respectfully. Tell them you don't mean them any harm, and ask them to let you pass. But talk with your thoughts. Speech only confuses them and makes them protective.

She tried it, and the mass of bees parted to give her a path through the orchard.

It was cool among the trees, among their dark, glossy leaves. The odor of citrus blossoms made her dizzy. She listed a little to one side.

Old Man caught her arm. Take it easy.

"It's the smell. It's wonderful. But overpowering."

He was apologetic. I forgot. You haven't learned how to deal with this intensity.

"But I didn't feel the cold, not really. Or this heat."

You can feel what you want to feel, and smell and taste, all the senses. Pretty good plan, huh?

"But how? I mean, that's not possible, is it?"

So many questions. So impatient. Slow down. You're still an apprentice.

An apprentice? She wasn't aware of signing on for any apprenticing. She was just looking for Aunt Hermione's soul.

My mistake. He sounded amused.

"I think," she said, "we should get the show on the road."

They arrived at the foot of the stairs leading to the front door of the palace.

"Now what?"

Go in. Ask to speak to the Princess. Tell her your problem and let her take it from there.

"Aren't you coming...?" She turned to look but he had gone.

"That figures," she muttered, and began to climb the steps.

Inside, the palace was dark and cool and smelled of sandy earth. The walls were covered with a plaster of adobe dust. The anteroom floor was tiled in more mosaics: the moon, stars and constellations against a cobalt blue background.

She was looking for the Big Dipper when a young man approached. May I help you? he asked with a barely perceptible bow.

"I'd like to see the Princess," she said, "if it's not too much trouble."

Indicating that she should follow, he led the way into a brightly lighted room. Long, unglassed windows looked out on the town. There was no furniture, but benches of stone against the walls. At the front of the room there was a sunken floor, setting that part of the room off from the rest.

Some kind of auditorium, she thought. A place where the Princess holds audience with her subjects? A stone bench with arms sat slightly raised, under a huge mosaic of a flying crow.

Crows. Everywhere I go, crows.

What do you wish from me?

A pleasant, soft female voice entered her mind. She turned to see a woman—a beautiful woman with dark hair and skin. Her eyes were the color of night, with flecks of gold. Stoner didn't want to stare, but she was certain those golden flecks formed the outline of the constellation Cassiopeia.

"You must be the Princess," she said.

Yes, I am. And you must be one of my subjects, though your hair and skin are an unusual color, and your clothes... The Princess smiled. Are you a traveler? Your clothes have such a foreign look.

Right. This Princess of Ancient Something-or-Other had probably never seen denim. "I guess I am," she said.

The Princess lowered herself to a step around the sunken floor and patted the space beside her. Stoner sat.

"If you don't mind my asking," Stoner said, "where are we?"

The other woman frowned perplexedly. You don't know? This is Shirpurla. She indicated the mosaic crow. Named for our Goddess Shirpur, the Raven.

Stoner said, "Oh."

Tell me your story.

She did.

The Princess of Shirpurla listened carefully. At the end she nodded, then clapped her hands three times. A young woman appeared.

Our guest, here, The Princess said, has need of your talents and the talents of your friends. Do you understand?

The other woman nodded solemnly and left the room.

That is my personal maid. She has certain...skills that will be of help to you. But I have to ask that you not tell anyone about this. If word got back to the King, he'd have them killed.

"Absolutely," Stoner said. "You have my solemn word."

The Princess rolled her eyes. *You know how men are. They hate a woman with powers.*

Boy, Stoner thought, some things never change.

How true. The Princess laughed. *Women's oppression is a universal language. Of course, according to my dear husband...she* mimicked a long face...*it's women's complaints that are universal.*

Stoner blushed. She'd forgotten they could read her thoughts.

The Princess rose to leave. *You'll grow accustomed to it. It's very efficient, you know. Not only quick, but when you can't find the right word, you can send a picture, or a feeling, anything you like. Be sure to try our dates before you go. They're famous throughout the civilized world.*

As she exited the room, she was nearly trampled by five young woman, barely in their teens, who poured through the doorway jostling and giggling. Seeing the Princess, they fell to their knees.

The Princess gave them a glowering look, which wasn't quite sincere and said, *Behave yourselves.*

The girls—they really were more girls than women—arranged themselves in a circle on the sunken floor. One by one they made eye contact with Stoner, nodded subtly, and dropped their eyes. One of them pulled a soft leather bag from beneath her robes and emptied its contents onto the floor.

Stoner leaned closer. Bones. Tiny bones, as tiny as the bones of a wren.

One by one, each girl picked up the pile of bones, shook it between her hands, and tossed it out in the center of the circle. Each time, money and giggles changed hands. It was a game, apparently a game of chance.

She tried to make out the patterns of wins and losses. It made no sense.

They started around the circle again. The first girl tossed the bones, then the second, the third...

They drew back, gasping. Not with fear, it seemed, but with delight.

"What?" Stoner asked.

The bones just told us who you are. It was the Princess' servant girl who spoke. *And what you need us to do. I'm to take you to the edge of the Great Sea, where the river waters run together.*

174

"I see. And did they tell you what I was supposed to do then?"

The girl shook her head. They say you know.

Sure, I do.

The girl stood up. We have to go. We haven't much time.

The others scurried to conceal the bones.

So, these weren't any ordinary servant girls playing a game. These were young witches, and their hummingbird bones told them what needed to be done. Aunt Hermione was going to love this.

Stoner followed the servant through a hidden back door. The girl led her among the palms, examining the plums, sweet dates, choosing the best for Stoner. Are you ready to go?

"Ready." The sugary taste still alive on her tongue, she threw herself on the wind.

She came to earth where the rivers dumped their brown silt into the sea. The servant girl was gone. There was no one there. She called, but there was no answer. Nothing around her for miles but sand and rock. The sun beat down white-hot. The sky was pale and empty. Nothing lived here.

Stoner was alone. The aloneness was so strong it was nearly tangible. And she had no idea where she was or what to do now.

"Aunt Hermione," she called, aloud and in her mind.

Not even the air moved.

Despair reached up from the dead, packed, lye-encrusted sand and grabbed her by the ankles. She sank to the ground.

This whole thing was a disaster. She couldn't find her aunt's soul piece. She didn't even believe in soul pieces. Souls weren't like jigsaw puzzles, put everything in its proper place and—behold!—a living, breathing soul. It was all ridiculous, and even if it wasn't, she was.

Stupid, she berated herself. Stupid and awkward and inadequate and unbelieving and unimaginative and ugly. A freak. Lesbian freak. Freak-freak. Aunt Hermione was going to die, and all because she'd entrusted her soul to her dear niece.

"Dear niece," she said aloud, sarcastically. The words and the tone echoed off of nothing.

Appropriate. Nothing echoing off of nothing.

"Hey, there, whatever world you are," she shouted. "This is Nothing talking to Nothing. How's tricks?"

And now, to make matters worse, she seemed to have sat down on a boulder. Well, maybe just a rock. It bit into her, all the way through her skin to her nerves and up her spinal column. It hurt, damn it.

She pulled it out from beneath her and stood up, furious, to throw it into the sea.

The rock seemed to move a little in her hand.

Startled, she dropped it.

That was truly disgusting, she thought, and shook her hand rapidly as if she could shake off the experience.

Curious, she bent down to look at it.

It was just an ordinary, sedimentary, striated sandstone rock. The kind of rock you'd expect to find in a place like this, where life was just one ocean after another, rolling in and dumping all kinds of debris and rolling out again, leaving behind dry, hot, uninhabitable land.

She poked it with one finger, half expecting it to scurry away from her. It didn't budge.

This whole situation gets weirder by the minute, she thought.

Then she remembered what Siyamtiwa had said, about even the rocks having messages. Maybe that was why it had—

No. That kind of thinking was nuts.

Given that you're on some kind of Shamanic type Journey to an imaginary place called the Upper World, where people read your mind… Given that you've been asking advice from an old Hopi woman who's been dead for at least for three years, one way or another… Given that you've been letting yourself be led around by a donkey… Do you really think you're in a position to make judgments about weird?

She held her breath and gingerly picked up the rock, ready to toss it at the first sign of independent life.

The rock lay on her hand utterly motionless, just the way good rocks were supposed to behave.

Fine. She studied it more closely. It was kind of pretty, really, with its shades of sandstone red and sepia. An interesting texture, gritty and solid. And warm, the way rocks grow warm in the sun.

Well, she thought to the rock, if Siyamtiwa's right and you do have a message for me, now's the time to come out with it.

The rock was motionless.

Guess it's not me you have the message for, huh?

Rock didn't reply. But maybe it was conserving its energy, given that it took a couple of millennia to recharge.

Listen, it's been swell chatting with you, but I really do have to get going. She hesitated. Trouble is, she thought, I don't know which direction to go.

She felt…not movement, exactly, but a gentle tug. Pulling her hand to the left.

176

Aha.

She looked. There was something in the distance. She couldn't quite make it out. Not much more than a mild swelling in the desert. But it was something to aim for. She took a breath and hurled herself into the air.

This out-of-body flying was really quite interesting. Too bad it didn't work that way in Ordinary Reality. But there'd be the usual drunks on the highway, and old men in golf caps who couldn't see any more but still had their licenses God only knew how. And lost tourists. People carrying young children who bounced and screamed and pounded on each other. Road rage. All the usual traffic hazards.

She circled the low hill and settled back to the ground in a perfect landing. She waited for Rock to give its next direction.

Forward this time.

Reaching the base of the hill, she saw that it wasn't a hill after all, but a man-made mound encasing what looked like a burial chamber or under-ground storage area. She poked her head into the darkness to get a better look.

It was only a dark cave. Shadowless and empty. By standing to the side to let in a flicker of light, she could barely make out a large hole in the floor.

"I suppose I'm expected to hurl myself down that," she said aloud.

Rock pulled her hand downward.

Okay. Alice in Wonderland time.

She stepped into the darkness and fell.

Even before she left the tunnel, she knew this was a bad place. Through the entrance she saw fog. Nothing but fog, silent and unmoving.

She hesitated to step out into that thick grayness. Two steps from the tunnel entrance and she wouldn't be able to find her way back. Rock was gone, her hand empty. The sun was polarized. Her senses were useless.

She tried calling to Burro, to Old Man, to Siyamtiwa, to anyone. Nobody answered. It didn't surprise her. More than at any time in her life, she felt her utter aloneness.

Maybe she could go back up.

She sent her mind back up the tunnel, back to the Upper World. But no matter how hard she tried, how carefully and completely she envisioned it, she didn't move.

Well, she couldn't stay here forever, neither here nor there. Carefully, keeping one hand on the cave wall, she moved forward and slipped side-ways into the fog. The rocks that formed the entrance to the tunnel were solid against her back.

And what now?

She could stand here and hope some troop of Girl Scouts working on their Rescue Merit Badges would happen by. Somehow she didn't think that would happen.

It was becoming hard to breathe in the fog. Every lung full felt like half air and half water. Like July back in Massachusetts, when the low pressure systems and the heat and the inversion layers and the humidity and the pollution grew thicker and thicker, hanging like a bell jar over the state.

Siyamtiwa had told her to turn to the things in nature for her answers. Except the things in nature were on strike.

I must be pretty awful, she thought, when even rocks won't talk to me.

Finally she couldn't stand it any more. She had to do something, to move even if she got lost. She was lost now anyway. What difference did it make? What difference did anything make?

Three steps and there was nothing on any side but fog. She couldn't even see her feet.

She forced herself to wade blindly through it. Sooner or later, she was certain, she'd find herself back where she'd started. But there might be something interesting along the way.

For a full hour she trudged through the pale white light and dampness. She'd seen nothing, heard nothing, touched nothing. This must be what Purgatory is like, she thought.

The ground beneath her feet began to turn soft. She must be getting somewhere, then. She hadn't crossed marshy ground before, and this was definitely marshy.

A moment of exhilaration.

And then the ground, the ground she still couldn't see, began to suck her down, mud grasping at her ankles. She wasn't just sinking into swamp or quicksand. This stuff was alive, and pulling at her.

Horrified, she stepped back. A shoe came off and disappeared into the fog.

Stoner stumbled backward toward the solid earth she'd left. Her back foot sank into mud.

In a panic, she turned in circles, searching with her feet for something she could stand on.

The ground all around her had turned soft and grasping.

The little patch of firm earth where she was standing was beginning to shrink. She was certain of it. She tried calling again. Called her Guides. Called the people she knew in Ordinary Reality. Called Gwen and Aunt

Hermione and Elizabeth and even Marylou. Even Mogwye would be better company than this terrible loneliness. The crows could come and pick ants from her brain to their hearts' content. At least she wouldn't be alone.

She was surrounded by absolute silence.

She sank down on her tiny island of solidity. Out of friends, out of strength, out of time, and out of ideas.

"All right," she said, holding her hands out and upward in supplication, "I give up. If there's any Great Spirit or God or Cosmic Consciousness in the universe, I'm yours. I won't try to do it myself any more. It's all in your hands. But there's one thing I have to insist on. Please, please don't expect me to have Faith."

She wasn't sure how long it was before she had the feeling there was someone...or something...there. It wasn't that she saw it or heard it. It was a sense of life. And movement.

"Who is it? Help me. I'm lost."

The feeling of movement stopped, but the entity was still there.

She tried to read its intention, good or malevolent. If it was anything, it was neutral.

She waited and listened.

Off to her right it seemed as if the fog had congealed a little. She stared into it.

Yes, there was something there.

She studied it until her eyes ached. She could see it, but it wasn't moving.

Waiting for her to make the first move, maybe. Waiting to pounce.

Maybe it couldn't see her if she didn't move.

She tried to hold herself very still, to stop breathing. Because whatever this entity was, if it wasn't harboring dark thoughts toward her it would have made itself known by now.

She heard a sound like rustling. At least, if fog could rustle this is what it would sound like.

It seemed to be coming from behind her. She started to turn...

...and found a hard, masculine hand clamped over her mouth. Another hand held her shoulder, keeping her to the ground.

"Don't move. Don't scream," a male voice whispered aloud.

Heart pounding, she did her best to nod agreement.

He released her mouth, eased the pressure on her shoulder.

Slowly, she turned to look at him and nearly screamed despite his warning.

The man was grotesque, a character from a slasher movie. His face was entirely covered with patches of green and black and khaki paint. Dark eyes glittered from white rings. His clothes were dark and torn. His mouth was closed around a razor-sharp hunting knife.

Stoner was frozen with fear.

He took the knife in one paint-covered hand and lowered it to the ground. He smiled. The smile was horrible.

They stared at one another for a moment.

The smile faded from his face, replaced by bewilderment. "Don't you know me?" he asked. His voice was tinged with disappointment.

She knew him. "Cutter," she said, and began to laugh and cry all at once.

Chapter 13

He sat on the ground opposite her, their knees touching. "I'm sorry," he said in a low voice. "I didn't mean to scare you."

Stoner waved one hand in what she hoped was a "no problem" gesture but which ended up making her look like a nineteenth century lady about to swoon, and tried to get control of herself.

"Oh, God," Cutter said helplessly. "Oh, shit."

She managed to find her voice. "It's all right. You startled me. Your face…"

"Shit, I forgot." He pulled a rumpled handkerchief from his pocket and scrubbed furiously at his face. "The camouflage stuff. Damn."

His knees were still pressed against hers. That was strange. The Cutter she knew would never have allowed that.

"I used to get off on this stuff," he explained. "When I was a kid. Playing soldier. Maybe because my dad was in the war." He wiped the backs of his hands. "Or maybe all boys do."

"I think they do," Stoner said. The way he was talking… That wasn't like him at all.

"My dad wouldn't talk about it," he said. "I mean, he told me where he'd been and all, but not what it was like. I didn't understand that until 'Nam."

Stoner looked him in the eye, dead on. "How do I know you're who you say you are?"

"Oh." He quickly pulled a chain and dog tags from beneath his t-shirt and handed it to her.

It identified him as Cutter, all right. David Cutter.

"David?"

"Yeah. That was my name. Before." He ducked his head in an embarrassed way. "Mom called me Davy."

"I never knew you had a first name."

"That was…you know. I dropped it."

"Why?"

He shrugged. "Reminded me too much of the past, I guess. It made me feel weak."

It wasn't just that he was talking so openly, she thought. There was something else different about him. He looked like Cutter, especially without the camouflage make-up. But a younger, much younger Cutter.

She mentioned that.

"Whoa." He whistled and ran a hand through his crew cut. "That's a tough one to explain." He thought hard, wrinkling up his forehead. "Tell you what. You come back to my place, and you'll understand."

Stoner couldn't resist. "Why, Mr. Cutter, are you making an improper suggestion?"

He blushed. Cutter actually blushed. "Oh, my God, no. I mean, if you…why…"

"I was only kidding." She touched his hand. He didn't flinch. Very, very strange. But she was glad for his company, terribly glad. Even if he wasn't quite…well, not quite himself.

"Listen," he said, glancing around, "I think we'd better get out of here."

"Suits me." She got up. Cutter scampered to help her. "I wasn't particularly fond of it, anyway."

"Trust me," he said. "It's a really bad place." He closed his eyes and seemed to be scanning the terrain with a sixth sense.

Stoner waited.

At last he said, "Hah," and started off to his right.

When she tried to follow, her feet sank into the fog. "Cutter? I'm going to drown in here."

He turned back. "Just pick up your feet."

"I tried that earlier."

"Step on top of the fog."

Okay. Step up. On top of— She reached out tentatively with one foot and froze.

"You gotta do it like you know what you're doing," he said. "It'll do what you expect it to do."

She hoped the fog was easy to fool, and mentally crossed her fingers for luck. She repeated "the fog will hold me" over and over to herself in her mind, fast and loud so nothing else could get in. Then, in a show of bravado she hoped would intimidate any and all self-respecting vapor, she jumped up on it with both feet.

The fog held.

"See?" he said.

"Uh-huh. But why can't we just sort of levitate to wherever we're going. That's what I've been doing."

"Doesn't work in here," he said. "Now hurry up."

They walked quickly in an unknown direction. Once or twice Cutter signalled to her to stop, opened his senses to the air, then started off again with the assurance of a beagle picking up a rabbit's scent.

He was at home here, she thought, in ways he would never be back in Ordinary Reality.

"Okay," he said. "Here comes the hard part." He turned to her. "Things are going to be kind of ugly from now on. We'll get through it, but you can't break stride or make noise or you'll never get out."

She just looked at him, having no idea what he was talking about.

"Things can get you," he explained.

It still made no sense.

"They like new souls."

"Who does?"

"The ghosts." He looked at her curiously. "You know where you are, don't you?"

"No."

"Then what are you doing here? People who come here always do it because they want to."

"I might have, though I doubt it." She'd had just about enough of this enigmatic talk. "Where are we?"

"This is the Place of the Dead." He dropped cross-legged to the ground. "Jesus." He shook his head. "Man, this is so fucked up."

She stood over him. "Cutter, will you please explain what's happening? Or do you want me to turn into a raving maniac right here and now?"

Cutter pulled a roll of licorice laces from his shirt pocket and offered her some. She shook her head. He wrapped a foot of it around his finger, making a little coil and knotting it, and popped it into his mouth.

"Cutter…" Stoner repeated threateningly.

"Okay, okay, let me think." He thought and chewed. "Here's how it is. People come here when they think they want to die. You know, like suicides. Or a piece of them does. So what we—the guys and me—what we do is find them and get them out so they can think it over. If they want to go back in…well, we did our best." He glanced up at her with an expression that begged her to believe him. "That's what we try to do, save people's lives. That was what we thought we were doing when we went to war, but they lied to us."

Her heart flooded with compassion for him. For him, and for all the other kids who thought they were going to save the world and found out—after it was too late—that they'd been tricked and used. "I'm sorry," she said softly.

He shrugged it off. "This isn't about me. It's about you."

"What's about me? I still don't know why I'm here. I certainly don't want to die."

"Part of you does."

Stoner shook her head. "Really, I don't. Someone made a mistake."

"Nobody brought you here but you," he insisted.

Something inside made her uncomfortable. She brushed it away. "Well, if I did," she said lightly, "I would like to withdraw my original request. If I didn't, I'd like to leave as soon as possible."

"Fair enough." He got to his feet. "Remember, follow me, keep moving, and it's Quaker meeting from now on."

"Quaker meeting?"

"'Quaker meeting has begun,'" he quoted. "'No more laughing, no more fun. No more chewing chewing gum.'" He grinned. "My mom used to say that to me. When I was getting out of hand."

For a moment he looked as if he might cry. Stoner reached out a hand and rested it on his shoulder. He let her.

"Jesus," he said, "sometimes I miss my mom."

He straightened and wiped his eyes on his sleeve. "Let's saddle up," he said in a John Wayne imitation, and plunged off into the mist.

Stoner follow, trotting to keep him in sight. She wanted to call out, to ask him to wait. But he had told her not to speak.

At first she didn't see anything but whiteness. Flat, silent, unmoving mist. Then shapes began to appear. Slender, broken silhouettes of trees. Dead trees. Black, scorched skeletons posed in the mist like the ruin of a forest fire. She could smell them, too. Wet ashes and rot.

It reminded her of a picture she'd once seen, of the city of Hiroshima after the bomb.

Trotting along, keeping pace with Cutter, she caught movement from the corner of her eye. One of the trees had moved. Or had it? She wasn't sure. And that one up ahead, hadn't it been on the other side of their pathway just a second ago?

She glanced behind and saw another, huge trunked, with broken limbs and twigs like fingers. It hadn't been there when she'd passed. Well, it had been there, but at least five yards to the right. She was certain of it.

Now she saw movement everywhere. Branches appeared from

nowhere and darted at her face. Tendrils combed at her hair.

She wanted to scream.

She bit her lip and kept running.

A stump, high as her waist, loomed in her path. She put on the brakes.

A hand grabbed her and shook her roughly.

Cutter. He gestured to her to keep going.

She gulped a lung full of decay-saturated air and pushed herself forward.

It seemed as if they'd been running for hours, days. Her knees burned. Her hip joints stabbed with every step. She couldn't get enough air into her lungs.

A stitch caught her side and nearly pulled her to the ground with pain. It felt as if her ribs had grabbed a nerve and were grinding it between them. She'd never known pain like this before.

If she could only stop, just for a minute. Stop and stretch and spread her ribs enough to release it.

But she didn't want to die, she told herself.

Don't you?

It was her own voice in her head.

Of course I don't.

Think about it.

She thought. About all the good things in her life. Marylou, Gwen, Aunt Hermione. Their home together. Her friends in a dozen different places all across the country.

And the emptiness? That little pocket of emptiness that makes things not quite right and not quite real.

That's only life, she argued. Existential. Knowing where I end and other people begin. Being human means…

Being lonely.

It bubbled up inside her like a black ocean. Aching, hollow, utter loneliness. Loneliness so terrible, so complete she could…

Die.

Yes.

She nearly said it aloud. And it was true. She wanted to die, not carry this terrible burden of emptiness one step more.

"Stoner!"

She jerked as if she'd been struck by lightning.

Gwen's voice.

"Don't you dare stop," Gwen said in her most intimidating accent. "If you don't come back to me, by God I'll…I'll…you won't like it."

Stoner nearly sang out loud. She lengthened her stride and caught up with Cutter.

He gave her a look of surprise, and gestured forward.

The mist thinned. She could see shapes. Shapes with color.

Not black, not gray...

Green!

She raised one eyebrow questioningly.

Cutter flashed her a V-for-Victory. Or maybe for peace.

She made a dash for the finish line.

And smashed right into something invisible, firm, and wall-like.

Cutter ran up her heels and bounced her off the wall again.

They sprawled on the ground, twisted together.

"What the hell was that thing?" Stoner asked.

He seemed as bewildered as she was. "I dunno. It was never here before."

Stoner dragged herself to her feet and brushed dirt from her jeans. "What do we do...?" She glanced up.

Someone was standing on the other side of the wall. A woman, and all too familiar.

"Mogwye," Stoner said.

"Brilliant," Mogwye said sarcastically. "What do you do for an encore?"

"I figured you were behind this."

"Not me. Look to yourself..." She paused for emphasis. "Dear."

Stoner was too angry to try to understand the subtleties. "I don't know what you have against Aunt Hermione, and I don't care. That woman would never hurt anyone and I know you would because you already have. So I'm telling you to stop it right now."

That little tirade had worn her out. She thought it might be nice to sit down.

"Your aunt is a lovely person and an asset to the coven," Mogwye said. "It's a privilege to know her."

The woman actually sounded sincere.

"Then why are you doing this to her? What's your problem? Is it me? Have I done something to offend you? Tell me what it is and be done with it. Call it off. For God's sake, this isn't doing anyone any good."

More of her energy left her. She really, really wanted to sit down.

Mogwye grinned. A tight, nearly-clenched-teeth grin. It made her smile look black, as though there was nothing inside her but infinite darkness. "My sweet Stoner. You are such an ass." She drew out the final 'ss,' making a snake's hiss of it.

"You know what? I don't much care." She turned her back on the woman, to focus her attention on Cutter.

Except that Cutter wasn't there.

"Looking for something?" Mogwye asked.

Stoner ignored her.

Think about what to do. Plan. Chances are Mogwye controls the wall...

"Very good," Mogwye said, reading her mind. "Care to try a two-hundred dollar category?"

"Mind your own business," Stoner muttered.

"Oh, I think this is my business. Very much so."

What was it Elizabeth had said? Bargain. Fight.

Mogwye sighed heavily.

Stoner had to sit down before she fell down. She could barely keep her eyes open.

Hand-to-hand combat out of question, since she couldn't even get up, much less reach the woman through the wall.

Damn it, Cutter, where are you?

"Cutter's gone home," Mogwye said. "It's just you and me. Your move."

"Look," Stoner said, trying to sound reasonable, "all I want is my aunt's health. Certainly that can't be any threat to you."

Mogwye pursed her lips. "No threat."

"Just that little piece of her soul. That's all we want. You don't need it. What good would it do you? A tiny piece of someone else's soul. What in the world would you do with that?"

"Remains to be seen," Mogwye said. "Maybe hang it on my tree at Christmas."

"Yes, I figured you for a Christian. Because of the clothes."

Mogwye laughed.

"Unless the church has changed a lot, I don't think Christians consider soul stealing a very Christian thing to do."

"Stop this nonsense and figure it out."

That was caustic.

"I'll give you a hint," said Mogwye. "Nobody can steal your soul unless you give it away."

"Aunt Hermione would never do that."

The woman shook her head sadly, and Stoner really wanted to lie down.

She's draining my energy, the way she did at the potluck. I can't fight that.

It seemed as if the fog was growing a little thicker on her side of the wall.

"Right again," Mogwye said. "On both counts. And when that fog gets thick enough...well, you just won't have any choices any more. If you get my drift."

She got it.

"Out loud," Mogwye snapped. "Say it out loud."

She felt her mouth forced open, her tongue forming the words. "I get your drift."

"Excellent." Mogwye crossed her arms and looked at her sadly. "You should have paid more attention to your aunt. See how much my powers do for me?"

"They don't do much for your personality," Stoner said.

"I'm not so bad, once you get to know me."

This seemed like a good time for a Power Animal. She gathered all her strength to a single point and called out. Power Animal. Burro. Anyone, help!

"Spirit doesn't go in there," Mogwye said. "Didn't you notice?"

She hadn't, but now that it had been brought to her attention... The air was utterless lifeless. Not even a psychic eddy to change the energy. If there had ever been any spirit in there, it had abandoned the place. The way it abandoned places where unspeakably terrible things had happened.

The fog thickened.

Stoner felt desperate. Time was running out for Aunt Hermione. Maybe it already had run out. Maybe for herself, too. She had to stall for time, to figure this out.

Figure what out? She didn't know where to start. All she knew was, she was in a totally strange place, where the only rule of nature that worked was gravity.

"Listen," she pleaded, tears filling her eyes. "I'll give you anything you want for her soul. Anything."

"Ah," said Mogwye. "Let's make a deal. Okay, if the price is right."

Game show talk. This had to be hell.

"You can have a piece of my soul. In exchange."

"That dried up old thing? What would I use it for? Scrubbing out the sink?"

"It's a decent soul," Stoner said pettishly.

"An empty soul. A soul that wants to die."

"I don't want to die."

"But you don't want to live. Do you?"

She didn't have an answer to that. Because, whatever she thought consciously, she was here in the place where you went when you wanted to die.

"Maybe part of me, but—"

"I certainly don't blame you," Mogwye said. "Your life looks flat to me, flat as a balloon with the air sucked out of it."

"It feels that way, sometimes." Perhaps she could trick her with the truth, play for sympathy. Assuming the woman was capable of sympathy. "But that doesn't mean—"

"Doesn't it? Are you telling me you like to feel flat?"

"Of course not, but—"

"Then what do you want?"

"I don't know." She tried to think and her brain turned to pebbles.

"Come on, come on," Mogwye said sharply. "Answer the question."

Stoner tried to search through the rubble of her thoughts. "I... I don't even remember the question."

"Useless. Absolutely useless." Mogwye turned away in disgust.

"Look, I—"

Mogwye dismissed her with a flap of her hand.

"Okay, I give up." Tears escaped her eyes and trickled down her face. She didn't care. "We can play this game forever and it'll take us nowhere. Just tell me, what do I have to do to get out of here?"

"Say 'please.'"

Anything to humor her. "Please," she said.

Mogwye laughed and started to walk off.

The rage she'd been holding, so tightly in check she didn't even know it was there, erupted.

God damn you, she thought, all her consciousness clear and focused as only rage can make it, DON'T YOU DARE WALK AWAY FROM ME.

Mogwye stumbled and nearly lost her balance.

Stoner was shocked. Did I do that?

The woman took a shaky step toward her.

THAT'S FAR ENOUGH.

Mogwye stopped.

She's playing with me, Stoner thought. This is a trick. SIT!

"Not on your life," the woman said. "I'm not your pet poodle."

So it really was a trick. Stoner felt her brief moment of optimism fade away.

And the fog grew thicker.

Mogwye narrowed her eyes to slits and seemed to withdraw into herself. She took a deep breath, held it, and let go suddenly.

Stoner felt her strength flush away like water.

"That's where arrogance'll get you."

She could see the woman gearing up for another blast.

She tried to duck, but there was nowhere to go.

This jolt sent her flat onto the ground again.

Damn it, she couldn't let it end like this. To die in the fog with no company but a nasty old woman in a Baptist collar.

But what could she do?

She glanced over at Mogwye, who had her eyes shut, recharging her batteries.

Well, enemy or not, she was the only teacher in town.

Stoner let her vision fuzz, the way Aunt Hermione told her to when she wanted to pick up something intuitively.

She felt Mogwye bring her consciousness to a tiny point, and center it first on the crown of her head as she drew in a breath, then on her solar plexus as she exhaled.

Stoner tried it. It gave her a real jolt, kind of like espresso first thing in the morning.

Mogwye took another breath and held it, narrowing her focus and aiming it in Stoner's direction.

Incoming, Stoner thought. She hugged the ground.

This time the energy drained out of her very cells.

"Don't fool around with experts," Mogwye said.

All right, make her think she's done me in, so she won't prepare herself.

She lay on her stomach, as still as she possibly could. My Power Animal should have been a possum, she thought, and concentrated. Breathe in through the top of the head. Out through the solar plexus.

She could feel herself returning to three dimensions. She pretended to be numbed.

"When you see Hermione again, if you see her again, tell her not to send a girl to do a woman's job next time."

Stoner took a deep breath, focused, and let her have it.

The woman dropped to the ground like a wet towel tossed on the bathroom floor.

Yes!

The fog made it hard to breathe. But she had to be ready, to hit her harder this time, hard enough to knock her out.

She took a breath.

Mogwye looked up, confused.

Don't rush it.

She took another breath.

Mogwye rubbed her forehead.

And another breath.

Mogwye swiveled her head in Stoner's direction. Turned her gaze inward.

"Geronimo!" Stoner shouted, and fired a SCUD missile of energy directly at the woman's forehead.

Mogwye went down, and this time she wasn't moving.

Maybe I killed her, Stoner thought. Anxiety crawled up her spine.

And just what did you think she had planned for you?

Stoner got up and felt for the wall.

It wasn't there.

"Tell your people," she said as she stepped over Mogwye's limp body, "next time don't send dirty laundry to do a witch's job."

Mogwye twitched.

Stoner didn't look back.

Trees ringed the clearing where she stood. Familiar trees. Live trees. Trees whose name she knew. Oak and maple and beech. Pine and sycamore. Hop hornbeam and basswood and sassafras.

An oriole had built its nest in a willow, and sang its ear-shattering song.

Stoner thought it was the most beautiful music she'd ever heard.

From the distance came a soft, cadenced thumping that could only be Burro's hooves.

Over here, she called.

Patience, he called back.

While she waited, she made a bouquet of the freshest grasses she could find. The sky was blue and bright. Fluffy clouds were edged with silver so brilliant she had to shield her vision against the glare.

She closed her eyes and tried to take it all in through her pores. The warmth, the freshness, the sheer joy of the place. She listened to Burro's footsteps. To the whispered flutter of birds' wings. To the miniscule 'tick' of an insect against tree bark.

There was running water nearby. The dreaming sound of it calmed her.

All the things around her were speaking. To themselves, to one another. To her. One by one, she focused in on each and listened for its message.

The stream told her this moment was only a drop in the flowing of time. This moment, already gone, would dissolve and flow back into time and return some day. Because time didn't have a beginning or an end, it merely was.

The oriole told her to stop worrying so much and get on about her business. My motto? said Oriole, Que será, será. Carpe diem. Seize the day.

Clover let her in on the fact that clover was Burro's all-time favorite treat, and begged to be eaten. A distant relative invited Stoner to pluck a few of her petals and suck the sweet nectar from the base of them.

It was the most miraculous taste she'd ever experienced.

Burro appeared at last, taking his own time. She greeted him with grasses and clover, and while he ate told him what she'd been through and done since she'd left him.

When she'd finished, she realized she'd been talking his furry ears off. "I'm sorry," she said. "I guess I was running off at the mouth."

Burro thought her a smile. 'S okay. You Shamans love stories. Especially your own.

She was surprised at how much the word pleased her. "That's very flattering, but I'm not a Shaman. Probably won't ever be one."

Not a bad life. Plenty exciting.

"Too exciting."

More exciting than the travel game.

"True. But I'm not ready for a career change."

You like those Native people. Shamans meet a lot of them.

"I've noticed that," Stoner said. "Is there a reason?"

It's what those people do. Go between one world and another. They claim the Great Spirit picked them for it. Even your bad-tempered friend Siyamtiwa.

"What about you…?" She hesitated, reluctant to call him an animal in case it was a term of disrespect.

Animals? It's okay to call us that. You guys thought it up in the first place. Wordy bunch, if you ask me.

Stoner smiled. "Do you get to go back and forth a lot?"

If we're told. We do what we're told. He chewed thoughtfully. Guess that's why they call us jackasses.

"You're not a jackass," she said indignantly.

Am too. Look it up. He snorted and shook his head and blew air out through his nose. Thank you for the snack. Time to hit the road.

The trees were beginning to take on a different look. Not strange, but brighter, their green leaves and brown and gray trunks more intense. The ground had softened and gentled underneath her feet, as if she were walking on moss.

No astroturf here, I'll bet.

Burro flicked his tail. Don't even mention that stuff. Did you ever get a mouthful of it?

"Never. I'm not likely to, either."

Good plan.

Somewhere in the distance she could hear shouts and laughter. And a radio playing.

"Is that where we're going?"

It's off the trail, but we can drop over if you like.

"I don't know. I'm a little worried about the time."

Still thinking in Ordinary Reality time. He sighed and belched. You're right. You're not ready to be a Shaman. We have all the time you want.

"But Aunt Hermione…"

She'll keep. That old lady's been making her own time for hundreds of incarnations. He nudged her off the path only he could see and toward the voices.

"You know," Stoner said, "it's kind of strange. I mean, Aunt Hermione's been around so many times. You'd think she'd be ready to go on to the next level or whatever."

She could. Any time she wants. She likes your particular world. Likes people. Must be related to us jackasses.

Stoner laughed. "Well, we're grateful for her foolishness. Don't you like people?"

Depends. There's good ones and bad ones. He nudged her with his shoulder. If you ever decide to come back as an animal, don't be a useful one. Being useful to humans is one pain in the neck. He trudged along silently for a minute, thinking. House pet, that's where the soft life is. 'Course, you could draw the short straw there, too.

She could make out the voices on the radio. An announcer, with a background of crowd noises. The kind of sound that only comes with a professional baseball game.

"That's strange," she said. "Do you mind if we check it out?"

I live to serve, said Burro.

Climbing a hill, she looked down on the largest Boy Scout Camporee anyone could possibly imagine. The tents stretched for miles, to the horizon and beyond. Young men scurried about below, building cooking fires, hanging out their laundry. Others lounged under palm trees or pine trees or against sand dunes.

The odd thing was, they were all in costume. Some wore US Government issue, Army, Navy, Marine, Air Force, representatives of any branch of service from revolutionary times to the present. Others were dressed in World War II Nazi and Japanese uniforms. There were Roman Legionnaires and Knights from the Crusades, African Tribal Warriors in straw and feathers, and hundreds of others she didn't recognize. Some were just plain naked, which made them even more frightening. A few women wandered among them, or sat in small groups at the entrances to tents sewing or chatting. All races, all colors.

And all young.

"What is this?" Stoner asked Burro.

They call it the Warriors' Camp.

"But there are so many of them."

Been a lot of wars.

"Hey!" It was a familiar voice. "You got out okay."

"Cutter."

He had cleaned himself up and changed into fatigues and a newly-laundered t-shirt. "You gonna hang around?"

"I don't know. We have things to do. What are you doing here?"

"I live here. Come on, there's someone I want you to meet."

They went down the hill in the direction of the radio. Words came into focus. Names. Ashburn and Hamner and Connie Mack Stadium.

Cutter saw her puzzled frown. "That's the guys from Korea," he explained. "The Philadelphia Phillies are playing the Brooklyn Dodgers. They're really into it."

"Cutter, what sort of place is this?"

But he didn't hear her, running on ahead to a tent perched under a clump of trees.

Burro gave a little snort and drew back.

"What's wrong?"

Over there. He pointed with his muzzle. Civil War soldiers. They used to eat us.

"They ate you?"

Twice. Once at Antietam, and once after the war, out on the frontier.

"Oh, Burro," she said, "I'm so sorry."

Usefulness comes in a lot of different packages. Watch your step.

"They don't look very hungry now." She put an arm over his back. "Anyway, I'd never let anyone harm you. And I'm very powerful."

So I hear, Burro said.

Cutter came running up, pulling another young soldier along by his belt. "This is my Dad," he said. "Dad, meet Stoner."

They shook hands.

There was a resemblance, but this man was much too young to be anyone's father.

She said as much.

"He wasn't my dad when he came here." The two men beamed at one another. "In fact, I wasn't even born yet. But he was here when I got here, and he's my dad, all right. The spitting image, only nicer." He gave the other young man a poke in the ribs. The other grabbed the back of Cutter's neck and they wrestled for a moment like puppies.

Stoner ran her hand through her hair in confusion. "I wish someone would explain this to me."

"When you're in a war," Cutter's father, who told her his name was Dave, said, "and you see the Beast, then a part of you has to leave. This is where we go."

It made sense. They all seemed to be young. And probably idealistic. Like Cutter, thinking they were off to do something glorious and life-affirming. And then reality hit them between the eyes.

She looked at Cutter. Such a likeable kid. Laughing. Optimistic. He had a scrubbed look about him. Add him to the Cutter she knew, and he'd be charismatic. "When I finish here," she said, "you can come back with me."

"I can't go back," he said, shaking his head. "Not ever."

"You came here with me, didn't you? I can't let you..."

He interrupted her. "I came here on July 17, 1970, when all my friends were killed because I made a mistake. When I saw the Beast. You don't go back from this place."

"Not ever?"

"Not ever. But it's not so bad. Not bad at all. I have my Dad, and we're really good friends. And all my buddies from 'Nam."

"They all saw the Beast, too?"

"They felt him."

So this was what happened in war. This was why they returned so silent, why the light was gone from their eyes. This was what they wouldn't talk about. They'd seen the Beast, and the Beast was human evil. The evil in the enemy, the evil in their friends, and ultimately the evil in themselves.

"Cutter, that place we were in back there, the Place of the Dead?"

"Yeah?"

"Did you happen to see Aunt Hermione in there?"

"Nope." He glanced at the sky. "You better get moving. Time's moving, and you have a long way to go."

"Cutter, I–"

He touched her lips with his finger tip. "Don't. Just go. And tell Marylou I love her."

He turned away.

"Why is time moving?" Stoner asked.

It's hard to tell. It usually means you're about to be called back. I think we'd better keep our minds on our business. Burro looked at her steadily and sympathetically. No more diversions, if you know what I mean.

She knew. Moving time meant time running out for Aunt Hermione. "We don't even know where to look," she said.

Call her with your mind.

She did, but there was no answering call, no sense of someone present, not even a feeling she should go in this direction or that.

You give up too easily, Burro said. I'll bet when you phone someone you hang up after four rings.

Not usually.

Burro said, Humph, and plodded on.

"Will I ever see you again after this?"

If you want to. He began to hum, "You just call out my name, and you know wherever I am…"

Stoner had to laugh. "Are Power Animals ours for life?"

It depends, Burro said. Some folks are most comfortable with a spirit they can get to know and make part of the family, like the family doctor. Others want a different spirit for every occasion–a specialist, you might say. Some, like your Native peoples, name a clan after you and you're stuck with that assignment for generations. That takes a Power Animal who's really not afraid of commitment.

"Have they ever named a clan after you?"

He snickered. I can just see it. The Burro Clan. Going into battle for the Burro Clan. They'd be laughed out of the Nation.

"Burro Clan sounds just fine to me," Stoner said. "I'd join in a minute."

Well, that's mighty nice of you to say. I'll take it as a compliment and thank you for it. He nodded his head in a little bow.

"I mean it."

I believe you, he said. I'm having a self-conscious moment, that's all.

Stoner laughed. "For a spirit, you're awfully…human."

We can be, said Burro. For all my griping, I do enjoy your race.

"And I admire yours," Stoner said.

The trees thinned out, and soon they entered a field of cropped and harvested wheat. There was no visible path.

"Excuse me," Stoner asked a little apprehensively, "but how do we know we're going in the right direction?"

How do we know we're not? I'll let you in on a secret: when the chips are down, just lay back and put your faith in the Big One.

"God?"

Personally, I prefer Great Spirit. Less gender bias.

"I don't believe it," Stoner said with a laugh. "A politically correct Power Animal."

Comes from spending too much time inside human heads.

The wheat stubble grew higher and thicker as they walked along. First to her calves, then her knees, then her hips. Her anxiety grew with the wheat.

"Burro, tell me the truth. Do you really know where we're going?"

No, I don't know. But it feels right.

Stoner groaned. "Just like a man."

The wheat had reached her waist. It swished and crackled with every step. She couldn't see the ground any more, and tried not to think of what else she might be walking on.

When it began to prickle her chin, she had to stop. "This is making me really nervous. It'll be over my head in a minute."

Burro turned around and came to stand beside her. Hop on. I'll carry you.

"No," she said, her imagination conjuring up visions of large, heavy men straddling the little animals, their feet nearly scraping on the ground. It was supposed to be funny. She'd never found the humor in it. She'd always felt sorry for the donkeys, being forced to undergo that humiliation. "It wouldn't be right."

Why not?

"I'm too big and too heavy for you."

We carry heavy loads. That's why we're built this way.

"I can't do it."

It was good enough for your Jesus.

There was no arguing with that. Still she hesitated.

What?

"I'm kind of afraid of horses."

I'm not a horse. Am I gigantic like a horse? Am I a thousand hands high like a horse? Am I a speed demon like a horse? Am I arrogant like a horse?

Against her better judgment and to avoid hurting his feelings, she climbed onto his back. With a long-suffering sigh, he plodded off into the lengthening wheat.

This wasn't so bad. Burro was sturdy, and careful, and sure-footed. And she didn't have to think about what might be underfoot that she wouldn't see until she'd stepped on it. Birds wouldn't suddenly fly up in front of her face. Snakes wouldn't slither out from under her feet in their startling, sudden way. There was just the nice, slow, rocking motion.

"So," she said after a while to make conversation, "have you been a Power Animal for many people?"

Now what? You want references?

"I was just curious."

Thousands.

"Did they treat you well?"

You bet. I have the power to disturb their dreams.

The wheat was so high now it nearly blocked out the bit of cloud and blue sky she could see. And it was still growing. Some of the awns at the tips of the wheat heads were already touching.

She watched, darkly fascinated, as they began to knit together.

"Burro?"

Uh-huh.

"Are we going to be trapped in here?"

Maybe.

"Then shouldn't we turn around and go back out?"

And which way is 'around,' please? Show me 'around.'

She was silent for a moment. "You don't know where you are, do you?" she asked in a small voice.

Of course I do. He took a few more plodding steps. On the other hand, if you have any suggestions...

"Burro!"

He gave a snorting, inhaling laugh. It sounded like marbles being sucked up into a vacuum cleaner.

"I AM NOT IN THE MOOD FOR PRACTICAL JOKES!" Stoner shouted.

Sorry, Boss.

"Stoooo-ner."

The voice came from a great distance, but she knew whose it was. "Aunt Hermione!" She sat upright, straightened her shoulders. "Burro, it's Aunt Hermione!"

Son of a gun, Burro said.

"Well, go to her. Hurry." She grabbed a handful of his mane.

Burro set off at a trot.

"Come on, faster."

Calm yourself, he said, and drew a wheezing breath. I'm not Man o' War, you know. But he did manage to do an awkward imitation of a gallop.

Stoner wrapped her legs around him and buried her hand in his mane. We must look like a couple of puppets in a high wind, she thought, flying in every direction.

Just doin' what you asked, Boss.

"And very well," she granted him.

Her aunt's voice came again, closer this time, and stronger.

They broke through the wheat and into a clearing of sorts. It was no larger than a living room, with brilliant green moss underfoot and walls of cattails and wild grasses. Two benches faced each other across the clearing. One was empty. On the other sat Aunt Hermione, holding a small child.

Chapter 14

Stoner was stunned. Her aunt looked healthier, more vibrant than she had seen her in years. Her eyes sparkled, her skin was like peaches. And she was smiling, a smile of pure delight.

The child took one look at Stoner and buried her head against Aunt Hermione's chest.

Aunt Hermione stroked her hair and whispered to her soothingly.

"Is she afraid of me?" Stoner asked.

"It's the two of you. Together, you're rather large."

Burro snorted as if he were tremendously pleased.

"I'm sorry." She slid off his back.

The child sneaked a peek at her and hid her head again.

Stoner ached to run to her aunt and throw her arms around her. But it was clear the child was very shy. "Is this her? The one we were looking for?"

"It is. She was hiding in the Void." She kissed the child's head. "Weren't you, sweetie?"

The little girl nodded into Aunt Hermione's shoulder.

Stoner went and knelt in front of them. "How old is she?"

"Just three."

She touched the child's wrist with one finger, lightly. The child held as still as a whisper.

"What's the Void?"

"A place some soul parts go, to run away from pain. It's very dark and very empty. And very, very lonely."

Stoner felt tears come to her eyes. "And that was better than what she left behind?"

"Yes, it was."

The child ventured another glance in Stoner's direction. This time she didn't turn away but gazed at her curiously. She was tow-headed, with deep aquamarine eyes and eggshell skin. Her forehead was creased in a small worried frown, as if she'd looked at life and found it unsafe.

"Do you have a name?" Stoner asked softly.

The child nodded.

"Would you tell me what it is?"

The child looked up at Aunt Hermione, as if to ask if it was all right to tell. The older woman nodded.

"Tony," the child said.

From deep inside her, Stoner felt anxiety awaken. There was something...something familiar... Not déjà vu, exactly, but familiar.

"Say her name," Aunt Hermione suggested. "She likes to hear her name."

Stoner said, "Tony," and felt even stranger.

"They won't call me that," the child said. "They don't like it. But I don't care because then they can't ever take it away from me."

"What do they call you, then?"

The child pursed her lips together tight.

"She won't say the name," Aunt Hermione said. "She thinks, if she does, she'll be giving in and her parents will get control over her."

"Good, don't say it," Stoner said to the child. "Don't ever, ever say it. Stay with the people who really, truly know you, Tony, the people you can trust. They won't hurt you."

Tony turned and looked at her again. She was the most precious child Stoner had ever seen.

"Cover your ears," Aunt Hermione murmured to the child. "I'm going to tell her what they called you, and I promise you she'll never use it. Okay?"

Tony thought it over for a long minute, then raised her hands and pressed them against her ears.

Aunt Hermione covered Tony's hands with her own, pretending to help her block out the words. "They called her Antonia," she said. "It's not her name at all. Never was."

Her anxiety quickened. "Antonia? I think I once knew someone named Antonia. A long time ago. It must have been grade school."

But something told her it wasn't.

"She's so tiny," she said, to divert her attention from her inner prickles. She turned to the child and smiled.

Tony put her hands in her lap.

"What made you have to come here, Tony?"

"Auntie Her told me to come."

"Auntie Her?"

Tony pointed up at the bottom of Aunt Hermione's chin. "Her," she said.

"Hermione's too much of a mouthful for her." She looked down lovingly at the child. "Isn't it, sweetie."

The child nodded with great seriousness.

Something about this was making Stoner increasingly uncomfortable. She tried to pin it down, but couldn't. "But this is such a lonely place," she said.

"Not now," the child said happily.

Aunt Hermione rocked her. "She's an unusual child," she explained to Stoner. "She hears voices in the trees and grass, and talks to spirits. She senses things most other people don't. She knows what magic is. At first her family merely ridiculed her for it, if you can call ridicule mere. They called her odd and told her she'd end up locked away in a mental hospital. They even took her to one of the worst state hospitals and made her look at the patients and the locked wards. They told her this was where she'd end up. When that didn't work, when she still insisted the spirits were real, they beat her. It was only a matter of time before she'd believe them, and think she was bad. The light was fading out of those beautiful eyes. I couldn't bear to watch it, and there was nothing I could do. There weren't many laws to protect children in those days. I told her to leave, to come here, and I'd come back for her when the coast was clear."

"So," Stoner said. She felt sick and there was a funny buzzing in her head. "This is your missing soul piece."

Aunt Hermione and the child looked at one another and giggled.

"But why couldn't she come back sooner? You've always believed in magic, as long as I've known you. And all those other things. You aren't afraid of them. Surely she could have come back before this. And…" The buzzing increased, and she began to get a cold, creepy feeling. And Aunt Hermione told the child… So she couldn't have been the child.

Stoner's chest felt tight. "This isn't you, is it?"

The child and Aunt Hermione shook their heads together, very slowly.

"Oh," Stoner said. And that was when she remembered. Their cruel laughter, the terror of that trip to the mental hospital, the smells of urine and vomit and disinfectant. The beatings, her parents' refusal to call her by her real name, the name her Auntie Her had given her and which she loved. They called her Antonia. Taking the name Tony, privately and to herself, because that could stand for 'Stoner,' too, and if she accidentally told someone 'Tony' was her name, no one would guess. Other people could call her Stoner if they were safe people, but she'd never, ever let her parents call her that again.

But she couldn't make the spirits go away. They were real, and they had feelings, and she couldn't bear to hurt them.

So Auntie Her had told her to come here, where she'd be safe. She forgot about the spirits, and magic, and Tony. After a while, her parents stopped calling her Antonia. They didn't call her anything at all.

Stoner burst into tears, putting her head on her aunt's lap while Tony patted her and tried to comfort her.

She cried for a long time, for the years of emptiness, of knowing there was something missing in her life and in herself, of wanting but fearing to believe the world could be a magic place if you looked beyond the obvious. That it could be beautiful beyond all the beauty she knew.

She cried until she thought her body would turn inside out with the shaking, then rested and cried again. With her aunt stroking her arm and the child patting her head.

After a long while she couldn't cry any more. Not now, though she knew she would again many times. She got up, scrubbing at her eyes with her hands, and walked over to lean against Burro's warm, solid, comforting side.

She felt a tug at her pants leg and looked down.

The child looked back at her with pleading eyes. She recognized the eyes. They were her own eyes.

"Please," the child said, "will you take me home with you?"

Stoner knelt and pulled Tony into her arms and held her tight. "Yes," she said. "Oh, yes."

When she looked up again, Aunt Hermione was gone.

The child's body was warm and cool and firm and soft all at the same time. Holding her was like coming home to someone you love. The release of tension you didn't even know you had. The feeling of completeness. The sense that 'everything's all right now.' And the joy. Mostly the joy.

There was only one problem. She had no idea how to get back.

She stood, the child Tony perched in the crook of her arm and beginning to drift off to sleep against her shoulder. Beyond the clearing there was nothing but the tall wheat, taller now, and tangled. A wall of woven wheat.

Anxiety set her heart to quickening.

It seemed as if the clearing were fading. The benches were still benches, but insubstantial, like unfinished sketches. The grass was graying.

The wheat moved closer.

"Tony," she whispered, "I think we're in trouble."

The child roused, looked around. "It's all going away."

"I don't know how to get back."

"Wait for the drums," Tony said with a sleepy yawn.

Of course. The call-back.

It better come soon. No one had told her what happens when you leave Ordinary Reality for Non-Ordinary Reality, and Non-Ordinary Reality deserts you. What was beyond that? Really, Really Non-Ordinary Reality? Bizarre Reality?

It was deathly silent. Whatever atoms and molecules were around had grown absolutely still. She could feel herself beginning to fade.

And then the drums began. Seven sharp, loud beats. Demanding. Compelling.

"Come on," she said to Burro.

But Burro had disappeared.

Home, she willed herself.

Miraculously, before she could even wonder, they were at the entrance to the tunnel. At last. It seemed as if she'd been away for years.

"Ready?" she said to Tony, putting her down and taking her hand.

The child nodded.

They stepped forward, looked up into the tunnel, waited.

And nothing happened.

Okay, sometimes you just have to take a step back and start over.

She stepped out, and back in.

Nothing happened.

Maybe if they went in a little deeper…, she thought as uncertainty fluttered at the edge of her mind. She took another step.

It was very dark in here. Darker than she'd noticed on her way down. She could barely make out the walls. She started forward.

"Not that way," Tony whispered, her voice small and frightened. "There's something really bad that way."

Stoner pulled back. But there was nothing the other way except to go backwards. Back there didn't get them out. And this was certainly the entrance.

"We won't go in the real dark place," she reassured Tony. "Hang on and we'll zip right up this tunnel to my world. You'll like it there."

At least I like it there, she thought to herself. I like a place where things are the same one minute as they were the minute before. It makes me calm.

She focused her attention on Elizabeth's living room and all the friends waiting for them, and took a deep breath.

Slowly, they began to rise.

It's over, she thought, and closed her eyes with relief. It's finally over.

Something soft and warm and damp and altogether unpleasant grabbed her ankle. She tried to shake it off.

It gave a hard tug and slammed her to the ground.

"What?" she said.

Tony screamed. Stoner held her tight.

She was being dragged away from the tunnel, back out into the Lower World.

The drums took up a soft, quick-paced rhythm.

Stoner clung to the sound. They moved forward a little, then were dragged back.

The light outside was too bright. She couldn't make out what was tugging at her, saw only a shadow mass.

She kicked her feet, struggling to break away, but the thing was as strong as a draft horse.

Tony shrieked. "Monster. From the cave." She wriggled out of Stoner's arms like a panic-stricken kitten and disappeared.

"Tony! No!"

The black mass jerked her across the ground. Pebbles and twigs dug into her back and arms. She kicked again, and it dropped her to the ground.

She scrambled to her feet. "What the hell is going on?"

Then she saw the creature for the first time. It was a dark, amorphous shape that seemed to ooze rather than walk. Slowly, it resolved itself into a human-like Entity in a dark brown cape and hood. Its body was in constant shifting, forming and reforming motion. Where it had passed over the ground, the grass and wildflowers lay crushed. Red blood seeped from their stems.

She couldn't see its face.

"What the hell are you?"

The oily brown mist swirled angrily.

Exasperated and frightened, she turned her back and started after the child.

Two hands clutched her throat, cutting off her breath.

She reached up to claw at them, but there was nothing there. She could touch her own skin, feel her own nails on her skin.

It was still choking her.

She began to feel dizzy. Could feel the veins in her scalp as her heart pounded. The pain in her throat was like needles.

Still she struggled, until she began to lose consciousness.

The invisible hands dropped her to the ground. The Entity hovered over her, dark and swirling.

"You're trying to leave me again," it snarled. Its voice was like a dentist's drill.

"What?"

"You know what I said," it whined in its shrill, nerve-rotting tone, and moved closer.

Stoner tried to press herself into the ground. "What are you?" she repeated.

The Entity laughed. It was a terrible laugh. Hard, mocking, evil. It cut through her mind. "The Ghost of Christmas Past," it said. "Or Christmas Present? Yet-to-Come? Your choice."

It swirled its cape across her face. It felt like the wings of a thousand bats.

She wanted to curl up into a ball and die. The thought of Tony, alone in this place, kept her going. "Where's the child?" she forced herself to ask.

"The brat, the brat, the brat. There's more to life than that." The Entity snickered. "I'm a poet and I don't know it. My feet show it. They're LONGFELLOWS!"

She had to get out of this, but the Entity kept her pinned to the ground. Think, she told herself. Think, think, think.

The Entity smiled. Not that she could see a face, but she could have sworn the black fog in the hood smiled. It wasn't a friendly smile.

"I don't like to be left," it hissed. It placed its soft, damp hands on either sides of her head. She had the horrid feeling it was going to kiss her. Every cell in her body cringed.

Instead, the Entity smashed her head against the ground. Pain like fire shot through her brain.

It grabbed her hair. "Do...you...get...it?" it demanded as it punctuated each word by slamming her head against the stones and gravel. "I...don't...like...to...be...left."

She tried to say something, but couldn't form words around the pain.

At last it shoved itself away. Stoner rolled over onto her stomach and draped her hands over her head protectively. She hurt. Everywhere. All kinds of hurt. Aching hurt and burning and cutting and cracking. More than she'd ever hurt before in her life. She groaned.

"Are we beginning to reach a consensus?" The Entity sneered.

"I don't understand," she said.

She felt herself lifted and hurled against a tree like a rag doll.

"DON'T TELL ME YOU DON'T UNDERSTAND!" The Entity raged. "YOU UNDERSTAND IT ALL. FUCKING LEZZIE!"

Sharp gravel rose from the ground and pelted her like a swarm of bees. She tried to hide her eyes, but her right arm wouldn't work. She had the feeling it was broken.

"Want to see what else I can do?" The Entity asked.

She couldn't answer.

"DO YOU?"

A cluster of pebbles sucked themselves up into a whirlwind and hovered near her, waiting for a signal.

She managed to nod.

The Entity made a short gesture, and the day went to night.

The sky was black and cold.

Cold suns, like frozen sparks.

Constellations, but they weren't familiar.

There was a large star in the center of it all. Larger than the moon, but dimmer than Earth's sun. Its cold light locked tightly inside.

Even as she watched, it began to shrink. Stars appeared where they had been blocked before. They seemed to slide toward the dead sun. Faster and faster they swept toward it, disappearing into its silver light. Suddenly the star winked out, but the sky behind was still blocked from view. The star became a deep black circle, edged with sparkling light. Beautiful, but evil.

The Entity swung its arm in an arc and the dark circle came closer, picking up bits of iridescence as it drifted through the sky. Slowly it rotated, then became a disk, approached, and settled like a plate at Stoner's feet. She could see that it was a deep hole. There was a foaminess surrounding it, glowing faintly, like the glimmer of breaking ocean waves under a half moon.

She knew she should back away.

The scene in front of her was captivating.

She didn't know if she had fallen, or was pushed, or even pulled by a force within the hole itself. All she knew was that she was going down, inside the darkness. Fast at first, sickeningly fast. She tried to cry out, but her downward motion shredded the sound of her voice. She grabbed for the sides, but there were no sides.

Hours must have passed, and still she fell.

Somewhere down below there must be a bottom, and when she

reached it...

Or, worse, there was no bottom, only eternal falling through emptiness.

Her descent appeared to slow, then slowed some more.

She didn't seem to be moving at all. There was no way to tell, of course. No landmarks, no sound. She tried to twist around, to look, but there was nothing to push against. It was like trying to balance under water, only worse. No water for friction here, not even a molecule. Not an atom of air. She was caught, suspended in space. Nothing to do but wait, but nothing to wait for.

She didn't know how long it had been. A minute, an hour, a month. Nothing around her. She couldn't even hear the beat of her heart. She wondered if she was dead, then thought she might go crazy. It would be better than this.

Help me. Please. Somebody remember me and help me.

She thought she felt motion. But that wasn't possible.

But she was moving. Gently, barely perceptibly moving. Upward. She looked around, as if she could see the source of the drift.

It could well be a hallucination.

But she really was rising, she thought.

Rising as if being lifted with great effort, with great care. As if she were heavy, or fragile.

Someone was pulling her out of the hole. But with what? She didn't see or feel ropes of any kind. Then, far above her, faintly, that strange, glowing foam.

As she was drawn closer, she tried to grab it. Her fingers passed through nothing.

Looking up to the top, she caught a glimpse of dim, human-like figures.

The walls began to take form. Soft as gelatin at first, then hardening. She reached out...

And felt her fingers touch dirt.

With a sob, she clung to the edge. Her heart pounded.

She looked down. It was like being suspended by her fingertips over the Grand Canyon, except that the Grand Canyon had a bottom, and this...thing...didn't. She thought she might be sick. Her fingers ached.

"Whoa," someone said. "Look at that."

There were faces peering over the rim. Twelve young women's faces floating above bluish tee-shirts.

The Twelve Virgins.

"Cool," said one.

But they weren't looking at her, they were looking down into the vortex. She felt her grasp begin to slip and said, "Hey!"

"Oops," said one of the Virgins. "Yo, all of you, give me a hand."

Together they heaved her onto solid ground and left her and went back to studying the hole.

"Thank you," she began, "you saved my life. You must be the search party."

"Yeah," said one Stoner vaguely remembered as their best shortstop and worst catcher. "We got your call."

"Yes, you certainly did, and I couldn't be happier."

"You know what I'll bet this is?" one of the Virgins said. " A Black Hole."

"I remember that from high school," said another. "Like, a star falls in on itself."

Stoner had an uneasy feeling and looked behind her. The Entity was moving toward them. "Excuse me," Stoner said.

"See this shiny stuff? That's space-time froth." The Blue Shirt scooped up a handful. It wilted, shrank, and winked out. "That's the stuff that's left over when there's nothing left."

"Does it suck you in?" another asked. "Like on 'Star Trek'?"

"No, but if you go in there you get stretched thin like spaghetti and time stops."

They all glanced at Stoner as if expecting her to be thin like spaghetti.

"When you come back out," the expert explained, "you're normal again. Except I think maybe you don't ever get out. You stay there forever all skinny."

"Excuse me," Stoner repeated.

"Hey," said another, "the perfect weight-loss program."

"Way cool." They all laughed.

The Entity was nearly on them.

"Women!" Stoner said in a commanding voice. They looked at her. "This is very interesting, but if you'll direct your attention behind me, you'll see that my Fog Faced friend is coming our way. And it is not happy. I suggest you make yourselves scarce."

One of the Virgins nudged another and said, "She called us 'women.'"

"I know," the other said. "That is so cool."

Stoner waved her arms in their direction, damned if she was going to be responsible for these lives, too. "Go!" she shouted. "Out! Go!"

They looked at her with that blend of fear and pity usually reserved for raving madmen. "Listen," one said, as they backed away from her windmilling arms, "it's cool, okay? Chill, okay?"

"I will not chill. You're in serious danger."

One of the women—Stoner thought she might be the team captain, or maybe the manager or scorekeeper—approached her. "Look," she said firmly, "in the first place, we're not in danger, you are. In the second place, you called us. And in the third place, that's why you wanted us to come to this event in the first place."

The rest agreed noisily.

"I'm sorry," Stoner said. She really was ashamed of herself for trying to protect them when they were there—eagerly—to protect her. "That was ageist of me."

"Whatever," one of them said.

The Entity was coming closer. "Very impressive," it said. "Your own private little army."

"And not to be taken for granted."

She scanned the area, looking for Tony. The child was still missing.

Stoner felt guilt like a foot on her chest. She hadn't taken care of her. "What'd you do with the child?" she demanded.

"Too bad you missed lunch," the Entity taunted. "Baby Bisque. Yum-yum."

"Oh, man, that is too gross," said one of the Blue Shirts.

"Watch out," Stoner said to them. "It's homophobic."

"Fuck that," said the captain-manager-scorekeeper.

The Blue Shirts formed an angry protective barrier in front of her.

It seemed to slow the Entity down.

Maybe, with their help, she could... "Okay," she said, "I'm going to find Tony. If it starts to get to you, get out of here. Agreed?"

"Cool!" said the team.

They circled the creature.

Carefully, Stoner slipped around them. With every step she breathed a little more easily. The Entity seemed incapable of moving against the energy of twelve angry young women.

When she'd cleared the circle, she took off running, amazed that she could even move, much less run—toward where she'd last seen Tony.

"Tony!" she called. "It's okay. We can get out now. Hurry!"

"Stoner," the childlike voice came back.

She followed the direction of the voice. There, at the edge of a clearing, was Tony. She was playing with a tortoise twice as big as herself. "Are you all right?" Stoner called to her.

"Sure." Tony crawled up onto the tortoise's back. "He's mine. Isn't he pretty?" She bent forward and whispered something into the animal's ear—or where its ear probably was. It turned and began lurching toward them. Stoner figured its ETA at about the year 2010.

"Could you ask Tortoise to pick up the pace a bit?"

In a second they were beside her. Ah, yes, she'd forgotten about instant travel.

"Isn't he pretty ?" Tony insisted.

"Absolutely," Stoner said. "He's the most beautiful tortoise I've ever seen."

Tortoise seemed to puff out his armored chest with pride and vanity.

"He's kind of stuck on himself," Tony whispered.

"And with good reason," Stoner said. Flattering this Power Animal struck her as a wise move. They were going to need all the help they could get. "Now we have to hurry, okay?"

She sprinted back to the cave entrance, Tony and Tortoise right behind her.

The Entity was still being held at bay.

"Now!" Stoner said, snatching the child from Tortoise's back. "Run!"

The child scampered into the cave.

"Thanks!" Stoner yelled to the Blue Shirts. She waved. They waved back.

She turned to the cave...

...and found her way blocked by a gigantic Falcon.

Its claws were sharp as harpoons. Its eyes were red. It had spread its wings across the cave opening.

A heavy oak limb fell directly in her path. She could feel the bark scrape against her leg as it landed.

She looked up for the tree, but of course there was none.

She watched helplessly as the Entity sent out a furious wind that stripped and shredded a dozen random maples. Branches piled up deeper at the cave entrance. Large rocks poured down on top of the branches. The entrance to the cave was sealed.

From inside, she could hear the child's terrified screams.

Furious, Stoner began tearing away at the branches and rocks that blocked the entry to the tunnel with her good arm. "I've had it," she said over and over. "Had it, had it, had it."

Within minutes her hands were cut and bleeding from the rocks. Her shoulders and face were scored with the scraping of sharp twigs and branches. Sweat poured out of her hair and into her eyes.

She felt herself beginning to cry from frustration and hopelessness, but she didn't care. If she never did anything again, she was going to undo this one piece of the creature's mischief.

Something shoved her gently to the side. Calm down, Burro said. I can do this better than you.

She threw one arm around his neck. "I thought you'd deserted me."

Nope. Kinda slow, that's all. He shrugged her away apologetically. You go sit over there and rest. You're in the way.

"Look out for the Falcon," Stoner said. "It works for that thing."

Nope, Burro said between mouthfuls of branches. Works for you, same as me.

"That's impossible. It won't let me leave."

Falcon has his job. I have mine. He pushed a rock aside with his nose and took a limb between his teeth. As I told you before, I do what humans want.

"Then what does Falcon do?"

Takes the long view. Sit. He won't let the creature harm you.

Burro hummed a little under his breath and went about his business.

Time had slowed again. The child was silent. The Entity smoldered, held immobile by Falcon and the Blue Shirts.

It was a very odd feeling. There should be chaos, and screaming and yelling and name calling and trying to grab things out of one another's hands.

But it was still. And that was the eeriest feeling of all.

Then she heard the drums again. The rapid tapping that said "Hurry, hurry."

Stoner's heart began to pound with the beat of the drums.

Burro pulled aside the last branch blocking their entrance.

She ran for it.

Out of the corner of her eye, she saw the Blue Shirts evaporate, saw the Entity start their way.

She found a little more speed in her legs.

Only a couple of feet now…

And something grabbed her by the shirt collar.

Stoner whirled on the creature. "NO MORE!" And twisted out of its grip.

"Take me with you," the Entity moaned.

"Never."

Time to get a move on, said Burro.

"Go back to whatever pit you crawled out of," Stoner said, taking a

212

step backward toward the cave's darkness.

"Please."

"NO!"

Again Falcon blocked her way. "Are you nuts?" Stoner screamed at it. Falcon merely blinked.

The Entity touched her. It was a light touch, no more than a pleading, apologetic stroke on her arm. It felt like the touch of a nest of squirming maggots.

Something in her broke."Don't touch me!" she raged, and hurled herself against the creature. "Goddamn it, show yourself!"

She snatched back the Entity's hood...

...and found herself looking into a mirror.

She gasped. Same chestnut hair, same blue-green eyes. Same sanguine skin.

They could have been twins.

But the other Stoner looked older, harder, bitter. Her eyes were flat and steely, her lips tight with anger. Lines of disapproval cut across her forehead. Her lashes were so stiff and bristly, she seemed to be wearing plastic mascara. Her skin was stretched and dry.

"What the hell is going on?" She looked around at her Power Animals. They seemed to have found something absolutely fascinating to watch anywhere but here.

"Don't you know?" the Entity asked. The anger seemed to have gone out of her. Instead she sounded hurt.

"I know her," Tony piped up. "That's Antonia."

Light was beginning to dawn. Slowly. At first she didn't believe...

Then she hardly believed...

She believed.

"Are you...did I...when...?"

She didn't wait for an answer. She knew. Years ago, before she'd left her parents' home, she'd been Antonia. Not just in name, but in anger. Enraged by the way she was treated, furious at everyone around her. Sometimes she'd wanted to uproot the trees in her front yard and smash them against her parents' house until it was reduced to matchsticks. She wanted to scream at her mother until her mother shrank to the size of a spider, then flush her down the toilet. Wanted to dismember her father joint by joint, to hollow out his unfeeling, judging, demanding head and use it for a soup bowl.

The fury of her anger froze her with terror. Every day she woke wondering if this would be the day she'd lose control. Sometimes she shook so hard she couldn't hold a pencil to do her homework. She hated the sounds her parents made, the television programs they watched, the food they ate. Hated the odor of her mother's perfume and her father's aftershave. Hearing their voices, downstairs, while she lay in bed and tried to read, she fisted her hands and dug her nails into the palms until they bled. And when she heard them coming up the stairs, she flicked off her light and burrowed into her bed, pillow over her head, to keep herself from attacking them.

They despised her. Despised who and what she was, while telling her they loved her.

She couldn't bear the rage that burned in her brain. Or the fear. Or the longing to be loved, the damned longing to be loved.

So she'd left that house. Slammed the door on it and on them and on Antonia.

Left them all and didn't look back.

"You can't leave me here," Antonia said. "I'm part of you. You need me."

Stoner looked at her shadow self. Her angry self. Her strong self. A self she didn't want to acknowledge. A self she couldn't live without. "A person who doesn't cast a shadow," Edith Kesselbaum had once told her, "has only two dimensions."

She gave in. It didn't feel like a defeat, more like a letting go. "You're right," she said to Antonia. "I do."

"I can do a lot for you, you know."

"Not until you're housebroken." She took Antonia's hand. It turned firm in her own. "Wait until you meet Dr. Edith Kesselbaum," she said.

Hermione felt a jolt of energy like electricity. Her mind was strong, and clear. She saw it all. "She did it," she whispered.

Gwen reached over and gave her shoulder a squeeze.

The call-back drums increased in speed and volume.

As soon as Elizabeth had blown her soul pieces back into her head and heart, and they had welcomed her home and she had thanked them all, before the real celebrating and storytelling got under way, she went out to find Cutter.

He was waiting for her, eager to see her but hoping she wouldn't stay long.

"Are you okay?" she asked.

"Yep." He looked at the ground. "You?"

"Yes. Thank you for what you did."

He shrugged and wanted to sink into the ground. He hated people thanking him. It mixed him up, made him feel things, made him want to let them in. "Sometimes I do that," he mumbled.

"It was a pleasure to meet your father."

That brought an involuntary smile to his lips. "He's a good guy."

"If you ever find out who won that ball game, let me know."

"If it was the Phillies, it'll be a miracle."

There was a brief silence. Cutter traced designs in the dirt with his boot.

"Well," she said.

Cutter nodded and slipped his hands into his pockets.

Stoner wanted to embrace him, to show her gratitude. But she knew it would frighten him. The last thing she wanted to do to this man was frighten him.

He must have sensed her thoughts. "Thanks," he said.

She walked back to the house.

At the door, she turned. "See you around."

"Here and there," he answered.

It was good to remember again. Hermione lounged on the living room couch and listened to the rattle of plates and silverware and the intimate, everyday sounds of cooking, and let the memories, the clarity flow over her again and again. She recalled sending the child away, so long ago, knowing there would be an aching separation from her but knowing, too, that the child's very life was at stake.

For years she'd hoped Stoner would find her on her own, would come to believe in magic and the just-rain-washed beauty of life when seen through the eyes of Spirit. Sometimes it seemed she might come close, when things happened around her and to her that could only happen because of spirit. But Stoner always drew back, not hearing but sensing those echoes of long ago.

Well, it was finally done. She'd faced the Beast—her personal Beast, anyway—and lived to tell it.

Hermione nodded to herself. You did well, my dear niece. Almost took me down with you, but that was my choice to make and couldn't be helped. After all, we've been connected for centuries. She smiled to herself. I wouldn't have it any other way.

She stood and went to find Grace.

"That's it," Mogwye said, slamming her Christian dress into a heap at the back of her closet and slipping into comfortable paisley polyester slacks. "Made a damn fool of myself, thank you very much. Next time you want something done, do it yourself."

The cat regarded her with a superior air and said nothing.

"Of all the humiliating little bits of theater…" She stormed through the curtain door to the kitchen, opened a drawer, fished around in it, and banged the can opener down on the table. "You will never, ever volunteer my services without my permission again. Get it? Never. No volunteering. Not me."

The cat glanced up at her, yawned, and curled up in the potato bin to wait for his dinner.

"That's the last time I'll let you talk me into something like this."

She chopped furiously at the canned cat food, mixing it with crunchy and a touch of chicken.

"It was a nightmare."

"You're in a bad mood because you lost." He rotated his head, stretching the kinks out of his neck. "You should learn to chill out."

"Naturally." She rinsed his bowl and filled it. "All you ever do is chill out."

He caught a fly, impaled it on a claw, and watched it writhe. Humans, he thought. First they decide to do with only two feet, now they want to live with only half a brain. He crunched down on the fly. Tasty little morsel. He stroked his whiskers. It gave him a distinct feeling of satisfaction to know he'd tricked old Mogwye again. She called herself a witch! Her idea of a witch was about as deep as one of those kids who dressed as a witch for Hallowe'en. As much understanding of spirituality as a frog. A couple of two-bit tricks and a touch of conjuring… He could have shown her a few things, back in the burning times. There were real witches then. But now… Amateur night.

He yawned.

Maybe it's time to move on, he thought. Could erode the self-esteem, living with this one. Too high a price to pay for her cooking, which is what the attraction had been in the first place. That and the supply of chipmunks and mice you could find at the edge of a woods. And she was dangerous, too. Calling up those Aknobes, the little ebony ghosts. They were serious troublemakers. Did she think you could stuff them back in the oven like undone cookies? Problems down the line with them, for sure.

"I know I could have stopped her," Mogwye muttered. "If they hadn't found out about the reading glasses. If they hadn't brought in that High

Priestess. I ask you, how fair is that?"

"Not fair at all," the cat agreed. "You should ask for a rematch."

Great Saint Joan, the woman didn't even know what the whole thing had been about! That the venture had been a success. Didn't even remember the Siyamtiwa Spirit had handed out the assignments. Definitely time to start looking for new living arrangements.

Mogwye sighed. "Your dinner, your Highness. Now, get out of the potatoes, if you please." She put the bowl down.

Maybe Hermione. Now there was a witch you could be proud of. Keeps classy company, too. Wonder if she's in the market for a pet?

His tail twitched. He arose in a World Class display of dignity. "Wouldn't advise you to go back to the coven," he said, chuckling a little to himself. "Bound to be feelings. Messed with a sister. You know how they are."

She looked out the window, to where the paved-over yard met the trees. More and more, lately, she found herself dreading the twilight. Sometimes she thought she saw movement in the darkness, just at the edge of the forest. As if bits of night were darting, and crouching... "I don't need the damn coven."

"True," said the cat. He licked daintily at a morsel of food. "You'll always have me," he lied.

"Last call for coffee," Gwen said, coming out onto the darkened back porch and letting the screen door slam behind her. "Kitchen's closing."

"Thanks." Stoner reached for the mug.

Gwen sat beside her on the glider and joined her moon watching. "It's been quite a day."

"Sure has. How does Aunt Hermione seem to you now?"

"At the moment, she and Grace are upstairs worshiping the Goddess with rituals which are none of our business. With tremendous gusto."

Stoner grinned. "That's my Auntie Her."

The spring peepers were nearly gone, but the wood frogs were wide awake in the moonlight. Their insistent "clacks," like the slapping together of pieces of wood, filled the night.

"I wonder what they're thinking," Gwen said. "Pop into one of those little froggy heads and check it out."

"I don't have to," Stoner replied. "They're thinking exactly the same thing Aunt Hermione's thinking." She took a swallow of coffee. It tasted rich and dark, and a dozen shades of brown. "How's Marylou?"

"Still can't get all the food out of the forks."

"She needs a new dish brush. A real one. From a hardware store, not a super market. I'll pick one up at Aubuchon's in the morning." She loved the everyday ordinariness of this moment. Except it wasn't ordinary at all. Home was amazing. People were amazing. Hardware stores were amazing, the aisles and aisles of shiny tools invented just to make things easy were amazing. Dish brushes…rusty gliders…moonlight…

And love was so amazing she could burst.

"Do you think she's upset? About Cutter?"

"Not in the least," Gwen said. "She says he didn't have that piece when she fell in love with him, so why go ballistic over it now? She's not going to spend the rest of her life moaning because the circus left town last week when she didn't even know it was there. She also says, and I quote, 'We all shed a few flakes over the years.' As if parts of your soul were nothing more than dandruff."

And while we're counting up miracles, let's not forget the miracle that is Marylou. Nutty, outspoken to the point of embarrassment, sometimes irritating, and always lovable Marylou. Feet on the ground, head in the clouds, heart on her sleeve, and mind on the upcoming meal.

"I can never decide," Stoner said, "whether Marylou isn't playing with a full deck, or if she has a few extra cards up her sleeve."

Gwen nodded. "And all wild cards."

Stoner laughed. "I think Marylou is maybe the wisest person I know."

They were silent for a while, listening to the creak of the glider.

"Grace says Cutter's a Go-Between," Stoner said. "He travels between the visible and invisible worlds."

"So does Elizabeth."

"But she can choose when and how she goes. Cutter has to go wherever the pull's the strongest."

"That must be terrible."

"Grace says it was because of the war, the things that happened to him. And his personality. He's more sensitive than most, so it all hit him harder."

"No wonder he's kind of reclusive," Gwen said. "It'd be like walking around without skin."

They scraped their feet across the floor, making the glider go faster. The air was cool and soft, like a caress. The sky was cobalt blue. A dark pine stood against the pale silver moonlight, showing its misty aura.

"What are you going to do with Antonia?" Gwen asked.

"I want to keep her around. But she has to be leash-trained. I think I'll leave that to the eminent Dr. Edith Kesselbaum."

Gwen laughed. "Poor Edith."

Stoner shook her head. "Poor Antonia." She looked down at the mug she'd been drinking from. "The Tetons," she said.

"That was a different kind of journey."

"I suspect I'll be taking some strange journeys now. How will that be for you?"

Gwen rested her head on her lover's shoulder. "Lead on, Tony. I'm right behind you."

Back in his make-shift shelter of branches and cast-off monks' robes, Cutter gazed up at the moon, past full now. The ghosts were gone. He could feel their absence.

"Yeah," he said. "Yeah."